STUDYING SEQUOIA

ALSO BY HILARY DARTT

The Intervention Series

The Dating Intervention

The Marriage Intervention

The Motherhood Intervention

The Garden Club Series

Jasmine's Pact

Just Holly

The Seedling Homestead Series

The Order of Composition

The Architecture of Vision

The Structure of Perfection

STUDYING SEQUOIA

BOOK TWO IN THE GARDEN CLUB SERIES

HILARY DARTT

CHAPTER ONE

Sequoia Carr had a strange effect on men. She'd yet to nail down exactly why she had this effect, or whether she could change it.

Not that it mattered, she thought on this Monday morning as she came off her shift at the Seabreeze Police Department. Sequoia Carr was done with men.

In fact, she rarely thought about them. She hadn't been thinking about men while she stripped out of her uniform and examined the peeling paint on the walls of the department's locker room, thinking that it looked like moldy Swiss cheese. She hadn't been thinking of them as she pulled on her favorite fluorescent orange running shorts and inhaled the musty gym-sock smell that permeated every concrete inch of the place.

She'd been thinking about running.

Sequoia found it fitting that marathon running was one of the first Olympic sports. It was essential to human survival. Cavemen ran after their food. They ran away from predators who would turn them into food. And now, Sequoia Carr ran. Every single day, because it was essential for her survival.

She pulled on her tank top. After a quick examination in the full-length mirror, which revealed unusually toned thighs, nicely tanned shoulders, and a dark brown braid that reached her waist, Sequoia put on her shoes. In her hydration pack, she stowed the sandwich she'd bought earlier, along with some chips and a bottled water.

Even though she hadn't yet set foot outside, her body knew the routine. She could feel her heart rate picking up already, and she could taste adrenaline in her throat. The slam of her locker echoed in the empty room. She zipped her hydration pack and put it on, then exited the locker room and ran right into Elijah Sawyer.

He jumped back at the contact, and when he saw who he'd run into, he jumped back again. It was almost comical. It would have been comical, Sequoia thought, if she was the comic type.

She may not be the comic type, but she was observant. She'd spent twelve years being observant. She didn't miss the pine-and-citrus scent of Elijah's cologne or the interesting almost-brown, almost-green, almost-golden color of his eyes. She *definitely* didn't miss the once-over he gave her before stuttering out, "Good morning, Carr."

She expected him to say something like, "Nice outfit," because that's what her co-workers usually said when they saw her wearing anything other than a uniform, her hair braided and hanging down her back rather than tucked into a bun or twist.

But he didn't. Instead, the words, "Going for a run?" tumbled out of his mouth like he'd been trying to hold them in.

Before she could answer, he pressed his lips together, did an about face, and took off in the other direction.

"Morning, Sawyer," she called out after him. Even though he was no longer looking at her, she gestured to her outfit. "Yep, I'm going for a run."

Elijah's retreat did amuse Sequoia, but as soon as she noticed she was grinning, she forced her expression back to serious.

And now she was thinking about men and the strange effect she had on them. Well, one specific man. She stepped outside to warm up, and blinked to let her eyes adjust. Fall was her favorite season in Seabreeze. The air was cool and the sun was bright.

There was something endearing about Elijah Sawyer, she thought as she walked, fast, away from the police station. She couldn't quite pin down whether it was his striking, model-worthy good looks or his standoffish demeanor, or maybe a combination of the two. Not that it mattered. Sequoia Carr was a lone wolf, unfit for romance of any kind. If she weren't, though, maybe she'd give Elijah a roll in the hay.

Now she barked out a laugh, and the sound had her slapping a hand over her mouth. She'd never roll in the hay. It was unsanitary. And Elijah probably wouldn't want to roll in the hay with her, anyway. They'd interacted a maximum of four times since they'd worked together, and he was usually terse and nearly silent … which was probably her own fault.

Actually, Sequoia thought, her lack of people skills extended beyond men. She was unfit for relationships of any kind.

She stopped at the concrete flower planter on the corner of Beachside and Grove to stretch her legs.

She had built-in friendships with her sisters, Jasmine and Holly, but she bungled those on a regular basis by the careless throwing out of words in thoughtless order at precisely the wrong time. She almost always managed to offend either Jasmine or Holly, or both, when they spent time together, and hated herself for how frequently she deployed her go-to phrase: "I'm not criticizing," she'd say. "Just making an observation."

Which was true. Usually. But all too often, her words came out sharp-edged. With the mindfulness she'd been practicing, Sequoia shook off the negativity and reminded herself that each encounter provided a new opportunity for making positive change. At least, that's what the books said.

She took a sip of her water and began to jog, then started her watch. Just as she did every morning, Sequoia headed down Grove Street first. She had a stop to make.

During the workweek, Sequoia spent a lot of time at the Seabreeze Public Transit station on Grove Street. It was a hot spot for the city's homeless population, and the Seabreeze PD received innumerable calls about vandalism or fighting there. One of the regulars spent his evenings carrying an open umbrella, rain or shine, and a sign declaring the end of the world was near. He often sang nursery rhymes as he paced the platform.

Julie Sandusky sat in her usual place, on the bench under the overhang. Because it was their routine, Julie stood up as soon as she saw Sequoia coming down the street.

As always, she looked so serious, and Sequoia was reminded of the first time she'd seen Julie here. It was five years ago, after Sequoia left Walt Walters—another man on whom she'd had a strange effect. Julie was easy to recognize, with her bright red hair, the coppery orange so many women pay hundreds of dollars to replicate, and her vivid blue eyes.

Sequoia had just taken up running, not because she wanted to, but because her sisters insisted that exercise would make her nicer (of course, they hadn't put it that way. Holly had explained that exercise created endorphins, which made people more cheerful).

When she rounded the corner near the transit station and saw Julie sitting there, their eyes had locked, for the briefest moment of recognition. But in each of their worlds, knowing one another was frowned upon.

Julie had been beautiful in her past life. Five years of homelessness had chapped her lips and hands, cracked her cuticles, and weathered her face. Her worn-out appearance and equally shabby jacket made Sequoia unbearably sad. So that first day, she'd run to the deli on the corner and bought a sandwich for Julie. But when she came back, Julie was gone.

Sequoia ate the sandwich, herself, and returned the next day with another. This time, Julie was there, and she smiled with so much gratitude Sequoia nearly cried. She made a mental note to get her emotions under control, then blamed her instability on Walt, and then returned every single day with a sandwich for Julie.

In all this time, they never spoke to each other. So on this cool, bright fall day, Sequoia stopped for just long enough to remove the food from her pack and hand it to Julie. Then she kept running.

Ninety minutes later, Sequoia inhaled the scent of bacon cooking as she took a long draw on a cold Stella Artois.

"Another six miles in the books," she said to herself as she laid out the tortilla for her breakfast burrito. "That's seventy miles this month. I think I can hit one-fifty before November."

Jasmine made fun of Sequoia for talking to herself, but Sequoia found it much more ridiculous that Jasmine talked to her dog, Rosie —or was it Roxie? Remy? It didn't matter. Jasmine talked to that little mutt as if it were a person.

"You may as well get used to talking to yourself, Carr," Sequoia said. "Call it Fate, call it Destiny, call it whatever you want, but there's pretty much no way you'll ever be standing in this kitchen, cooking breakfast with a man, cracking open a beer at eight a.m."

Although her sisters seemed way too interested in her romantic encounters, or lack thereof, Sequoia was okay with being alone.

"Keep telling yourself that, Carr," she murmured.

Not only was she decidedly not relationship material, but she was also too observant to make living with her pleasant.

"Some people call it critical," Sequoia said. "I call it astute."

Sequoia surprised herself by sighing as she sat down at the dining room table. It hadn't always been this way. As a child, a teenager, and even a young adult, Sequoia had imagined herself falling madly, passionately in love with a real-life version of Clark Kent. Then she met him and those dreams died, dissolving into steam.

Walter Walters. His parents had doomed him from the start by giving him that ridiculous name. However, genetics had been kind to Walt Walters. He was tall and broad and muscular, well-endowed in every department. At the start, she would have sworn he could transform into a superhero. But choices—starting with his parents' choice of names for their only son and ending with his choice to seek out the companionship of another female right under Sequoia's nose —made him undesirable.

Walter Walters was Sequoia's first love. She fell hard, headlong, head over heels for him exactly two months after she graduated from college. Ambitious and full of hope for the future, Sequoia had just been accepted into the police academy.

She was happy. Elated. So much so that, acceptance letter tucked into her purse so she could look at it whenever the urge struck, she went shopping for essentials like boots and sweatpants that would make Holly, the chic, trendy fashionista, cringe.

"Although Holly's ever-changing choice of hair color makes me cringe," Sequoia said as she stuffed packages of plain gray t-shirts into the trunk of her car.

Sequoia decided to treat herself to pizza and beer at Bob's Pizza and Wings downtown.

Walter Walters, stunning in his solitude as much as he was in his physical appearance, sat at the bar.

And who was Sequoia Carr to ignore a specimen like that?

As all people with strange names learn to be, Walter Walters was charming. He was witty. He lured her in with a joke about beer—a joke she couldn't even remember now.

Knowing Walt, it was something about the size of his penis. Despite being tall and broad, he always felt the need to hint at the magnitude of his natural bounty.

For some strange reason, probably because she was full of uncharacteristic hope and excitement, Walt's joke delighted her. Instead of walking away like she should have, leaving him at the bar, she poured herself into a taxi with him that very night.

Half a decade after the fact, Sequoia realized they had almost nothing in common, aside from a deep love for cushy socks and a hearty dislike for the St. Louis Rams. Still, they hit it off spectacularly. The sex was amazing—the best she'd ever had. They knocked it out of the park—three times. Would they call that a turkey in baseball? Or was that bowling?

It didn't matter. She gave all the credit to this mysterious stranger she met over pizza and beer.

An avalanche of personality clashes and discrepancies in values took things downhill from there, she thought now as she dug into her breakfast burrito with unusual ferocity.

Because Sequoia's parents had taught her the value of work, she'd always been career-oriented (a euphemism for obsessed with work). Straight back to her days as a barista when she boasted the record for number of cappuccinos made (and drank) in an hour.

So she didn't even notice when Walt began acting distant just a few months into their fresh love. He later pointed out that he skipped dinners and went to lots of weekend conferences out of town, but she was so wrapped up in the police academy—counting pushups and studying criminal justice textbooks every night—that she didn't pay attention.

It was true: she spent most of her free time studying or running or working out or interviewing seasoned cops on their roadside investigation techniques.

Of course, now that she could see it in hindsight, it all made sense: Walt's later-than-usual nights, the phone calls he didn't answer, the way he started shaving his chest hair.

(Which, she reminded herself now, was totally weird.)

The modern-day Sequoia took another sip of her beer as she contemplated the reason Walt had strayed.

He blamed her. Obviously.

"A guy needs sex more than once in a new moon," he'd said one evening, and she'd pointed out that he probably meant *blue* moon, and a blue moon occurs roughly every thirty-three years, and they'd definitely had sex more often than that.

The blue moon comparison was more of an exaggeration than anything, but, Sequoia admitted to herself now, it was a reasonable complaint.

Some people were cut out for love, and some were cut out for work.

Obviously, she was cut out for the latter, not only according to Walt, but also according to herself.

She didn't even want to spend time with Walt, and when he started making fewer and fewer appearances, returning fewer calls, and canceling more dates, she knew it wasn't about him.

It was all about her: Sequoia Carr was meant to be alone. Fly solo.

CHAPTER TWO

────────

THAT EVENING—AND NOT FOR THE FIRST TIME—SEQUOIA FELT LIKE HER sisters had her in the interrogation room at the police department.

"What I want to know," Holly said, "is why you haven't talked about anyone you're dating in, like, forever."

The three of them sat at Jasmine's dining room table, snacking on vegetables Jasmine had set out. Eating together was a weekly tradition, a standing meeting of The Garden Club. Sequoia remembered with fondness how they'd given themselves that name the day they realized their parents had named each of them after flora.

Although she'd loved the meetings as a child, the adult Sequoia sometimes dreaded them. She couldn't put her finger on why, exactly, but it probably had something to do with the fact that the conversations always ended up veering toward her love life. This line of questioning made her heart race and her cheeks burn. Not having dated someone in, *like, forever*, was nothing to be ashamed of.

Only, Sequoia felt ashamed. She felt incapable. And she hated feeling incapable. Because she was the oldest of the three Carr sisters, her parents had constantly reminded her that she had to set a good example for Jasmine and Holly. She must work hard, try and try again, and then succeed, not only for herself, but as a role model.

This, right here, was a perfect illustration of why she sometimes lashed out. Tonight, though, in the spirit of mindfulness and new opportunities, she'd remain calm.

New start, she chanted silently. *New opportunity.*

"I want you to know that this is where I would normally say something like, 'I don't understand why you insist on changing your hair color as often as you change your underwear.' But I'm not going to."

"What?" Holly said. "Don't you like this shade? Jessica—that's my hairdresser—said it's called Auburn Sunset."

"It's better than the last one," Sequoia said. Jasmine kicked her under the table, but she steamrolled ahead: "What was that? Cotton Candy Throw-up?"

"Shut up, Sequoia," both of her sisters said.

"Hey, I thought we'd agreed not to use 'Shut up' during The Garden Club meetings."

"We founded The Garden Club when we were kids," Jasmine said. "And we only banned the term, 'shut up' because we didn't want Mom and Dad to hear us saying it."

Sequoia shook her head. "Fine. Let's get back on topic. First of all, asserting that I haven't talked about a date in 'forever' is unrealistic. Forever means forever. Not a month."

"It's been way more than a month since you said anything about romance," Holly said. Jasmine nodded for emphasis before putting a raw cherry tomato into her mouth.

"Well," Sequoia said, grasping at thoughts in the back of her mind before she finally got a firm grip on one. "I don't tell you lovely ladies everything, now, do I?"

That sounds good, Sequoia thought. It implied that her love life was more interesting and bountiful than parched, cracked desert soil.

Holly shrugged it off, and Sequoia had the shortest moment to experience relief and to come up with a subject change. But Jasmine, the newly-dogged newspaper reporter who wouldn't let go until she had an answer, pointed at Sequoia's face.

"I knew it!" she said to Holly. "She's hiding something."

Well, that backfired.

"Actually, I'm not," Sequoia said. "There's nothing to hide."

"Did you run today?" Jasmine asked.

Sequoia nodded. "Just six miles."

Every once in a while, she got the urge to tell Holly or Jasmine, or both of them, about Julie Sandusky. But she felt like that was a whole separate component of her life, and she didn't want to mix it with the sisters component.

As usual, Jasmine scoffed at Sequoia's use of "just" preceding six miles. But she didn't let the topic of romance slide.

"You know, you could find a running partner or running buddy," Holly said. "Then you might meet some new people. You know, people you could date."

Sequoia exhaled, loudly, hoping that signaled the conversation was over.

"You know, you could go on one of those dating websites," Jasmine said.

"Um, no thanks," Sequoia said. "Those sites are filled with felons and the very desperate."

"I don't know about that," Holly said. "But I do know that you're lonely."

"Don't project your feelings onto me," Sequoia said. "I rarely feel lonely, and even then, it's just because I use up the toilet paper and wish I had someone to bring me more, or because I can't decide what to make for dinner and wish someone else could make the decision. So don't worry about me. I'll either find that person or I won't."

"I just think it would be nice if you had someone," Jasmine said.

Sequoia rubbed her forehead with the tips of her fingers. "You guys are so weird," she said. "You're crazy weird. I'm not sure if this is the best idea."

"What?" Holly said. "We didn't even come up with an idea."

"The idea of me dating," Sequoia said. "Seriously, all this feeling lonely crap is your thing, not mine."

"Do you even have any friends?" Holly said.

"What is with you today?" Sequoia said. "I have you two. And my co-workers."

"Your co-workers don't count," Jasmine said. "You don't even talk to them."

"Yes, I do," Holly said, mimicking Sequoia. "We talk all the time. Like, 'Hey, did you see that box of donuts in the break room?'"

"Look," Sequoia said. "I'm an introvert."

"When is the last time you had a date?" Jasmine said.

Sequoia's mind flashed on a couple images of which her sisters wouldn't approve: her straddling Ryan Tucker in the bathroom at the Burger Stop during a casual sex encounter, and her bent over a stack of beer cases in the storeroom at Bob's Pizza and Wings, Dustin Myers standing behind her, during an even more casual sexual encounter.

A girl—even Sequoia—had needs.

Those were pretty recent, but she liked to keep them under wraps. And anyway, they didn't exactly qualify as "dates."

"I can't remember," Sequoia said. "Anyway, I think my relationship with Walt proved that I'm not capable of maintaining long-term romance."

Holly rolled her eyes. This time, Jasmine (ever the peace-maker) kicked Holly under the table, but she set her jaw, as if she, too, had a thought on the matter but was making a conscious effort not to reveal it.

"What?" Sequoia said. "You know it's true."

Actually, they didn't know. She'd never told them the demise of her relationship with Walt was her fault. Yes, she'd revealed Walt's affair with the long-legged, platinum blonde Barbie, and they'd defended her valiantly, promising to crush Walt's testicles with their bare hands if they ever saw him again.

But she'd never told them why he had an affair, which was because she was a cold, heartless woman who refused to think about anything other than her career.

"Whatever you say," Jasmine said. "But I don't think it would hurt to date once in a while. Keep your skills from getting rusty, you know?"

"Oh, I've got skills," Sequoia said.

Her sisters giggled, and Jasmine went into the kitchen to get the casserole out of the oven. This transition provided the perfect opportunity for a subject change, and Sequoia grasped it.

"Aside from the fact that there's nothing to talk about when it comes to my dating life," she said, "Jasmine's exploits with Hudson have trumped my stuff, anyway."

"True," Holly said. "How's it going, redecorating his place?"

Sequoia expected Jasmine to start glowing as she talked about wall sconces and curtains, and then morning coffee and late night pizza with Hudson Stover, her boyfriend and the photojournalist she worked with at the *Daily Trumpet*.

Instead, her sister sighed. "We can't even agree on a paint color for the living room. He thinks my choices are too ethereal and I think his are too industrial."

"Hm," Holly said. "Maybe you should start with a focus piece, like a throw pillow, and go from there."

"That's actually a good idea," Jasmine said.

She stood up and rummaged around in her purse until she found her notebook and a pen. When she returned to the table after having written down *focus piece - throw pillow?*, she sighed again. "And I really want to get rid of his gross couches. I mean, who buys black velvet couches?"

With the spotlight finally trained on someone else, Sequoia breathed a sigh of relief.

That night, walking out the door of Jasmine's house, Sequoia felt like she'd escaped from Alcatraz, swam across the San Francisco Bay and dragged herself onto the shore.

"Being on the receiving end of interrogations is exhausting," she said as she drove home to get ready for work. "I'll have to remember that the next time I'm questioning a criminal."

An hour later, she walked into the police station thinking about black velvet couches. Who, indeed, would buy such a thing? Sequoia had always liked Hudson but she had to go with Jasmine on this one.

Distracted, she came around the corner, narrowly missing another collision with Elijah Sawyer, who was finishing up his shift and on his way out.

Usually, she'd make some snarky comment about how he really should watch where he was going. But something happened. An unfamiliar feeling took root low in her belly and she knew she'd stutter if she tried to speak. Which, of course, was unacceptable. And weird.

They were almost exactly the same height. This typically turned her off, but at the moment, it gave her a chance to notice (again) that his eyes were the most interesting color. He smelled so good, like pine trees and citrus, that she wanted to nuzzle his neck and maybe even hug him. If she'd been alone, she would have said to herself, "Totally weird, Carr. Totally weird." But he was still standing there, frozen.

So she nodded curtly at him. "Excuse me, Sawyer."

He jumped into action, nodded back, and mumbled, "Morning," as he walked away.

For the second time in as many days, Sequoia had to force the smile off her face.

Elijah Sawyer had made his first appearance on Sequoia's radar a few months before, thanks in large part to Jasmine and a series of unfortunate events.

First, Liza, the cops reporter at the *Daily Trumpet*, noticed a bunch of expenditures unaccounted for in the Seabreeze PD's budget. This set off a string of press conferences, hosted by Seabreeze PD's public information officer, Earl Little, a rat-faced man with beady eyes.

It was simply bad timing that Liza's daughter had her first child (a little girl) at that same time. Liza flew across the country, leaving Jasmine, a features reporter, to cover the police beat. (It was supposed to be temporary, but Liza ended up staying on the East Coast, and Jasmine had surprised everyone, even herself, by asking to stay on the police beat.)

Almost immediately upon Liza's departure, Earl Little turned up dead. Actually, Sequoia thought with a snort, "turned up dead" was a bit of a euphemism. Someone shot the guy. Elijah Sawyer had the dubious honor of standing in for Earl Little. It was likely a wrong place, wrong time scenario, but Elijah took it like a champ.

It only made sense that Jasmine and Elijah crossed paths, and when they did, Jasmine noticed how "prickly" he was (and, of course, how good-looking). Thanks in part to his prickly factor and in part to the fact that she was already engaged in some kind of weird love triangle with Hudson and her high school sweetheart, Parker, Jasmine decided Elijah would be the perfect match for Sequoia.

Sequoia wondered if Jasmine would have snapped Elijah up, if circumstances hadn't been what they were. Probably not. He wasn't really her type. Not outgoing enough.

Anyway, Sequoia thought, it was only then—after Jasmine asked Sequoia if she knew or fantasized about Elijah—that Sequoia took any notice of him. She'd noticed him, to be sure. How could she not? He was good-looking in the tough, manly way that made her believe he could handle her. His face, chiseled perfection with a strong jaw and a cleft chin, belonged on the pages of a magazine, maybe in an ad for cologne. Or fast cars. But, there was the thing about her flying solo. And he was her co-worker. So she'd always observed him from a neutral perspective. But once Jasmine met him, Sequoia let her perspective shift, just a little. And she realized she found him border-line fascinating.

Next—and she blamed Jasmine for making her think this way— she did begin to fantasize about him! She often imagined him naked. Sequoia had seen him at the end of his shift a few times, his t-shirt stretched tight across his chest. Elijah Sawyer had nice muscles.

Finally, he smelled so good.

Fortunately, she thought as she approached her desk today, the two of them rarely crossed paths. Except, of course, during the past two days. She felt that silly smile forming on her mouth again and shut it down as she sat at her desk to check her emails and read through the day's call log.

Recently, the shenanigans of her new boss, Beth Hardwick, had kept her distracted from thoughts (and fantasies) about Elijah. But their two near-collisions had brought him back into focus.

The computer finished booting up and Sequoia logged into her email, trashing junk mail and scanning the rest.

Beth Hardwick seemed to have something to do with the money

the police department was missing, and for some inexplicable reason, she seemed pissed off at everyone else about it. She also seemed to have something to do with Earl Little's death. Not that the world was missing out on much now that he was gone, but he'd been in charge of sharing information with the newspaper and it seemed he was doing a good job of it. Too good.

And, of course, Jasmine had decided to morph from fluff reporter to serious journalist at the very moment things were spiraling out of control at Seabreeze PD. Her stories hinted that the missing money and the dead public information officer were inside jobs.

Sequoia tended to agree … but she hadn't said as much to Jasmine. Jasmine was doing just fine on her own. Seabreeze was a small town. Everyone knew Jasmine was Sequoia's sister.

Which is why Beth Hardwick now hated Sequoia.

Email-checking complete, Sequoia moved on to the call log. She didn't see anything particularly interesting, but found herself scanning the list of responding officers for Elijah's name. She wondered whether he drank coffee.

Beth Hardwick's entrance cut Sequoia's musings short.

"Morning, Carr," she said, sidling up to Sequoia's desk. She leaned against the corner of the desk and crossed her arms.

Sequoia checked the time on her computer before clicking out of the call log. Five minutes until the official start of her shift. She stood up.

"Morning, Hardwick," she said. "I was just heading out."

"I need to talk to you."

"Can it wait? My shift starts right now."

"Your shift starts in five minutes."

Conscious of Beth Hardwick's ability to make her life miserable, Sequoia suppressed a sigh. Didn't the woman know that starting your shift five minutes early was actually starting your shift on time? Apparently not. Beth pushed herself away from the desk and stood with her feet set wide apart, her arms still crossed. She was blocking Sequoia's path, and she knew it.

Sequoia nodded. "What do you need?"

"I don't need anything. I want to tell you that I'm making some shift changes in the department. These changes may apply to you."

Feigning indifference, Sequoia shrugged. "Okay. Thanks for the heads up."

Beth inhaled as if she were about to say something, and Sequoia pushed past her. "Have a good day."

CHAPTER THREE

Sequoia didn't let out the breath she was holding until she arrived at the driver's side of her patrol car in the parking lot. She was absolutely not indifferent to a change in shift. Graveyards were perfect for her because they were conducive to her lifestyle.

So what if her sisters called her a hermit? She was an introvert. Working overnights allowed her to spend most of her awake time alone in the car, while sleeping (alone) when everyone else was awake.

It was perfect. Day shift would be miserable. Swing shift would be even worse than miserable.

But if Sequoia had learned one thing in her quest for mindfulness, it was that stressing over what she couldn't control didn't change anything. For now, she'd enjoy her alone time.

She got into the car and with more force than was strictly necessary, she slammed the door, sealing herself in. She took another deep breath and began setting up her workspace: coffee in the cup holder, patrol bag on the passenger seat, and lucky pack of gum in the cell phone compartment. She turned on her radio, and checked on with dispatch.

She started the car and pulled out onto the road. In the foggy dark, the streetlights glowed orange and the traffic signals sparkled. The evening began to thrum. Sequoia was in her zone.

Working nights was a mixed bag. The city slept, its people settled in just like the fog. Some nights, she drove around in the silence, the traffic signals changing from green to yellow to red, her car's blinker loud against the smooth backdrop of the slumbering town.

Other nights, though, the scenery was totally different. Family fights, bar fights, lovers' quarrels. Shouting, the crashing of ceramic lamps against walls, sirens blaring and lights flashing.

Sometimes Sequoia would be floating through the midnight quiet like it was a pool of soothing, medicated water, and she'd get a call from dispatch. Within moments, she'd be dropped out of her pool of serenity into a boiling vat of stress.

Sometimes she went through a whole shift in silence, talking to no one, not even herself. And sometimes she walked in on a drug deal and talked a million words per minute.

In her personal life, Sequoia thrived on order, on schedules, on lists. But for forty hours each week, she thrived on the quick pivots, the sudden turnarounds, the fast changes and the snap decisions. And she was good at it.

Would things be the same if she had a lover to come home to each morning? Would she still thrive on the adventure and the adrenaline? Or would she wish for something more predictable, something that would give her a better chance of living through the end of each shift?

Not that she didn't have anything to live for, Sequoia thought as she pulled onto the shoulder of the highway to patrol for speeders, but she often heard of cops who thought of their families on every call. She often wondered if those thoughts impaired their judgment, caused them to behave differently than they should.

Without any warning, her thoughts drifted to Elijah Sawyer. What did he think about when he was going through a door on a call? Who did he think about?

She'd always thought of him as single, but was he? Did he have a family? She wasn't even sure whether he wore a wedding band, and couldn't believe she'd never bothered to look.

"Why am I thinking about Elijah Sawyer right now?"

Suddenly, something occurred to her that had never crossed her mind before: would anyone ever think of her when that time came?

"Huh. Never thought of that."

Fortunately, some jerk in a lifted pickup truck blazed past her at about ninety miles per hour, and she flicked on her lights and sirens to follow.

Sequoia's shift turned out busy, which kept her mind off romance and other such nonsense. But all good things must come to an end, including her shift. After clocking out, she changed into her running clothes and put a sandwich for Julie in her hydration pack.

Although running was a good release for her physical stress, it also provided the inevitable opportunity to go over (and over and over) the thoughts she otherwise attempted to push out of her conscious mind.

So, of course, Elijah Sawyer's was the first face to materialize as she finished her warmup and began running towards the Seabreeze Transit station.

Elijah was probably just waking up. He probably wore underwear to bed. Boxer briefs, no shirt. At this very moment, his skin was probably still warm from sleep. Maybe he had silk sheets. Or satin. Or did those fall into the same category as black velvet couches?

Sequoia had always enjoyed morning sex, but since Walt, she rarely participated in it because she usually left the scene before anyone did any actual sleeping.

Julie sat on her normal spot, on the bench at the transit station. Although Sequoia's normal routine was to drop Julie's meal in her lap and keep running, today she found herself slowing to a stop as she pulled out the sandwich.

"Hi, Julie," she said.

Although they'd gone through this routine almost daily for the past several years without Sequoia ever asking questions, Julie looked wary.

"Hi," she said.

"How are you today?" Sequoia said.

Then she realized that was a stupid question. Julie Sandusky, with her sunburned nose and chapped cheeks, was homeless. It's not like she could say, "Great! I'm having a great morning. When I woke up on the concrete at five a.m., it was only fifty degrees, but it's a great day so far."

Julie looked at her like she was crazy, and Sequoia shook her head. She felt like she should apologize, but realized that would only make things worse. She began to zip up her hydration pack, and Julie finally answered: "I'm doing well, thank you. And you?"

Julie had always had such formal speech, but it had been so long since they had a real conversation that Sequoia had forgotten.

"I'm doing well, thank you," she said. "Just, you know, going for a run."

She kicked herself again. No, Julie probably didn't know what it was like to just go for a run.

"Enjoy," Julie said. "And thank you for the sandwich."

Sequoia nodded. "You're welcome."

Despite the awkwardness of the conversation, Sequoia felt a bit lighter as she jogged away. For the first time, she wondered what Julie did all day. She probably didn't sit on that bench. Where did she go? Who did she talk to?

She always seemed to be alone. Sequoia picked up her pace. When did a person realize solitude was the status quo? When did she just accept that?

When Walt broke things off with Sequoia, she fought against solitude. She was positive she was meant for a long-term relationship. A marriage and kids. A family. Every day, she obsessed over her loneliness, cried about it, wished for someone to sit on the couch with at night, in socks and sweatpants.

Then, she'd gone through the five stages of grief. Not over the loss of Walt Walters himself, but over the loss of her capability to be in a long-term relationship. It ended with acceptance. Now, she could accept that she'd end up alone.

At the corner where the ice cream shop sat opposite the coffee shop, Sequoia ticked off a mile in her mind. A flock of seagulls flew overhead, one of them cawing loudly.

Yes, she'd thought Walt was The One, but in addition to his penchant for infidelity (she later learned he'd dated several different women during their time together), he harbored some pretty annoying habits that undoubtedly would have driven her crazy over time.

Take, for example, the way he blew snot rockets into the garbage can each morning. Her stomach turned even now, five years after she'd seen that last shining glob of snot.

Walt blamed Sequoia for his sideshow trysts, and although she agreed that her lack of warmth probably contributed, she figured most other men would have simply broken things off.

She remembered one conversation in particular, when she'd questioned his growing number of out-of-town business trips.

"You work at a bank. You can't tell me they're sending you out of town every week," she said.

"Are you accusing me of something, Sequoia?"

"Nothing specific," she said. "It just seems strange, that's all. Plus, the restaurant bills on those trips are pretty high. Are you eating for two?"

"It's all about schmoozing, Sequoia. You know that. I take clients out to dinner."

He always ate at chain restaurants, and it never occurred to her to look more closely at the bank statements. One day, she realized he was eating in Seabreeze when he said he was out of town.

"It's only natural for me to have questions when you say you're out of town, but you're spending money locally," she said that night in her calmest, most reasonable voice.

"You don't trust me. Why do you jump to conclusions? What if someone had one of those machines, you know, those credit card scanners, and they stole my debit card number?"

True. He wouldn't be so stupid as to use the card from their shared bank account, would he? Unless he wanted her to catch him.

When she pointed this out, he stormed out of the house, muttering about how she was putting him on the line like a common criminal, using her interrogation skills, playing cop in their kitchen.

Now Sequoia followed the running path down to the harbor, where she ran along the water's edge. Sleek, shiny yachts and square, complicated-looking fishing boats bobbed against rubber buoys. The smell of diesel fuel and bilge pumps and the ocean felt like home to Sequoia, and as she ticked off her second mile, she decided to head down to the shoreline to tack some extra distance onto today's workout.

Denial was strong medicine when Walt first left. It blocked all the uncomfortable feelings of despair. It was all she could do to trudge through each day, but she managed. Although Jasmine and Holly had known about Walt, they hadn't known quite how serious Sequoia considered the relationship. So even though they noticed she "seemed down" (in Holly's ever-descriptive language), they didn't understand the depth of her sadness. She'd skipped out on a few of their lunch and dinner dates, saying she had extra work to catch up on. They believed her. Of course.

Then anger set in. Although she knew she should direct her anger at Walt, he was gone. So she poured it over everything else in her life. She pulled drivers over for speeding, even if her radar showed them traveling just three miles per hour faster than the posted speed limit. She chastised her sisters for their choices in sunglasses and socks. Yes, the socks Holly insisted on wearing—toe socks with flip flops—were really stupid, but Sequoia knew she didn't have to turn them into a symbol of Holly's own life. What had she said then? Something scathing about indecisiveness and rainbow socks on an adult. If she remembered correctly, Holly had cried. Even now, Holly's alligator tears over a rainbow socks comment made Sequoia roll her eyes. She even chuckled a little as she ran along the shoreline and watched the incoming waves.

Sequoia would flip from bargaining ("If I'm more patient with Jasmine and Holly, maybe Karma will match me up with a nice boyfriend") to anger and back again.

The depression stage felt like it would last forever. How sad to think she'd be alone for the rest of her life. Sequoia found her eyes tearing up at the most inopportune times, like when she was in the break room at work and the coffeemaker quit. Fortunately, anger, her own personal superhero, always made an appearance during those times. So what if she smashed the coffee carafe into a million tiny pieces? Okay, she'd only done that in her imagination as she set it back into the broken machine, the whole vision wavering behind the stupid tears.

Finally, she found acceptance. In fact, she thought now, she found acceptance through running. Holly had been talking a lot about getting her personal training certification, and Sequoia had to admit she found the research her sister did pretty interesting.

"Did you know exercise produces endorphins?" she said to Sequoia at dinner one night. "So it will be my profession to make people happier. Hey, did you ever think about exercising?"

Sequoia was always in decent shape, especially because the Seabreeze Police Department required her to pass an annual physical test. But she'd never exercised regularly.

So she took up running, and didn't miss Holly's self-satisfied expression when she admitted she'd done so because of Holly's research.

Physically, running did erase some of the stress that made Sequoia's shoulders tense and contributed to her tendency to fly off the handle at any given moment. Mentally, too, it gave her something she'd never given herself before: time to think.

Out of habit, Sequoia often kept herself so busy she didn't have time to think about work, her love life … anything, really. Running forced open some mental space, and Sequoia found it refreshing. Surprisingly so.

Because it gave her time for reflection *and* solitude, she was able to accept that being alone wouldn't be so bad. She could enjoy her own company. She didn't need Walt or any other man to find happiness.

Sequoia Carr was a loner, and that was okay. Preferable, even.

Eight miles had rushed by under her feet during the past hour and ten minutes, and as she rounded the corner to approach her starting point—the police department—she saw Elijah Sawyer getting into his patrol car. Why did she suddenly see him everywhere? And why did the sight of him make her shiver?

"Just because you're a loner doesn't mean you can't find a man attractive, Carr," Sequoia said to herself.

She went into the locker room and took a cold shower.

CHAPTER FOUR

"Whattup, Tree?"

Sequoia raised her hand to high-five Tony, the manager of the soup kitchen at the city's homeless shelter.

"Hey, Tony," she said. "What's cooking?"

"I got bean stew and French bread today. Want to ladle stew or butter bread?"

"I'll ladle. Double time, too, since I missed my last shift."

Tony nodded and handed Sequoia a hat, an apron, and a pair of plastic gloves.

"Yeah, you skipped out on us last week. What was it, that murder thing?"

It had been a murder thing. One of the less-quiet work nights. But Tony knew Sequoia couldn't talk about it.

"I know you can't talk about it," Tony said. "But if you ever need help with a case, just ask me. I got skills."

Volunteering at the city's homeless shelter was risky for a police officer. In so many cities, the lives of police and the lives of the homeless intersected, and badly. It was likely she'd cross paths with some of her repeat customers. But Sequoia's reason for seeking a new kind of interaction was twofold.

First, she'd always gotten along reasonably well with the homeless population. There was the singing Armageddon guy who'd punched her in the shoulder once, but otherwise he pretty much ignored her, even as she herded him back to the shelter. She'd quickly learned to stay just past the reach of his right hook.

Second, Sequoia's limited interactions with Julie Sandusky had given her an epiphany. Before Julie Sandusky, Sequoia thought most homeless people chose homelessness and hopelessness. But Julie taught Sequoia that wasn't so.

Sequoia stood behind the counter with her ladle ready.

"Hi, Sally," she said to her first customer. Sally grunted in response, and Sequoia made a mental note to arrange for a new pair of gloves for the old lady. Hers were tattered; pieces of thread stuck out at random angles, and two of the fingertips were completely missing.

"Tree lady," said the next man in line. The boom of his voice echoed through the room, and Sequoia grinned at him.

"Robert," she said. "Soup?"

"Well, I ain't here for the ambiance, woman," he said. "Give me some soup."

"What've you got for me today?" she said, holding up the full ladle. "Before I give you soup?"

"I ain't got nothing for you. You're here to give me something, woman."

The banter was the same, week after week, and Sequoia settled into the rhythm here just like she did on a shift at work. She served stew to seventy-two people, most of whom she knew by name. One of them was Julie Sandusky.

When the line finally cleared out, she got herself a bowl of stew and sat down across the table from Julie, who shrank into herself and glanced around.

"I've never seen you here," Sequoia said. "Did you like the stew?"

Julie's eyes continued to flick from one side to the other, but her shoulders relaxed.

"You get a job yet?" Sequoia asked.

Julie shrugged, and although the movement could have come across as insolent, Sequoia knew it was frustration.

"I've tried everything. I'm not sure what I'm going to do."

Sequoia tried the stew. It wasn't the best she'd ever had, but it was far better than the shelter's meatloaf.

"I know," Julie said. "Not that good."

Sequoia wrinkled her nose. "How can I help you, Julie?"

Julie sighed, and her shoulders slumped. "I just don't know. The good news is that I'm already at rock bottom, right?"

Her laugh came out harsh and bitter.

Sequoia was unaccustomed to the tight feeling that closed off her throat. She swallowed, and then did something else completely unusual for her: she reached across the table and took Julie's hand.

"Something will come up," she said. "It has to. Keep looking, okay? Don't give up."

Julie's eyes were free from makeup, but intense in their light color and glare. Sequoia felt like Julie had something to say, but she pressed her lips together before nodding and inhaling so her chest rose.

"I won't," she said.

Sequoia helped clear the buffet line, and by the time she was done, Julie was gone. As she often did with cases at work, Sequoia assigned her subconscious the task of figuring out some options for the woman she'd come to respect over the past several years. She also made a mental note to do some research when she got home.

She could only imagine what Beth Hardwick would say if she used work resources to research job opportunities for a homeless woman with a criminal record.

Not that the criminal record was Julie's fault, but still. Sequoia and Julie went way back, further than the sandwich deliveries at the transit station. Just as things got tumultuous with Walt, Sequoia had worked a case on Trenton Washington, a big-time drug dealer with a small IQ. He'd used his girlfriend, Julie Sandusky, as a mule for his product. Although detectives knew what he was up to, they needed proof. That's where Julie came in. Detectives asked her to inform on him, and when he found out, she turned up with a bruise on her cheek the size and shape of a piece of toast.

Washington went to prison, but not before trashing Julie's apartment and beating her to within an inch of her life.

A passerby heard the noise and called police, and that's when Sequoia showed up.

When Sequoia met Julie, Julie's face was swollen, bruised, and bloody. She agreed to an interview, but was so weak she had to put all the details together over the next couple of weeks.

Washington went to prison.

Julie took a plea on her drug distribution charges, along with a short stint in jail.

A year later, Julie emerged from jail and started her new life. All the trauma led to a drinking problem, and Julie had since struggled to hold down a job for long enough to get back on her feet. So she hung out at the transit station, accepting handouts from a police officer.

ALL WOMEN HAD NEEDS—EVEN a woman who was designed for solitude. So Sequoia maintained a short list of high-quality men from whom she sought companionship when she needed it.

No one needed to know she'd asked each of them to get tested for sexually transmitted diseases, or that she picked and chose when she saw each one, depending on her moods.

Her meeting with Julie at the homeless shelter earlier this morning made her pensive, and for a pensive mood she needed an independent man, a man who would get the business done and not expect her to cuddle or stay for a nightcap or even do more than roll out of bed, mutter, "goodnight," and run out of the apartment.

Alex Light was tonight's pick.

Alex was a construction worker, a brute of a man who, surprisingly, shared her complex taste in books. If she wanted to talk to him, she could, but the truth was that each of them was so exhausted most of the time that their communication consisted of nothing more than pleasantries and necessities.

When she opened the door to her apartment, he immediately wrapped his arms around her waist, and she leaned into his muscular body, relishing the feel of his stubble against her face.

"Well, hello," he said to her.

"Hello," she said back.

Under certain circumstances, normal daily events might make it difficult for Sequoia to concentrate on sex. She'd be mid-kiss and wonder if she'd remembered to sign off on a ticket or whether she'd locked her patrol car.

But not with Alex. Never with Alex. He was exactly what she needed tonight: competent, efficient, and ruthless.

Within a matter of seconds, he had her undressed on the bed and she could feel his whiskers between her thighs.

Then, suddenly, from out of nowhere, she imagined those were Elijah Sawyer's whiskers.

"What the hell," she whispered.

In a move Sequoia normally would have found comedic, Alex popped his head up to look at her. "Everything okay?" he said.

She nodded and pushed his head back down. "Everything's fine. Just got a little distracted. Sorry. Carry on."

Alex carried on, and Sequoia let herself drift along, enjoying the sensation of his mouth on her lady parts and his hands on her breasts.

But then—and this time it wasn't out of nowhere, obviously, as she'd just had a similar thought—it was Elijah's hands on her breasts.

She managed not to say anything out loud this time, but she gasped, which, fortunately, could be mistaken for a sign of pleasure. Alex groaned as if her gasp had turned him on, and she had to work hard against the urge to giggle. That never turned men on in bed.

For a few moments, Sequoia tried to dissolve Elijah's image from her mind. But when Alex asked, again, whether everything was okay, Sequoia decided to go ahead and let Elijah into her mind. Alex would never know she was thinking of Elijah Sawyer, and neither would Elijah Sawyer.

The trouble, she thought as she finally reached the release she'd been craving, was that *she'd* know … and she'd likely think about it the next time she saw Elijah at the office.

Oh, well, she thought. *When you're a confirmed lifelong bachelorette, there is absolutely nothing wrong with letting your imagination take over.*

Because Sequoia was such a reasonable person, she knew this theory would be tested at some point. She just didn't know how soon. Not that it mattered. Her needs were satiated, and, apparently, so were Alex's.

After he pumped himself dry—which took only about three minutes—he rolled off her and went into the bathroom to clean up. When he returned, he immediately pulled his jeans on. He leaned down to kiss her as he buttoned them, and then stepped into his boots.

"I've got to go," he said. "We've got to be at the site early tomorrow."

He left, and for the rest of the evening, Sequoia found herself wrestling with a strange combination of guilt and longing.

"What the hell is wrong with me?" she said.

And because she was alone, no one answered.

THE NEXT DAY, Sequoia met Jasmine and Holly for lunch at the beach. They sat around a little, bright red table with a white umbrella. Holly had brought them all drinks; a lemonade for Sequoia, a coffee for Jasmine, and a "green power smoothie" for herself.

It always started the same way with Jasmine and Holly. One of them would ask the other a question about romance. Holly might say, "So, Jasmine, how are things going with Hudson?" and Jasmine might respond, "They're going great! We had a lovely dinner last night at his place. We cooked together while drinking wine and it was very romantic. He even bought special bones for Ruby."

It all sounded innocent enough, although bones for the dog didn't seem like a big enough deal to mention. Nevertheless, Sequoia always cringed when her sisters started talking romance, because things would inevitably head south from there.

Her sisters couldn't help but ask her about her own romantic prospects or conquests (or failures). Why they felt obligated to include her in this strain of each conversation, especially since her answer was always the same, she didn't know.

Sometimes she tried to head it off, by completely changing the subject: "I had a totally disgusting call yesterday," she'd say. "It was a dead body that had been lying in bed for a week. The smell alone made me sick, but I just about lost my lunch when I realized I couldn't tell where the body ended and the mattress began."

But not even body decay could set them off course.

Sure enough, Holly asked Jasmine, "So, how's it going with Hudson?"

Jasmine blushed.

"Oh, my goodness gracious," Sequoia said. "You're actually blushing. Things must be going spectacularly. Wait. Don't tell me: you guys decided on a new color scheme for his place."

Jasmine looked down at her lap. "Things are going well," she said.

"Spectacularly?" Holly said.

Jasmine cackled, wickedly, and twisted her hands together. "Define 'spectacularly.' If you mean, 'Hudson has amazing oral sex skills, then ...."

"Stop there!" Holly said.

"We did decide on a color scheme," Jasmine said. "Blues and grays. And he agreed to get rid of the black leather couch, admitted he was holding onto it only because it was a throwback from his college days. Although now we're trying to decide whether to use my bedding or his."

She looked up at the ceiling and groaned. "Anyway. Let's talk about something else. Sequoia."

Even though it was kind of fun watching someone else squirm,

Sequoia had mercy on Jasmine. "Just buy new bedding," she said. "Just my two cents. Anyway. Work's going great."

Holly and Jasmine exchanged a glance.

"What?" Sequoia said. "It is. My boss is going to be making some shift changes, she said. So I may get a different shift. I could spend more time with you two lovely ladies if that happened."

She should have known Jasmine would twist a work-related comment into an opportunity to talk about men.

"Ooh, doesn't Elijah Sawyer work the day shift?"

"How do you even know that?" Sequoia said.

"Because," Holly said, "they had to work together when he was public information officer. And she works the day shift."

Sequoia nodded. This was a surprisingly astute answer coming from Holly.

"That's right," Sequoia said. "How is your work coming, Jas? Are you still feeling like a very serious reporter?"

Jasmine nodded, emphatic. "Yes. I'm feeling very much like a serious reporter. So much so that I won't let you derail me from my original line of questioning, which was asking you if Elijah Sawyer still works the day shift."

"Ugh," Sequoia said.

"So does he?" both Jasmine and Holly said.

"Yes," Sequoia said, drawing out the word. "But that doesn't mean we'd cross paths any more than we do now."

"So, you guys cross paths?" Jasmine said.

"Ooh, now Sequoia's blushing!" Holly said.

"Oh, my God," Jasmine said. "She's blushing over a *man*! I have never seen this happen before. Mark down this date on the calendar. It should be a new holiday. Blush Day."

Although she'd never admit to her sisters that she'd pictured Elijah's face, his hands, his body, his—well, all of him—when she was having sex with Alex, it couldn't hurt to tell them how he'd looked at her when he saw her in her running tights.

She cleared her throat.

"Spill it, sister," Holly said.

Suddenly, Sequoia felt stupid. Elijah Sawyer giving her the once-over didn't signify anything other than some primal, manly reflex. On the other hand, her imagining Elijah naked signified her serious desperation.

"Never mind," she said. "It's nothing."

"Woooow," Jasmine said. "I don't think I've ever seen you like this. Over a guy."

"Stopit." Sequoia ran the words together and realized her mistake immediately.

Of course, her sisters dissolved into giggles, and they were right back in their teen years, sitting on Sequoia's bed, under New Kids on the Block posters, magazines spread on their laps.

The quizzes. They always took quizzes, and the quiz results always made Sequoia angry. Whoever wrote the damned quizzes must be some kind of a moron. She'd decided that from the start. But her sisters took the quizzes—and the results—so seriously.

They'd tease Sequoia after tallying up her points.

"You're a gentle kisser," they'd say. "Does Ryan Thomas like that?"

"Stopit," she'd say. "Stopit right now."

This, of course, they always found hilarious, and mimicked her nonstop.

"Stopit," they'd squeal. "Stopit right now."

Yes, twenty years had passed, and they were all grown up. But her sisters couldn't resist a good opportunity to make fun of her. She felt her face burning even hotter, starting in her neck and spreading to her ears.

Rather than giving them the satisfaction of repeating herself, she sighed.

"It's nothing. Okay? I mean, Elijah is handsome. And we crossed paths. It was just an embarrassing moment, that's all. We literally bumped into each other." As an afterthought she added, "He smelled nice. He—well, that's all."

"He what?" Holly said. Her voice became a shriek. "He *what*, Sequoia?"

Sequoia dropped her head into her hands. She took a deep breath, making a conscious effort not to deflect by talking about

Holly's hair color. "Nothing. It was nothing. Okay? Let it go. Stop it."

As they'd done so many times before, her sisters looked at each other and had some private, silent conversation while she sat there and watched.

"You know we're going to find out eventually," Holly said, and Jasmine added, "You might as well tell us."

Sequoia opened her mouth to protest, but Jasmine held up a hand and Holly, her eyes alight under that Auburn Sunset hair, said, "It's okay. We know you don't want to. And we can respect that. But just know that when the time comes, I will choose lingerie for you to wear when you have hot, steamy, incredible, mouthwatering sex with Elijah Sawyer."

CHAPTER FIVE

MONDAY NIGHT. SEQUOIA WAS RELIEVED TO GO BACK TO WORK. NOBODY there questioned her (well, nobody sane anyway). Nobody mimicked her. Nobody forced fairy tales down her throat. Fairy tales that eliminated black velvet couches and involved bedding choices.

Sure, she had to wrestle half-dressed, completely drunk people. She had to counsel half-crazy people. But none of them actually knew her. Which she considered very refreshing.

Just as she put her bag and phone on her desk, Beth Hardwick approached. If Beth wasn't a police officer, Sequoia imagined she would be wearing a tight pencil skirt and high heels, which would be clacking on the linoleum floor right now.

Only, Beth Hardwick was a police officer, and she was wearing a pair of thick-soled black boots with her khaki pants and button-up blouse. Her heels didn't clack, but she strutted towards Sequoia, her hips jutting out alternately like she was on some kind of catwalk.

"Carr," she said.

"Beth," Sequoia said.

"Made some changes tonight. Put some different guys on nights with you. Sawyer, for one. Just wanted to let you know."

Sawyer? As in, Elijah Sawyer?

"But—" Stammering? Sequoia Carr was stammering over a man. "What about him being the public information officer?"

Beth raised an eyebrow and Sequoia wondered immediately if she didn't want Elijah to be the public information officer.

"What about it? I'll have someone else step in. Anyway. That's it."

She rapped her knuckles on the desk, two quick taps. Sequoia nodded, her eyebrows raised. She was sure her face gave the impression that she didn't care, even while her heart started beating a crazy rhythm in her chest.

Beth Hardwick shrugged one shoulder, then sauntered off.

Sequoia had just assumed Beth would be moving her to day shift, just to make her uncomfortable. But this? She hadn't anticipated it. She had read somewhere that it's impossible to feel stressed when you're taking deep breaths. So she took a few deep breaths. It was fine. She probably wouldn't even see him, much less have the opportunity to think about him in his uniform, doing a strip tease.

They'd be out on the road, separate. She could get through this.

Then Elijah walked in.

The way Sequoia swung away from him in her desk chair was not childish at all. At least, that's what she told herself.

"Morning," he said to her. Before Sequoia could remind him that it was actually nighttime, he was walking away. "Evening," he called over his shoulder.

She grinned at her computer screen, realized she'd forgotten to turn it on, and then wondered if Elijah had noticed she'd forgotten to turn it on. The computer took centuries to boot up. Elijah returned before it was done.

"I like you better in your running outfit," he said.

This caught her off guard. Not only did it light up a strange awareness in her lower belly, but also, he was her co-worker and it was extremely unprofessional for him to comment on her choice of outfit. Especially when her choice of outfit featured tight running pants.

Because her strange sense of pleasure and satisfaction conflicted with her sense of moral rightness, she had no idea how to respond.

She could just say, "Thanks," and he would probably move on. Or she could say, "I like those uniform pants on you," which was true, and again, totally inappropriate.

So, she shrugged, kept her eyes glued to the computer screen, and didn't say anything. Elijah stopped next to her desk and planted his feet far apart as if he meant to stay awhile.

"'Thank you, Sawyer,' would have been an appropriate response," he said.

"Thank you, Sawyer," she said, still not looking at him.

"Do you run often?" he said.

What is this, coffee hour? Sequoia thought. *Doesn't he have something better to do?*

"Every day, pretty much," she said. She finally turned to look at him, and noticed immediately that his eyes were smiling. Was he doing this on purpose? "I usually go right after work."

"How far do you go?"

Are we still talking about running? "Somewhere in the four to eight range."

Elijah's mouth dropped open. "But, *why*?"

Sequoia laughed before she caught herself. Laughing at a man's joke was just leading him on.

"I like it," she said. That was simple enough. He didn't need to know that it was the only pastime she'd found that eased the nervous, jittery energy that was constantly zipping around in her body, and the barrage of thoughts that bombarded her consciousness twenty-four hours per day.

"I used to run," he said. "But then I took up drinking."

She laughed, again, and wished she could kick herself under the desk.

"No, seriously," he said. "I kind of tapered off. It was one of those things where I got sick, and then when I felt better, something else came up and I didn't have time. I think I moved or something. And I just never got back into it. Maybe I could join you one morning, now that we're on the same shift."

Warning bells and alarm buzzers went off in her mind. Loud ones, probably equipped with those spinning lights. Running was her time. Her alone time. It was the only time during a given day that she could dramatically reduce the number of inputs her brain had to process. Someone tagging along would undoubtedly take away from the peaceful feeling she so looked forward to.

"I kind of like the solitude," she said.

"I get that," he said. "Let me know if you ever change your mind."

Then, he walked away.

"I won't," she muttered.

As she went through the motions of opening her email and scanning through the call log—without actually reading anything—she evaluated this new situation.

So. Elijah Sawyer was an early arriver just like she was. Respectable. But, it was also inconvenient. It meant they'd be in the office together at the beginning of every shift. And at the end of every shift. Which meant he would probably still be around to see her every morning after she changed into her running clothes.

She groaned and made a mental note to buy some looser running pants. Then she looked at the clock on her computer and realized it was time for her shift to begin. Which meant she was late. She should be in her patrol car, pulling out of the driveway.

Elijah Sawyer was messing with her.

Working for a small police department meant officers spent most of their time alone. Nobody worked in pairs, and backup was sometimes several long minutes away. Fortunately, working for a small police department also meant working in a small town, where crime rates were lower than average and repeat customers were the norm.

Almost as soon as Sequoia did pull out of the parking lot, two minutes after her shift started, she got a call about a family fight at the Peaceful Breeze apartment complex. She sighed.

The Peaceful Breeze was a shining example of a misnomer. She spent half her working hours there. She broke up fights and scooped up drunks outside the dingy apartments. She followed aggressive drivers into the parking lot and arrested them for DUIs. It was like a second home.

The U-shaped building squatted low and gray, its paint peeling and its concrete cracked in so many places it looked like a roadmap or the bottom of a dried up lake.

Sequoia pulled up along the curb and used her car radio to tell dispatch she'd arrived. They'd given her an apartment number, but she could have found the fight without it. Screaming and the sound of hard objects hitting walls came from an apartment in the back corner of the second story. Denny and Shelly Marvin. Repeat customers.

She shook her head. Why couldn't people just talk it out?

As she approached the stairs, someone came rushing out of the apartment directly below the one where Sequoia was headed. It was Barb Green, the Peaceful Breeze's resident gossip and mother hen. Based on her outfit—a pink robe with one pocket hanging by a thread and purple pajama pants frayed at the ends—Sequoia guessed Barb had been about to go to bed when the Marvins started fighting.

"They've been going at it all night," Barb said. "I think Denny's finally done it this time. Evidently, he came home late and Shelly's pissed. I think she finally caught him cheating on her. With some skank from the dollar store."

"Thanks, Barb," Sequoia said. "I guess Denny had it coming, didn't he?"

Barb chortled, a pig-like snuffling sound that had Sequoia smiling, too. This conversation followed the script of many before it. Barb had invited Sequoia in for coffee a few times, but Sequoia always turned her down.

Someone screamed from upstairs, and Barb said, "Well, you'd better get to it, Missy."

She watched Sequoia walk up the stairs, and then disappeared back into her home.

Even though the Marvins' apartment door stood wide open, Sequoia banged on it. "Seabreeze PD, can I come in?"

Instead of an answer, Sequoia heard another loud crash, and Shelly Marvin screamed, "Get out, Denny! This was the last time! Go on and live with your white trash mother!"

"Shelly!" Sequoia said. "Seabreeze PD. Can I come in?"

Suddenly, someone came thundering up the stairs behind her. Sequoia did an about-face so her back was against the wall next to the open door. The new arrival was a slightly overweight woman wearing too-tight leggings and a button-up flannel, which was hiked up over her love handles. She stopped short when she saw Sequoia standing there, and her ample cleavage heaved.

Before Sequoia could offer any kind of greeting or introduction, Shelly Marvin came flying out of the apartment, leaped onto the back of the woman in the flannel, and put her in a headlock.

Shelly was a tiny woman, and apparently, this brute of an intruder barely registered the presence on her back. That is, until Shelly started choking her.

"Shelly!" Sequoia would start with reason.

The woman in the plaid was yanking on Shelly's forearms, but Shelly was holding on tight. She was also screaming in the woman's ear: "You knew he was married. You *knew* it! You've met me! You're worse than a two-bit whore. I'm gonna kill you and then you're going straight to Hell for this!"

For her part, the woman in the plaid just grunted, leaning forward, trying to loosen Shelly's grip. It wasn't working. Shelly only became more frantic, her skinny legs flailing behind her.

"Shelly, you're going to go straight to jail for assault," Sequoia said, her voice loud but calm. "You'd better get off her."

"I don't give a shit!" Shelly screamed. "She seduced my husband! She seduced my man! I'll kill her!"

Looking at the woman in plaid, Sequoia wondered how in the world she had seduced Denny Marvin. The only thing she had going for her was a full set of teeth (where Shelly's were rotten from drug use) and a generous bosom (where Shelly's was practically nonexistent). Other than that, Shelly had her beat.

"I understand," Sequoia said.

"You married?" Shelly grunted at her, now using one hand to pull her chokehold even tighter

Sequoia shook her head. "Not relevant."

"If you were, you'd understand," Shelly said, yanking her grip tighter with each syllable. "You'd be helping me kick her big, fat ass right now."

"You're breaking the law," Sequoia said. "Regardless of whether she seduced your husband."

"He's breaking a contract. A marriage contract. It's legally binding."

"Then kick *his* ass. Quietly. Later, when no one's here to call the police. But if you don't get off her, right now, you're going to jail."

For a moment, Shelly seemed to concede. She let herself slide down the big lady's back, and the instant her feet touched the ground, the big lady spun around, arms raised in attack mode.

Shelly punched the lady right in the face and she went down like a sack of potatoes. Only for a second, though. Then she was up on the balls of her feet, fists raised. Sequoia felt amusement rising in her chest. This woman reminded her of the cowardly lion in "The Wizard of Oz," and she half expected her to start chanting, "Put 'em up, put 'em up."

Sequoia stepped between them. Even though she wasn't a rookie, it was a rookie mistake. Flannel Girl hurled a meaty fist at Shelly, and Sequoia barely managed to duck out of the way in time.

"That's enough, you two," she said, spreading her arms to push them apart.

"This she-man stole my husband!" Shelly's arms went windmill style, and Sequoia was grateful for her own longer-than-average arms, one of which held Shelly at just the right distance.

Sequoia didn't bother telling Shelly she was sure Denny wouldn't have gotten stolen by anyone, she-man or otherwise, if he didn't want to be stolen.

"I understand," Sequoia said. "But this is no way to solve it."

"Oh, I beg to differ." Shelly's arms flailed and her voice deepened.

Suddenly, the Flannel Girl swerved away from Sequoia's other hand to take a new run at Shelly.

Then, out of nowhere, someone tackled Flannel Girl, taking her straight down. Her body hit the floor with a thud, and she grunted. Shelly stood back, hands on her hips, breath coming fast.

Sequoia was a little flabbergasted. Who in the world had tackled Flannel Girl? The mystery tackler was still tangled up with Flannel Girl on the concrete. His identify revealed itself one sexy limb at a time.

Elijah Sawyer.

"What are you *doing* here?"

She knew her tone came across abrasive, even though, along with intense annoyance at what was obviously a savior complex, she felt immense gratitude for Elijah's tackling Flannel Girl.

He grunted as he rolled Flannel Girl over and handcuffed her.

"Just giving you a little backup," he said.

Before Sequoia could come up with a witty response, Denny Marvin, the man himself, finally ambled out of the apartment he shared with Shelly. He wore flannel pajama pants that looked way too similar to Flannel Girl's shirt, and he scratched the skin under his waistband as he approached the scene outside his door.

"Real prize," Elijah said.

Sequoia chuckled, even though she knew it wasn't an appropriate response. Why did everything about Elijah Sawyer make her want to behave inappropriately?

"SO WHY DID you show up at the Peaceful Breeze tonight?"

Sequoia had arrived back at the office a few minutes before Elijah. After citing and releasing Shelly Marvin and Flannel Girl (who Elijah escorted back to her own place), Elijah and Sequoia had parted ways, and hadn't seen each other again for the rest of the shift.

"Just giving you some backup," Elijah said, again.

"I didn't need backup."

Elijah sat in his own chair, then spun towards his desk so his back was to her. "You did, too. You almost got punched in the face. More than once."

Sequoia plopped down into her chair. "I did not."

"Yes, you did."

"Okay, fine. I did. But I was fine."

"Look," Elijah said. "Don't get your panties in a bunch. I know you're perfectly capable. I heard your call on the radio, and figured you might need backup. I'd do it for anyone."

Although something inside her bristled, she tamped it down. "Thank you," she said. "But I had it handled."

"I'm sure you did," Elijah said. "Right up until you got punched in the face, knocked unconscious, and sent to the ER. After those three tweakers killed each other in a brawl."

"That wouldn't happen," Sequoia said to the back of his chair.

"That's what you think," Elijah said. "But I've seen it happen."

Sequoia shrugged, even though she knew he couldn't see her. "Wouldn't happen to me."

"So you say."

"Oh, my God. Do you think I'm a crappy cop, or what?"

"Not at all," Elijah said. Now he spun his chair around so he was facing her. She continued facing the computer so he had to look at her profile.

He went on, "But what would you have done if I didn't show up? Keep standing there, holding the two ladies apart, hoping not to get the crap beat out of you?"

He had a point.

"I'm not sure," Sequoia said. She took her fingers off her keyboard and turned her own chair so they were face-to-face. "I admit, I was feeling like I was in a bit of a pinch."

Now, Elijah laughed, and her belly reacted. "In a bit of a pinch," he said. "Definitely. Look, I heard the call come out and I knew it was going to be a cluster. I didn't have anything going at the moment, and knowing how the Peaceful Breeze can be, I didn't like the idea of you, or any cop, being alone there, with at least two criminals. So I backed you up. Just in case. And for the record, I'd do it for any of my co-workers. Not just for you."

"Sounds reasonable," Sequoia said. "Thanks for being there. But for the record, I didn't need you. I had it under control."

"Okay," Elijah said, drawing out the word in a way that reminded her of one of her sisters. Probably Holly.

"What?" she said. "I did have it under control."

"Yeah," Elijah said, "I could tell."

She could probably never prove to him that she had a plan for making things work. But there would be no point. He'd never believe her, until he saw it in action.

"No, you couldn't," she said.

"You almost got punched in the kisser. Not once, but twice," he said.

"Keyword: almost."

"Why is it so hard for you to say thank you?"

"It's not," she said. "I already said, 'Thanks for being there.' Remember that?"

"You didn't want to," Elijah said.

"True," Sequoia said. "But I did, and isn't that what's most important?"

"I'm not sure. I think your gratitude is the most important, actually. You, like most lady cops, have that thing going on, where you feel like you don't want to admit you need help, even though we all need help at one point or another."

Sequoia had read an article once that said a person's pupils dilated when she was attracted to someone. Her pupils were probably dilated right now. All this banter turned her on, for some reason. Men didn't usually banter with her. Probably because she came across as a grumpy woman, not to be bantered with, ever.

"Yeah, I might have that thing going on." She shrugged, and then she did something she'd rarely—if ever—done before: she grinned at a man. She grinned at Elijah Sawyer.

And, to make things even weirder, he grinned back.

They remained there, grinning at each other, for quite some time before Sequoia finally realized it had been quite some time and said, "Wait. Did you just call me a lady cop?"

"I'd hold the door for you, that's all I'm saying."

Although Sequoia rolled her eyes and turned away from him again, muttering something about old-fashioned chivalry being sexism in disguise, she didn't mean it, not even a little.

She'd love for Elijah Sawyer to hold a door for her.

Sequoia and Elijah worked in silence for a few moments, and Sequoia had to fight with her brain to keep her mind off Elijah and his chivalry so she could type up her report on the Marvins.

She didn't even like chivalry. It was often a disguise for misogyny. Even as the thought formed, she knew it was a lie.

Not all chivalrous men were misogynists. Walt Walters was, and he had been the king of chivalry, opening every door (even the car door) when they were out in public. He always insisted on pushing the shopping cart at the grocery store, bargaining on car prices, and carrying heavy stuff.

Of course, these were all things of which Sequoia was capable, and it always irritated her, just a little, when he insisted on doing them. Walt was probably the exception to the rule, though. Chivalry was simply good manners.

Mindfulness.

Sequoia reminded herself then that her chivalry-related irritation resulted from her own fear of winding up alone. If she couldn't let a man open a door for her, she couldn't accept a small kindness. And if she couldn't accept a small kindness, how could she give one?

Which is exactly why she wasn't girlfriend or wife material.

"So, the Marvins are regulars?" Elijah's voice cut into her thoughts, and it was so smooth and sexy, like the strum of a guitar string, that she was grateful she'd just had that little talk with herself.

"Yeah," she said. "I see them at least once a week. I've broken up their fights, calmed them down when they've been disorderly, helped them jumpstart their car when its battery died in the middle of the road, you name it."

"Wait. You know how to jump start a car?"

"Shut up."

He chuckled.

"Funny guy," she said.

"It's a talent," he said.

Even though Sequoia didn't turn around when she heard the office door open, she knew right away it was Beth Hardwick. She could sense that woman's presence like she could hear the chop of a helicopter's blades overhead. Remembering her resolution to be extra nice to her supervisor, she spun around in her chair.

"Hey, Beth," she said. "How's it going?"

Instead of answering, Beth said, "I heard you were over at the Marvin place again."

As if Sequoia hung out there, rolling joints and taking shots.

"Yeah. Another domestic dispute. Denny hooked up with this husky lady in a flannel. Shelly was pissed. They fought about it. Husky flannel lady showed up, and she and Shelly fought over Denny. Who, I must say, is not much of a catch, himself."

To Sequoia's surprise, Beth snorted. "Yeah. No kidding. Anyway, I think you need to throw them both in jail the next time you see them."

This directive immediately put Sequoia on edge. She had spent a lot of time with the Marvins, but throwing them in jail wasn't going to help anybody. Right now, they may be losers, but they both held down jobs and paid their rent. They were a nuisance, but only to one another. They didn't belong locked up.

Still, Sequoia knew better than to argue with Beth, so she just nodded.

Then Elijah piped up. "I don't think they belong in jail, Hardwick. They're idiots, but they both have paying jobs. In jail, they're just a drain on taxpayers."

Beth snorted again. Sequoia imagined her stomping her foot like a toddler in the beginning stages of a tantrum. Beth said, "They're a drain on taxpayers now. Carr, your fellow officer here, spends so much time at their apartment I've started to think they're inviting her over for tea and crumpets every week. The taxpayers of Seabreeze are paying one cop's entire salary just for her to deal with this couple, who, as you've both just said, aren't actually that much of a problem. So throw 'em in jail and let Carr here deal with real crime."

"Agree to disagree?" Elijah said.

Sequoia snickered and turned away from him and went back to writing her report. She couldn't concentrate, though, because Beth said, "No. I do not agree to disagree. I'm your superior, which means you're my inferior. And as such, you're bound to do what I say. Is that clear? The next time either one of you crosses paths with either one of the Marvins, I expect at least one of those losers to go to jail. Clear?"

"Crystal," Elijah said. "Crystal clear."

Sequoia didn't answer at first, but then Beth was standing beside her desk, one hand on the back of her chair. "Carr?"

"I got it, Hardwick."

Beth went into her own office and shut the door. Sequoia hated that woman. She didn't usually feel so strongly about people, but Beth Hardwick was a dirty cop and a bad supervisor. She was definitely involved with the department's missing money scandal, and even though Sequoia had long since decided to put her head down, ignore the scandal (and all of Jasmine's splashy newspaper stories about it), and do good police work, her internal investigative sensors were going off.

Beth Hardwick was supervising an entire group of police officers, and she was leading them in the wrong direction. Someone had to stop her. The way the woman operated though—killing off people who got too close, like the old public information officer, Earl Little —Sequoia knew it was best to avoid being that someone.

She looked at her computer's clock. Twelve minutes left on her shift, and then she could go for a run.

CHAPTER SIX

At exactly six a.m., Sequoia turned off her computer. Tense and jumpy thanks to Beth's behavior, she felt anxious to lace up her running shoes. Elijah was just standing up, as well.

"Going for a run?" he said.

"Every day," she said.

He looked taken aback at her brusque tone, and although she wanted to soften it by saying something else, she didn't. No use leading him on.

"Want company?" he said.

So this man was not to be deterred.

"Um, no," Sequoia said. This time, she did lessen the blow as well as she knew how. "Thanks for the offer. It's not you. I like my alone time."

She liked it so much, in fact, that she was already walking towards the locker room.

"It's not like I'd be talking to you," Elijah said. "I can't run and talk at the same time, anyway."

"You'd probably slow me down."

As she walked away, she glanced over her shoulder at him. He stood there in his uniform, hands in his pockets, with the most interesting look on his face. His eyes were narrowed and his lips were pursed. He didn't look angry or upset or embarrassed, Sequoia thought. He looked puzzled, like he was trying to figure something out.

No, that wasn't it. He was trying to figure someone out, and she had no doubt that that someone was her. Now she gave him a genuine smile, one she knew bordered on devilish. He'd never figure her out. And even if he did, he'd be disappointed.

"Game on, Sawyer," she whispered. She walked into the locker room to change into her running pants, and hoped to hell he'd see her when she came out.

She got lucky. Elijah was in his car in the parking lot as she exited the building. Even if he wasn't checking out how she looked in her pants, he had the opportunity.

Just when she felt like gloating inside, she realized what she was doing and wanted to kick herself. Who cared if Elijah Sawyer saw her in her running pants? Who cared if he was trying to figure her out?

This couldn't end well. There was no way for either of them to come out of the situation satisfied.

Without looking back, Sequoia began her warmup, walking fast away from the police station and toward the Seabreeze Transit station.

She *could* enjoy Elijah's attention for however long it took for him to realize she was cold and incapable of changing. But she didn't want to deal with the repercussions that realization would bring. And even if Elijah enjoyed interacting with Sequoia now, that couldn't last.

So, she'd keep her running tights to herself. She started to jog, slowly, keeping her heart rate low. At the transit station, she found Julie, whose expression actually conveyed happiness and friendship. Surprised, Sequoia gave her a little wave and dug the sandwich out of her pack. Julie had never smiled at her before, and Sequoia slowed all the way to a stop as she handed her the food.

"I got a job interview!" Julie said.

Sequoia felt emotion rising up in her chest, and reached down to hug Julie. Then, embarrassed, she straightened up. "That's great," she said. "Where is it?"

"It's at Turn the Page, that bookstore downtown? Just stocking the shelves, organizing, that kind of thing."

"That's awesome," Sequoia said, and for once, she actually meant it. "When is it?"

"It's tomorrow."

Her reflex, born out of innumerable conversations with her sisters, was to fire a bunch of questions at Julie: What are you going to wear? How will you do your hair? Mascara only, or mascara and eyeliner?

These questions seemed intrusive, so instead of asking them, Sequoia gave Julie's shoulder a quick squeeze and said, "Good luck. I can't wait to hear how it goes."

As she jogged away, she felt moisture on her cheeks.

"Huh," she said to herself. "This is a strange, strange day."

Because things were already topsy turvy, Sequoia decided to change up her route, too. She ran down to East Cliff Drive and followed it up the coast to her favorite lookout spot. From the edge of the high cliff, she could see surfers riding waves, the bright, early morning sun sparkling on the sea, and boats bobbing here and there, tiny white dots against the bright blue-green water.

Then she looked down at the bronze sign next to the fence: "Lovers' Point."

She groaned, turned around, and ran back to the police station. Then she kicked herself for looking for Elijah in the parking lot.

Not for the first time in recent days, she said, "What the hell is wrong with me?"

SEQUOIA DIDN'T CONSIDER herself a needy person when it came to human interaction. The opposite was probably true. Walt Walters was her witness. He told her she wasn't needy enough. Which she thought was stupid.

But after the strange mix of feelings she'd experienced around her time with Elijah, and the strange emotional response she'd had to Julie getting a job interview, she felt like she needed some conversation with an unbiased outsider.

She didn't want to call Alex Light since she'd just called him a few days ago. So she moved down to the next person on her list: George Harrison. The two of them had established a friends-with-benefits relationship early on, when they met at Champs sports bar shortly after her breakup with Walt. Tipsy on half a pitcher of cheap beer, Sequoia had told him, "I'm not relationship material, but I'd sure like to take you home."

After an entire evening of great conversation that ranged in topic from gun control to contemporary art and holistic healthcare to life on Mars, the chemistry was building up to decent. They held conflicting opinions on every single topic, but enjoyed one another's company enough that the sex was satisfactory. They agreed that they could never last long-term because their fundamental values were so different, but that they'd meet up for great discussions and solid sex whenever they felt like it.

She truly enjoyed George's company, and sometimes wished she'd been more like Holly, kind of hippie-meets-beauty-queen. Holly would be perfect for George, if only she enjoyed debating (but she always got her feelings hurt).

For now, Sequoia enjoyed letting George scratch her itch. Scratching his wasn't so bad, either.

He showed up on her doorstep with takeout containers and a bottle of wine, and she greeted him with a corkscrew. They sat at her kitchen bar and ate spaghetti straight out of white Styrofoam containers with plastic forks. She poured the wine into plain glass tumblers, and they clinked glasses.

"So, it's been a while," George said. "Why tonight?"

He always opened their evenings with questions like that, questions that put Sequoia on the spot and opened the floor for discussions.

She shrugged. "Just wanted some human company, you know, beyond a bed buddy."

"I feel honored," he said. "Especially since you know I read the paper, and you know I'm going to grill you about that sister of yours."

Sequoia sighed. "I hadn't even thought about that. I should have known, but I was just thinking about what a strange day it's been, and I thought it would be nice to discuss it with someone other than that sister of mine. Or that other sister of mine."

"I'm intrigued," George said. "Do tell."

It might be awkward to delve into the details of her strange new relationship with Elijah, so she skipped that and instead told him about her emotional reaction to Julie's impending job interview. She told him about how she'd hugged Julie, and how she barely ever wanted to hug anyone.

"Wow. Your human emotions emerge," George said. "I never would have guessed."

She slapped his arm, and he tucked a strand of hair behind her ear. He stood up to collect their Styrofoam dishes, and leaned forward to kiss her on the nose before carrying the containers to the trash can. When he came back, he held out a hand and led her to the living room.

"Want to talk for a while?" he said. "Or are you all maxed out on the human emotions and ready to hop into bed?"

"This is why I so enjoy your company," Sequoia said. "Let's chat for a while."

As an afterthought, she went back to the bar to grab the wine. She refilled their tumblers and set the wine on the coffee table.

"So what's got you all ferklumpt?" George said.

Sequoia took a gulp of wine and took her time answering. "I have no idea."

"Is it related to that sister of yours?"

"Jasmine?"

"Yeah," George said. "Who's suddenly become a serious reporter determined to oust your boss as a thief?"

"Well, when you put it that way," Sequoia said. "I mean, the truth is that I feel like she's finally doing something respectable. Instead of writing about school picture day or the science fair she's writing about stuff people actually care about. And what's crazy is that *she* cares about it. You know? Like, it's important to her. Plus, she's got this new guy, Hudson. He's great. And I'm just here, doing the same old thing. Alone."

When it looked like he was going to respond, she held up a hand. "You know I don't mind being alone. I think it's my, you know, destiny or Fate or whatever. But I feel like I'm kind of missing that human connection. Or something. It sounds weird. But I think you know what I mean."

"Doesn't work give you that human connection?" George asked.

"Not the kind I want."

He laughed. "Well, I guess that's true."

"I mean, I feel like my work's important. I'm good at it. But is that—*this*—all there is? Anyway, enough about that."

"Wait. I've never heard you muse about whether work is all there is."

"I don't know what I'm saying," Sequoia said. "Maybe I've had too much wine."

George looked at her still-full cup of wine and raised an eyebrow. "You've probably had a total of half a glass. I hardly believe the wine's affecting you."

"You're probably right. I don't know where that came from. That was weird of me to say."

"That was weird of you," George said. "But I kind of feel like you meant it."

"Stop analyzing me," Sequoia said.

"I thought that's why you called me here."

"Maybe it is. Or maybe I just wanted you to scratch my itch."

"Are you lonely, Sequoia Carr?"

Out of nowhere, panic rushed in. It filled every corner, every crevice of her being. Was she lonely? Were her interactions with Elijah Sawyer making her lonely? Or, bringing existing loneliness to light? Or was it something else? Was she jealous of Jasmine's relationship with Hudson? Or did she really want companionship of her own?

"Maybe I need to get a dog," she said.

George guffawed. "That is the most ridiculous thing I've heard in quite some time. You don't even like dogs."

"Hate them." She nodded and picked at piece of dried spaghetti sauce on the leg of her jeans.

"But the fact that you're considering it makes me think you're lonely."

"Shit. And stop laughing. It's not funny."

"I knew the great Sequoia Carr would change, eventually," George said. "We all get lonely."

"But I'm too complicated to be with someone else," she said.

George motioned to her wine, and she took another drink. "Look," he said. "I don't want to tell you what to do. And more than most people, I understand that you feel like you're complicated. Shit, you *are* complicated. But I think that if you're lonely, you need to reevaluate your projected long-term status. You know? Like, you need to just go with the flow."

"There is no flow."

"What do you call this?"

"I mean, this flows," Sequoia said, "but, neither one of us thinks this is serious. Every time I say good-bye to you in the doorway, I almost expect it to be the last time. I expect you to find someone who wants something long-term, and to never come back."

George was silent for a moment. Sequoia took another drink of her wine.

"You expect me never to come back because you imagine I'll find someone better than you."

"Better for you," Sequoia corrected him. "I mean, I'm a great catch."

"You are a great catch," George said. "I think we agree that we wouldn't be compatible, over time. We'd probably fight over politics, religion, child-rearing, you name it. And honestly, I think that's why you seek me out. You don't have to worry about the future at all. We enjoy each other, but you don't feel any pressure. All I'm saying is, maybe it's time for you to branch out."

"Branch out?"

"Yeah. You know, like date some people. Go on real dates. As if you might actually keep dating them. Not some detailed friends with benefits agreement, or sex-only agreement, or whatever. 'Sign on this line,' you know? But, like, normal dating."

"Normal dating?" Sequoia said. "What's that?"

For the first time in their relationship, George left Sequoia's house without removing a single article of clothing from either of their bodies. As always, Sequoia found the conversation pleasant. And strangely, she didn't feel disappointed that they hadn't done the deed.

When George walked out the door—after giving her one more kiss on the forehead and pouring the rest of the wine into her cup—she felt filled up in a whole different way. She couldn't say why, but it was similar to the sensation she'd experienced after Julie told her about the job interview.

For a few seconds, she allowed a film reel to play in her imagination, one in which she went to the animal shelter and walked up and down the corridors looking for a dog to adopt. When her imaginary self stopped in front of a particular kennel and knelt down to the dog's eye level, she shook her actual self.

"You're crazy, Carr," she said. "You don't need a dog any more than you need a long-term boyfriend."

CHAPTER SEVEN

"How was your run the other morning, without me?"

Elijah had stopped by Sequoia's desk at the start of their shift, and now took what Sequoia recognized as his typical stance: feet set wide apart, arms crossed, as if to convey he wasn't going anywhere.

"Very satisfying, thank you," she said. She purposely avoided eye contact with him, pretending to take a deep interest in her email.

"Don't you get lonely?" he said.

That word again. Sequoia shrugged a shoulder. "Do you?"

"I would if I were you."

"How do you know? If you were me, you probably wouldn't."

"How far did you run?"

Why was he changing the course of the conversation? This seemed very suspicious. She couldn't remember exactly how far she'd run, only that she'd ended up at Lovers' Point, so she said, "I don't know, six or seven miles, probably."

He nodded, but didn't move. He was likely casting about for some random topic to discuss.

"What else do you do for fun?"

"I don't really do fun," she said, putting finger quotes on "fun." "Sometimes I watch a show or something."

"So when you're home, alone, what do you do?" he said.

"I don't know, projects or something," she said.

"Home improvement projects?" he said.

This elicited a dirty look from Sequoia, who was about as handy with a hammer as she was with a glue gun. She pictured the one wreath she'd tried to make, and the resulting web of hot glue stuck in her hair and to her fingertips. She shook her head. "No, usually research projects."

"Research projects?" he said.

"Did I mumble?"

"Do you hang out at the library?"

Sequoia turned her chair around to face him now. His expression held a little humor, but something else, too. Something she recognized from her own interrogations. Again, he was trying to figure her out. He was trying to dig deep, get an answer to a question he might not have identified yet.

"What is this?" she said.

Elijah's grin came fast. "It's a social conversation, Carr."

She rolled her eyes. "In social conversations, people use each other's first names."

"Do they?"

"Um, yeah. They do."

"Sequoia," he said, trying it on. "I like that."

For some reason she couldn't identify, hearing him speak her name sent a shiver over her skin. This reaction annoyed her. Fortunately, default mode kicked in.

"This isn't a social setting," she said. "Sawyer."

"Let me guess. You don't do social settings."

She thought of Alex Light and George Harrison. Did she consider her interactions with the two of them social? They were social on the surface, but they also fulfilled other, specific purposes. In that way, they were like business transactions. In a pinch, though, she'd consider them social relationships. She wasn't going to let Elijah Sawyer put her in a pinch.

"Not really," she said. "Which leads me to *my* question for *you*: don't you have work to do?"

"That was good," he said. "You're good."

"I am good. But seriously. Don't you have anything better to do?"

"Better than this? Nope. Can't say that I do. Do you have any pets? A cat? You seem like a cat person. Aloof."

"No pets. I'm not that needy. My sister, Jasmine, has a dog. Of course. And I'm not aloof. I'm just quiet. Again: don't you have anything better to do?"

"Nah. This is it," he said.

"Beth Hardwick would say differently," Sequoia said, "and I have a feeling she'll be in here, snooping around, looking for mistakes any minute."

"You're probably right." With that, Elijah dropped his arms, grinned at her again, and walked to his own desk, calling over his shoulder, "To be continued, Sequoia."

Sequoia didn't answer.

She could have said something childish, like, "It's Carr to you," but she didn't. Why did he want to carry on a social conversation with her? Why was he determined to change the way she'd been socializing for the past five years? It made no sense. What really made no sense, though, was why she was still thinking about it.

So she shifted gears. Instead of wondering about Elijah's motivations, she continued preparing for her own workday. When she looked at the computer screen and realized she'd never even opened —much less read—the first new email in the system, she rolled her eyes.

Elijah Sawyer was an unnecessary distraction. Already. And they hadn't even slept together yet.

Wait—is there a "yet"? Are we going to sleep together?

"Where did that come from?" Sequoia realized she'd spoken aloud and looked around to see if anyone else noticed.

The office was empty, aside from Elijah, and from what she could tell, he was busy typing away on the computer. Not that anyone would think twice about her talking to herself. She did it all the time.

Her computer dinged, signaling a private message from someone else on the network. She clicked the messaging program to open it, and couldn't help but notice the little shiver that ran up her neck when when she saw the note was from Elijah.

I'll show you where that came from.

She shook her head. So he had heard her. She'd been foolish to think he wasn't paying attention.

She clicked "Reply," typed, *Get back to work. You're distracting me,* and then clicked "Send" before she realized the implications of what she'd written.

Am I?

No. Leave me alone.

I'm working. You leave ME alone.

She'd ignore him. She'd finish checking her emails and the call log, and then she'd head out, without paying him another single iota of attention. After a few seconds of silence, her computer dinged again.

Are you ignoring me?

On a loud sigh, Sequoia stood up, turned off her computer, and headed out to her patrol car. If she could just get out on the road, she could settle into her rhythm and forget about Elijah Sawyer. Even as the thought formed, though, she felt something like a smile tugging at the corners of her mouth.

The shift squeaked by. Few stops and even fewer calls made it feel like twenty hours instead of ten. Sequoia spent most of her time sitting in the car, patrolling for speeders or drunks, waiting for dispatch to call her out. Fortunately, the citizens of Seabreeze were relatively well-behaved tonight. It was unfortunate, too, because the quiet overnight hours were empty of diversions, which meant Sequoia had lots of time in the dark to ponder the newest human distraction.

As she sat on the side of the highway, she wondered what Elijah was doing. She saw him cruise by, once in each direction, and wondered if he was checking to see what she was up to. She then kicked herself for thinking about him, for even *kind of* assuming that he was driving by her on purpose. This conundrum was precisely the kind of thing that got women in trouble. They became smitten, or as Jasmine's boss was so fond of saying, "twitterpated."

Finally, the shift ended and Sequoia sneaked into the locker room to change into her running clothes before sneaking back out to go for her run. Elijah was nowhere in sight. "Thank goodness."

Anxious to see Julie Sandusky, Sequoia did a short warm-up and then hit the sidewalk at a pace slightly faster than usual.

Julie was sitting at her spot on the bench, and she stood up when Sequoia rounded the corner. Sequoia could tell right away from her posture, from the way she tried to control her expression, that the news was good. Still, she resisted the urge to pump her fist or let out a war cry or a big cheer until Julie nodded and held her hands out to her sides, palms up.

Then something like joy overcame Sequoia, and she did raise her fist, whoop, and jump. She picked up her pace and was surprised when she found herself with her arms around an equally surprised Julie.

"You got it?" Sequoia said.

"I got it," Julie said. "I can't believe it."

"I guess you won't be needing my sandwiches any more," Sequoia said.

Over the course of her next five miles, she thought about how she and Julie had met, three years ago. Sequoia had always thought Julie seemed too wise, too smart, to end up with a loser like Trenton Washington. Those smarts had made her a superstar informant.

Until he caught her.

Yes, Julie had broken the law, transporting illegal drugs for sale. And even though she'd served her time, Sequoia knew Beth Hardwick wouldn't appreciate Sequoia doing Julie favors.

Now she was approaching the end of her run, and she pushed thoughts of Beth Hardwick out of her mind. She wouldn't let that woman ruin her good mood.

Sequoia couldn't hear the yelling from outside. So it came as a surprise when, still in her euphoric, post-run state, she opened the door to the police station and heard Beth Hardwick's voice.

"I told you to arrest at *least* one of them. I think I made myself pretty clear, didn't I?"

Before she came into Beth's line of sight, Sequoia froze.

Elijah's voice responded to Beth: "You did make it pretty clear. But neither of them were committing a crime."

"Their existence is a crime."

Sequoia nodded to herself. The Marvins' existence was a crime and in of itself, but not one for which any cop could rightfully (or legally) arrest them. What could possibly have happened? How could Elijah have crossed paths with them? She hadn't heard anything come out on the radio. Unless it had happened right at the end of shift, between her getting out of the car and walking into the office. Still, she should have heard it on her portable radio.

"You can't arrest someone for existing," Elijah said. He sounded testy.

"You could come up with a charge."

"A bullshit one."

A beat of silence.

Then Elijah spoke again. "Look, Beth. It wasn't even a call. I stumbled upon them when I stopped to grab a soda on my way back to the office. Wrong place, wrong time. Shelly was pissed at me because I pulled her off that lumberjack of a woman the other night. I'm not going to arrest her for calling me an asshole."

"I gave you an order."

Incredulity colored Elijah's speech when he responded: "Name-calling isn't against the law, Beth. Freedom of speech."

"Well, it's against *policy* to ignore a direct order," Beth said.

Sequoia, still pressed up against the hallway in the entry, rolled her eyes. The order had been stupid.

"You gonna write me up?" Elijah said.

Although Sequoia couldn't see Beth, she imagined her shrugging one shoulder. "I have to now, don't I? I said I would."

Sequoia stalked into the office. "Oh, get a handle on yourself, Beth," she said. "You can't write him up for not arresting Shelly or Denny any more than he can arrest Shelly for calling him an asshole."

Beth's head swiveled from Elijah to Sequoia. "Were you eaves-dropping?"

"Just dropped in."

Now, Beth's eyes raked over Sequoia, from her disheveled pony-tail to her sweaty tank top to her leggings. "Aren't you off the clock?"

"Just came back to change. I walked in and heard you guys talking."

Elijah, for his part, remained silent.

"Maybe I should write you up, too."

Sequoia shrugged. "I don't give a shit. I wouldn't write Shelly up for calling me an asshole. Especially if I were Sawyer. I mean, she's speaking the truth."

She'd been hoping this joke would soften Beth up, make her dismiss the whole event as ludicrous. But Beth's glare only hardened.

"Was I clear, or was I not, when I told both of you that at least one of the Marvins was to be arrested the next time you came into contact with them?"

"You were clear," Sequoia said. "Like I said. Crystal. And I think Sawyer's acknowledged that, too. But you can't expect him to arrest Shelly for being at the same convenience store where Sawyer was. That's a bullshit charge. The paper gets a hold of this and you're going to be sorry. You'll be worse off than you are now."

Mentioning the newspaper was a mistake, Sequoia realized within a nanosecond. A major mistake.

"How will the paper get a hold of this, Carr?"

Of course, she was insinuating that Sequoia would say something to Jasmine. Finally, Elijah found his voice.

"Sequoia's been very professional ever since her sister took the police beat, Beth. Everything Jasmine gets is public record. I don't like what you're implying."

"Either Carr's been leaking stuff to her sister, or you have," Beth said. "Did you hear how easily that rolled off Carr's tongue? She said, 'The paper gets a hold of this and you're going to be sorry.' That was a threat. Clearly."

Sequoia rolled her eyes.

"Is there some kind of secret love triangle going on here?" Beth had narrowed her eyes, and she was looking from Elijah to Sequoia wildly. "The two of you and that pesky *Daily Trumpet* reporter?"

"I'm not listening to this," Elijah said.

He would have walked out then, but Beth stopped him with a hand on his arm as he passed her. "Not so fast. I have a couple of papers to fill out before the two of you leave."

In the end, she wrote them both up; Elijah for disobeying a direct command, and Sequoia for insubordination. Then she marched into her own office, slammed the door, and drew the blinds.

Left alone in the main office, Sequoia and Elijah stared at each other.

"I think this calls for breakfast," Elijah said.

Too stunned to disagree, Sequoia found herself seated across from Elijah in a booth at the Jupiter Café fifteen minutes later.

"First write-up?" Sequoia said after the server brought them coffee.

"Yep. You?"

"Nah, it's my fourth," Sequoia said. "It's not such a big deal after the second time. You'll get used to it."

"That woman is insane," Elijah said. "It's kind of scary. I haven't told Jasmine anything that veers from the official script, yet, but Beth's behavior today makes me think I should."

A few minutes passed, during which neither of them spoke. The server came back to take their orders, and Sequoia resisted the urge to tease Elijah for ordering an egg-white omelet with avocado, especially after she ordered a lumberjack omelet with sausage and bacon.

Sequoia sipped her coffee, black, and Elijah doctored his up with sugar.

"You're ruining perfectly good coffee," she said to him.

"So, tell me about your other write-ups. Did you get written up for being a smart-ass?"

"Ha. Very funny," Sequoia said. "I'm just rebellious, I guess. I got written up once for taking Julie Sandusky to rehab. On the clock. That was the first time."

"Who's Julie Sandusky?"

Sequoia realized too late that she had just blurted out Julie's full name. Since being written up for taking Julie to rehab, she'd always been so careful not to mention her to co-workers, or even to her sisters. She'd realized that being too close to someone she met through work, especially in her line of work, could be dangerous.

"Oh, she's just this woman I know. An acquaintance, I guess."

"She the lady you bring sandwiches to every day?" Elijah said.

"How do you know about that?" Sequoia's first reaction was anger, mostly because she was afraid someone like Beth Hardwick would find out she still brought food to Julie. It was off the clock, but still. The wrong person might see it as a conflict of interest. Had Elijah been spying on her? Had he followed her on a run?

"Wow," Elijah said. "I can practically see the wheels turning. Why don't you want to talk about it?"

The server brought their breakfast, which gave Sequoia a moment to think before answering.

"It's not that I don't want to talk about it," she said after taking a bite of her eggs. "It's just that I like to keep the various components of my life separate. You're in the work component. She's not."

"So, your life is a drawer and you've got a really great drawer organizer in there?"

"Exactly."

"And it really bugs you when something gets into the wrong compartment," Elijah said.

"Finally. Someone who really gets me."

She'd meant it as a joke, but saying it out loud felt eerily true. He let her off easy on that one, and instead of calling her out on it, he moved on: "So, why'd you take her to rehab?"

"She needed to go. She asked for help, and she didn't have anyone else. So I took her. I mean, it was like a ten-minute drive or something. Not even an hour out of my day. How often do trouble-makers ask for help when we're arresting them?" Sequoia was quick to amend, "Not that she was a troublemaker originally, when I first met her, but she had a down swing. Hit rock bottom. I took her to rehab. That's that. I don't think it was worth getting written up for, but apparently Beth Hardwick did. She wasn't my supervisor back then, but she convinced our sergeant, Lester, remember him?"

"Guy with the underbite."

"Right. She convinced him to write me up."

Elijah nodded as he scooped some of his egg whites onto a piece of whole wheat toast. "She's a real piece of work. So, why do you bring this Julie person sandwiches every day?"

"You never told me how you know I bring her sandwiches every day. And it's not always sandwiches. Sometimes it's a burrito."

"I have eyes everywhere."

"Huh. I do it because we're acquaintances. And I don't have very many of those."

"Friends?"

"I wouldn't call us friends, exactly."

Then Sequoia remembered that moment a couple of hours before, when she'd celebrated with Julie over the job at Turn the Page.

"You're smiling," Elijah said. "Like you just realized you *would* call her a friend."

"Maybe I would," Sequoia said. "Don't put me on the spot."

"So what were your other two write-ups for, before today?"

Sequoia chuckled. In the moment, getting in trouble didn't feel even slightly humorous. But now time had passed, and she felt like she could defend herself against the letters in her file.

"Don't laugh," she said to him. "The second time I got written up was for shopping on the clock."

"You don't seem like much of a shopper," Elijah said.

"Tell me about it." She sipped her coffee. "Good ol' Hardwick acted like I did it for fun, like I went out on a spree and bought myself a bunch of nylons with the police department credit card."

"Do you even own nylons?"

"Exactly. No, I don't. I ran into that stupid superstore thing for ten minutes. Yes, it was on the clock. But it was in the middle of my shift and I didn't want to wait five hours."

"What were you buying?"

"Oh—you'll love this. I was buying some shoes for this homeless guy. He had really big feet. Save the jokes, please. He wore a size fifteen or something, and the shelter never could find him shoes. He was wearing these old boots with giant holes in the toes. He had these really expensive, fancy wool socks underneath, and you could always see them poking through. They were in really bright colors. I always imagined they came from Peru or something, you know? Llama's wool or something? Anyway, one day I was on a call at the Seabreeze Transit station and I noticed one of those beautiful socks had a huge hole in it. His toes were visible. It was cold, really cold, and a big storm was coming in. It was supposed to rain for days. So I bought him new boots. Seriously. Ten minutes in the store. Fifty bucks of my own money. Hardwick had Lester the Bulldog write me up for that, too."

Reliving the memory had Sequoia worked up again, so she paused to take a deep breath and an even deeper drink of her coffee.

"It was that Armageddon guy, wasn't it?"

Elijah's eyes sparkled over the rim of his own coffee cup.

Sequoia pictured the Armageddon guy, his tall, colorful socks sticking out of the tops of his boots under his pink tutu.

"Yeah." She nodded, paused. "I know. He's crazy. He punched me once. Right in the arm. He probably has no idea I bought him those boots. But he wears them. At least he didn't get frostbite."

"You're a very interesting person, Sequoia Carr," Elijah said.

"I hate to tell you this, but you're not the first to say so," Sequoia said.

"Why are you still single?"

Sequoia's back went up faster than she could stop herself from sneering at him. "And we were having such a nice time," she said. "How do you know I'm single?"

He gestured at her left hand. "You don't wear a ring. You use the same last name as your sister. And you're awful prickly. I'll bet you don't let anybody get close enough to carry on an actual relationship."

For some reason, his honesty—and the fact that he used the same word to describe her that Jasmine used to describe him (prickly)—smoothed her hackles. "All true," she said. "You should go into detective work."

"I know. I should. Which means I can't let you evade me. So why are you still single?"

Sequoia was so tired. She'd worked all night, gone for a run, experienced a strange moment of connection with Julie Sandusky, and argued with Beth Hardwick, all before actually enjoying this breakfast (which, she reminded herself, was absolutely not a date) with an extremely handsome man.

Pure exhaustion was the main factor contributing to her honesty. It was the only explanation, she thought. A tiny voice from somewhere deep in the recesses of her brain piped up to say that Elijah himself might be another explanation for her strange behavior, but she told it to shut up.

"It's pretty simple," she said. "I'm just not relationship material."

She was surprised—pleasantly so—when he didn't respond right away. His face took on that same contemplative expression.

Then he signaled for the bill. She was unpleasantly surprised when he looked her right in the eye and said, "That's bullshit."

CHAPTER EIGHT

Beth Hardwick was waiting for Sequoia at the start of her next shift. Sequoia wondered whether the woman ever slept, and then reminded herself that she lacked many of the characteristics of a normal human, including empathy and sanity, and was probably wired to run on little to no sleep.

"Hi, Beth," Sequoia said, infusing her voice with as much sugar as she could muster. "Is there a reason you're sitting in my chair?"

Beth, apparently not wired for pleasantries, either, skipped the greetings and said, "I'm moving you, Carr."

"To your office?"

Beth raised an eyebrow. "Funny. You're a real comedienne."

Although Sequoia's heart was beating fast and she wanted to demand, "Where are you moving me?" she remained silent.

"I'm putting you back on day shift," Beth said. "It's actually more like a promotion."

"What? You're promoting me after you just wrote me up for arguing with you about not arresting someone for not committing a crime? This really couldn't be any less confusing."

Beth smiled, a thin, humorless smile that made Sequoia want to hide under the nearest piece of furniture. But since that was her desk, and Beth was sitting at it, Sequoia stood her ground.

"It's simple," Beth said. "You're going to be filling that position in the K-9 unit until we can find a permanent replacement for Mack. As you probably know, he's retiring soon, and we need to get someone in and trained before then."

"The K-9 unit?"

"Did I not speak clearly?"

Beth's eyes were alight with malignant victory.

"No, you did speak clearly. It's just that I am positive I'm not the right person for that position. I think everyone here knows how I feel about dogs."

Panic, a strong and forceful tide, rose in Sequoia's chest. The way she felt about dogs was a running joke in the office. Most people assumed everyone liked dogs, and were surprised and alarmed when someone, especially a woman, didn't.

It all started when the department bought a new K-9 and the handler brought it into the office to show it off. It was a female, and someone had named it Xena, after the warrior princess. For some reason, the stupid dog ran up to her and sat down at her feet, wagging its tail. Xena's eyes were focused and bright, her pointy ears stood on end, and she tilted her head. And waited.

For what, Sequoia didn't know. So after a cursory glance at the dog, she went back to her work. Still, the dog sat there. Its tail made swishing noises on the carpet. All the other cops stopped what they were doing to watch. Sequoia, on the other hand, refused to stop what she was doing. The dog didn't distract her (too much), but the silence—as people waited to see what she'd do—did.

Finally, she looked up. She glanced at the handler. He stood back, grinning at her, then shrugged one massive shoulder as if he didn't know what to do. Sequoia looked at the officer standing next to him. He glanced at the handler, and then grinned at Sequoia as well.

She looked back at her computer, and then said, "Call it off."

Nothing.

Sequoia's ears started to burn. With anger or embarrassment, she couldn't be sure. And it didn't matter. They were making a mockery of her. What did the stupid dog want, anyway? Did it want her to pet it? Acknowledge it? She couldn't read dogs' minds. She looked at the animal again, and it licked its lips and snapped its jaws at her. But still, it didn't move.

Well, two (or three, if she counted the handler) could play this game, Sequoia thought. She turned her attention back to her computer and didn't look at the dog again.

Then the handler gave it a command in some strange-sounding language and it leapt to a standing position, then bounced forward and nosed her right on the cheek before turning away and trotting off.

Of course, this had the entire office in stitches, and out of reflex, she wiped the dog snot off her cheek … which only added to the hilarity.

Beth's voice brought Sequoia back to the present. "I don't care how you feel about dogs, Carr. I care about you making arrests when I tell you to. I care about you doing the job you're assigned, period. Next week, Monday, you're on K-9s. I'll have Mack get with you to schedule the exchange."

"The exchange?"

Jasmine would hate it that Sequoia had just rephrased the end of Beth's sentence as a question, and Sequoia cringed at it, herself.

"Yes, Carr. You'll have to bring the dog to your house. Obviously. We don't have a doggie condo here at the station."

"Obviously," Sequoia said.

"Any questions?"

"Nope. No questions. You've made yourself pretty clear."

"I thought so. Now, isn't your shift starting?"

Things really couldn't get worse at work. Unless Sequoia got fired. Although, maybe that would be a blessing. So when Elijah offered to ride with her for the night, she took him up on it. He'd walked into the office as Beth Hardwick walked out, and despite Sequoia's insistence that she was fine, that nothing was wrong, he pestered her until she finally caved and told him what Beth had said.

At first, Elijah acted like switching over to K-9s wasn't a big deal, especially if it was temporary. But when Sequoia explained her feelings about dogs, and the story about Xena, Warrior Princess, Elijah managed to work up a little indignation even though she could tell he found the situation slightly humorous.

"I mean, it will be kind of like having a partner," he said as they got into her patrol car. "Won't that be kind of fun? You can feed the dog pieces of your taco through the sliding window."

"I think that's against policy, actually," Sequoia said.

"Oh, right. Well, you can take it running with you."

"Have you seen those dogs in action? They're so hyped up. It'll probably take my arm off."

"Okay. I'm going to stop trying for positivity."

"Yeah, why don't you?"

She pulled the car out onto the street and took a deep breath. She was surprised when Elijah put a hand on her arm.

"It'll be okay," he said. "It's temporary, and I have a feeling you can handle it. You can handle anything."

"Let's hope you're right," Sequoia said. "Now, let's see if we can go get ourselves into some trouble tonight."

She thought she heard him say something about getting into trouble right here, but she tuned it out. This thing with the dog and this thing (whatever it was) with Elijah, were too much to take in. Just for fun, she drove downtown, to the row of bars and clubs that were at once a tourist destination and a hot spot for locals. This little section of road provided quite a bit of excitement, and Sequoia had a feeling they'd find something good to get into.

She wasn't disappointed.

Sequoia parked at the corner of Beach Street and Pacific Avenue. "Let's walk," she said.

"Let's hope we don't run into the Marvins again," Elijah said.

"Aren't they in jail?" Sequoia said.

"Nope. Damned cops won't arrest those two lowlifes."

Sequoia chuckled. A couple of people smoking outside The Sloop seemed to find this strange, and their heads swiveled to follow Sequoia and Elijah as they passed.

Elijah nodded at them, and they averted their eyes.

Downtown Seabreeze reminded Sequoia of Nashville or Las Vegas, on a smaller scale. Bright lights from neon signs cast colorful patterns on the sidewalk, and music poured out of doors for an audio buffet with tons of variety.

Jazz, country, rock, disco … for the first time in as long as she remembered, she wanted to run inside and dance. With Elijah.

It was probably because she was walking right next to him, able to smell his woodsy cologne. She could probably reach out and hold his hand. If she wanted to. What would that be like? Were his hands smooth, or rough? Were they blocky or long? What did he do with his hands, in his spare time? Woodwork? Poker?

Why the hell am I thinking about holding anyone's hands, especially Elijah's?

"You okay, Carr? Is all this music making you jumpy?"

"Shut up, Sawyer. Just got a chill."

"So did you ever actually explain why you believe you're destined for spinsterhood?"

"Uh, no," she said. "And I probably won't."

She wished she could walk faster, get ahead of him and away from this line of questioning. It couldn't end well. But they were out, together, and she couldn't leave him alone on foot patrol.

"But it doesn't make any sense," he said.

"If you knew me better, you wouldn't say that."

"Aha," he said, holding up a pointer finger. "I think if you knew you better, you wouldn't say you aren't cut out for relationships."

Trying for a new angle, she said, "Why are you taking such an interest in this? It's weird."

"Observer of human nature, that's all," he said, as calm and casual as could be. "And I think you're selling yourself short."

She said, "I'm selling myself short of a lifetime of hurt and disappointment, and that's it. Which is why I gave up on relationships five years ago. There's no turning back now."

Even though she'd meant that last part as a joke, her future suddenly looked a little bleak.

Elijah shook his head, and they came to the end of the street. They turned around, in unison, and when she looked into his face, she experienced a strange, foreign feeling. It wasn't romance. She didn't want to kiss him or anything that would be inappropriate while they were in uniform. But she felt this tug, a pull, from deep inside her body. And it freaked her out.

"Look," she said as they began walking back. "This is pretty much the end of your line of questioning. I've been living like this for five years, and I'm perfectly content. I'm not going to change my mind, and *you're* certainly not going to change my mind. So let's just drop it, okay?"

Before Elijah could answer, a pair of men tumbled out of the country bar, Wild West, arms flailing. A bar fight would serve as a perfect diversion from this dead-end conversation with Elijah, Sequoia thought, and she kicked into a jog to help break it up.

Just as they approached the brawling men, Elijah told her, "You can drop it. But that doesn't mean I will."

AT HER REGULAR lunch with Jasmine and Holly, Sequoia wondered whether she should cancel all future regular lunches with Jasmine and Holly. Maybe she wasn't cut out for romance *or* friendship. Not that her sisters were friends, but still.

"Oh, my gosh, *disaster*," Holly said, her voice infused with sarcasm.

She held her hands up and wiggled her fingers in what Sequoia assumed was supposed to be a spooky affectation.

"It's so *exciting*," Jasmine said, clapping her hands together. She was practically bouncing in her seat.

"It's only exciting because it's a disaster," Sequoia said. "It's like a bar fight. It's a disaster. It breaks things like barstools and glasses and beer bottles and probably even bones. But it's exciting. Which guy is going to land the punch that knocks the other guy unconscious? Is one of them going to make a wild swing and hook a bystander in the face? Will anyone go to the hospital? Me getting a dog, for work, and spending my entire day with it, every single day, is exactly like that. At every turn, every minute, I'll be wondering which type of disaster will strike next. Pretty exciting."

She took a big bite of her meat lovers' pizza.

"You're chewing very aggressively," Holly said. "I think you need some yoga or something."

"This will be really good for you, Sequoia," Jasmine said. "It'll help you with your relationship skills."

Sequoia continued chewing and didn't answer. Holly nodded, her head bobbing up and down way too fast.

Sequoia swallowed. "A relationship with a dog is not the same as a relationship with a human," she said. "When will you people realize dogs are not like humans?"

She thought of Jasmine's dumb dog, Roxy or Remy or whatever its name was. That dumb dog ate vegetables and snored on the couch, but it was still a dog.

"Ruby is like a human," Jasmine said.

"Ah, Ruby!" Sequoia said.

"I know, she's so sweet, isn't she? It's like having a child. I mean, I take her to doggie day care. I feed her vegetables. I talk to her."

"She doesn't talk back," Sequoia said.

"I know," Jasmine said. "It's the perfect relationship."

Sequoia rolled her eyes.

"I know what you're thinking," Holly said. "Animals are so needy. I can't possibly give an animal the attention it wants."

"Actually, I was thinking about how hairy and smelly and slobbery dogs are," Sequoia said. "I don't have to play with it, or anything. But it's going to stink up my house."

"I want to issue a challenge," Holly said. Jasmine clapped her hands together again, and Sequoia shook her head. Holly went on, "I know you like a good challenge, Sequoia. I want to challenge you to open your heart to the possibility that you might actually be able to enjoy working with this dog. Just open your heart, that's all I'm saying."

"Ugh," Sequoia said. "You are such a hippie."

"I know!" Holly said. "And that's why I'm so relaxed and happy. Which is what I want for you, my oldest sister. So just give it a chance. I'd hate to see you ruin any potential fun because you're so set on not enjoying it. Okay?"

"Yeah," Jasmine said, before Sequoia could answer. "I'm really looking forward to this. I've always wondered what it's like to work with, you know, a working dog. Hey, maybe I can come along with you one day and write a story about it for the paper. You know, like a day in the life kind of thing."

"That would be so fun!" Holly said.

"I have a feeling you'll be writing about how terrible I am at it," Sequoia said.

"Nonsense," Jasmine said. "You're good at everything. It's annoying, actually. And like I said, this will be good for you."

"Well, I guess we'll see," Sequoia said.

Her sisters echoed, "I guess we'll see."

"How's that certification process, Holly?" Sequoia said.

Holly looked at her lap. "Fine."

"You're lying," Sequoia said.

She was starting to wonder what was really going on with Holly, but her musings were cut short when Jasmine stomped on her foot.

"Ow!" Sequoia said. "What? She's avoiding eye contact. It's a classic sign of deception."

"Leave her alone," Jasmine said, folding her napkin into a tiny square.

"No, it's fine," Holly said. Now, she looked Sequoia directly in the eyes, holding her gaze for way too long. "It's going fine. I've been studying. I just need to sign up to take the tests."

"Okay," Sequoia said. "Great. Let us know if you need help studying. We can quiz you. Just like we used to quiz you on spelling."

"Thanks," Holly said, her tone way too bright.

After a pause, Jasmine pulled her phone out of her purse. "Now," she said. "Take a look at these curtains. We can't decide between the dark gray and the Navy blue. I like one, but I'm not going to tell you which one. Hudson likes the other. I just want your opinion. These curtains might lead to our first fight."

THAT AFTERNOON, Sequoia cleaned house. She figured she should vacuum the corners before a dog came and shed its fur all over the place. She might never see the house this clean again. AC/DC blasted on the stereo system, and Sequoia mopped in time to the heavy beat.

What if it was her trying to choose between gray curtains and Navy blue curtains? She'd told Jasmine she'd like the gray—it was a soothing, creamy gray—but when it came right down to it, would she really care about curtain color? Probably not. Which curtains would Elijah choose? Would he even care? Why was she even thinking about him?

"Change this line of thinking immediately, Carr," she said to herself.

What was going on with Holly? Why was she acting so suspiciously about the personal training certification? Maybe she didn't want to do it any more.

Now that she was thinking about it, Sequoia remembered Holly quitting the track team halfway through her freshman season. She'd applied for and gotten into several colleges, and ended up taking just a year's worth of classes at the community college before quitting to pursue professional golf. Okay, it wasn't professional golf. It was something else, but Sequoia couldn't remember what.

Sequoia's mind switched topics.

Why would anyone think assigning her a dog was a good idea? How could she possibly be of use with a canine sidekick? This was a disaster. She was headed straight for failure.

Where would she even put the dog's crate? The corner in the living room seemed like a good place. It would be out of the way. But she'd have to move the bookcase.

"Ugh. So much work for a dog."

The bookcase would fit by the front door. Moving her library of thriller novels and poetry collections might take all day, but she was confident she could finish it before tomorrow morning. As she took the books off the shelves and piled them near the front door, Sequoia marveled at how much she'd read as an adult. Possibly too much. Some of these books had to go ... especially the romance novels she'd tucked behind her work-related training manuals. She should probably burn those.

She had no idea what to do with her self-help books. Did she want anyone to know she was practicing mindfulness? Maybe she'd hide those under the bed.

Within a half-hour, the hundreds of books were separated into several piles, and Sequoia was sweating.

"This is where it would come in handy to have a man living here," she said. "He could help me carry all this shit across the house."

Someone knocked at the door. When Sequoia opened it to see Elijah on the doorstep, she told herself it wasn't Fate that had brought him here at this very moment.

He held up a six-pack of beer and a pizza box.

"Moral support," he said. "I figured you'd be getting ready for the dog."

"Is it strange that I'm almost crying with gratitude right now?" she said.

"What can I say?" he said. "I rock it with the ladies. I make them all cry."

She stepped back to let him in.

"Whoa," he said. "What is going on here? Is this Armageddon?"

She threw up her hands. "Practically. They're sticking me with a dog. It feels like the end of the world."

"Are those romance novels?"

Face burning, Sequoia herded Elijah into the kitchen. He set the pizza box on the table while she got out paper plates.

"What are you doing, redecorating to make it more dog-friendly?"

"Kind of. Not really. Just trying to find a place for the crate. I thought the living room would be a good place, but I had to move my bookcase. And then I realized how many books I have."

"Wait. So you're telling me you're beautiful *and* smart?" Elijah pulled slices of pizza out of the box and set them on plates.

"Funny guy," Sequoia said. They sat down at the table. "Obviously I'm smart. And well-read. But I don't have the strength. Want to help me move furniture?"

Over still-hot pizza, Elijah grinned at Sequoia and held up his beer. "I'd love to. Here's to moving furniture together."

Whether he really loved it or not, Elijah sped up the process considerably. Without too much commentary, he moved some books, put others in boxes, and dragged the bookcase across the room before restocking it with her library.

At one point, Sequoia said, "I can't tell you how grateful I am for your help. At first, I thought I could get this all moved by tomorrow, but I started to second-guess myself. I have way more books than I realized. And way less muscle."

"You're welcome," Elijah said. "I love putting muscle into a job."

Are we still talking about moving furniture?

"Blue or gray?" Sequoia blurted out.

Elijah looked surprised at the sudden change of subject, but his expression quickly turned thoughtful. "Gray, I guess. Yeah, gray."

He sounded so comfortable, so companionable, that Sequoia couldn't help but smile at him. The second she realized her smile was natural, relaxed, and maybe even inviting, she wiped it right off her face. Why was she asking him about curtains, for goodness' sake?

"Well, I guess I'd better get to bed," she said.

It was a lie and they both knew it. Sequoia never went to bed early. She'd spent too long on the night shift to fall asleep any time before midnight. Ever.

But for some reason—maybe because he didn't want to argue with her, or maybe because he knew he'd already pressed his luck by showing up and bringing pizza—he didn't argue with her.

Even though his leaving was her idea, when the door closed behind him, she felt lonely. The worst part: she didn't even know why. Well, not exactly, anyway.

CHAPTER NINE

Sequoia Carr had done this to herself. She'd actually thought, "Things can't get any worse." And why not? She was under the thumb of a corrupt, insane woman. She'd been taken off her favorite shift. And she was now going to be partners with a dog.

Then.

Mack, the Mac Truck of deputies, showed up at her house with said new partner. Her new partner was none other than Xena, Warrior Princess, the dog who had humiliated her just a few short years ago.

The dog leapt out of the back of Mack's patrol car and charged toward Mack, then came to an abrupt stop and sat down next to him, wagging her tail.

Bright-eyed and bushy-tailed squirrels had nothing on Xena, Warrior Princess.

"She wants to know if you remember her," Mack said.

Sequoia studied him for a brief moment: dark skin, twinkling eyes, huge muscles. Pretty handsome. He wasn't particularly tall, but according to the coffeemaker conversations she'd overheard, Mack had earned his nickname thanks to a serious weightlifting regime and lots of egg whites.

"Of course I do," Sequoia said. She walked over to Mack's car and lifted the lid of the trunk, which he'd already popped open. She removed the crate and carried it inside. When she came back out, Xena was still sitting next to Mack. Her tail was still wagging, and her eyes were hyper-focused on his face.

Mack held one of the dog's toys against his chest.

"I think I see a tear in your eye, Mack," Sequoia said. "Are you actually sad about getting rid of this dog?"

"I am. Even a woman with a heart of stone will be moved by Xena," he said. "I think you'll be surprised. Even *your* heart will soften, Carr. I promise you."

Sequoia rolled her eyes. "Doubt it."

"Any questions before I turn her over to you?"

Panic set in.

Sequoia nodded, then realized the movement was manic and froze. "I mean, does she have any food or anything? Does she like to cuddle with a certain toy at night? How much do I feed her? Does she chase cars? I guess I do have a lot of questions."

Mack's features transformed when he beamed at her. "That was a test, Carr. You just aced it. Flying colors and all that. I was worried you wouldn't even realize you had to feed her."

When Sequoia's mouth dropped open, he rushed to say, "Kidding. I knew you'd know to feed her, but I was afraid you would just throw some kibble in the bowl and call it good. Not because you're an idiot, Carr. But because you said yourself you don't even like dogs. I'm so relieved you thought to ask about her feeding. Now I feel better about leaving her in your capable hands when I retire."

Although Sequoia felt somewhat perturbed by this little test (wasn't she supposed to throw some kibble in a bowl and call it good?), she could understand where Mack's concerns came from. She decided to change the subject.

"You're retiring?" she said. "I thought Hardwick said you wanted to move to investigations. Maybe I heard her wrong because I was distracted by the tragedy of joining K-9s. How old are you, anyway? Twenty-five?"

Mack laughed. "Almost forty, Carr. I came on when I was twenty."

"Huh. What are you going to do?"

He shrugged a massive shoulder. "Find my way in the world, Carr."

She didn't know what she'd do when it came time to retire. She'd probably be one of those old cops, weathered and wrinkly, who died sitting behind her desk because she didn't have anything else.

Watching Mack with Xena, Sequoia felt almost guilty. His love for her was obvious, if strange. Sequoia would never be able to explain to a roomful of people how some humans became so enamored with their pets. Fortunately, she wouldn't have to, since most humans suffered from this weird mental affliction.

Mack helped Sequoia set up the crate, and filled Xena's food and water bowls before setting them in the kitchen. Sequoia knew right away that she'd move those somewhere more practical so the dog wasn't underfoot when she cooked, but she didn't want to say anything for fear that Mack would move the dishes right up onto the dining room table.

Xena paced around the house, sniffing every freshly vacuumed corner and every shining surface. Her toenails clacked on the hardwood floors as she went. Mack didn't seem to notice. He went on and on about how to get Xena to sit and stay and search for drugs.

"I made you a cheat sheet," he said. He pulled an index card, folded in half, out of his pocket.

"So I listed out all her commands, in German, and all the English phrases so you'll know what you're saying to her. She obeys really well. If she doesn't obey, just give her a correction."

"A correction? Like, with a red pen?"

"Ha. No, with her collar. Let me grab her box out of the car."

It turned out Xena really did have a favorite stuffed animal: a pig that crinkled when she chewed it. Mack put it in Xena's mouth before making a big production of saying good-bye to her.

"It's not like you're leaving the planet," Sequoia said to him. "You can come visit her any time. And I'm sure we'll see you at the station. When you retire, you can babysit her whenever you want. Besides, you and I both know this can't last long."

Mark snorted and Sequoia thought he might actually be a little teary-eyed. When he finally left, the dog sat there, facing the front door, for what seemed like hours, her ears straight up and her head cocked to one side. Every once in a while, she'd hear a noise outside and her tail would wag for a few beats.

Sequoia actually felt a little sorry for her.

Xena's front-door vigilance was finally rewarded an hour later when Jasmine and Holly came in. When the dog realized it wasn't who she was expecting, she leapt to her feet and snarled.

Holly and Jasmine froze in the doorway. Xena continued to snarl, her front lip bared to show an impressive row of perfectly white teeth. Again, Sequoia panicked. She hadn't been expecting this kind of behavior. Xena was supposed to be well-trained. Maybe Mack had used her as a guard dog when they weren't working.

Wasn't there a command for, "Shut the hell up"? Xena growled. Jasmine and Holly stood in the doorway.

"Just a minute," Sequoia said. "I'm looking for my cheat sheet. She's probably freaked out by your hair, Holly. That doesn't look like Auburn Sunset any more."

Holly murmured something that sounded like, "It's Fading Sunset," but Sequoia was too distracted to clarify.

Finally, she found Mack's index card on the kitchen counter.

Using her index finger, she scrolled down the list of English words until she found, "No." Wasn't "no" the same in pretty much every language? Sequoia sighed. Xena growled. So, the German command was … *pfui*? Mack had written in parenthesis, *pronunciation: "Fooey."*

"This has got to be a joke," Sequoia said.

Anger was a quick balm for the inadequacy she felt as she waited for the dumb dog to stop snarling at her sisters. Why would Mack give her a cheat sheet with jokes on it? Was he actually expecting her to fall for this and tell the dog to "Fooey"?

He'd probably planned this out so that when she brought Xena into the office she'd make a fool of herself saying nonsensical words that weren't even real commands.

"What does it say?" Jasmine said. Her tone bordered on frustrated. "Just tell her to stop it."

"Stop it," Holly said to Xena. Jasmine laughed and repeated, "Stopit."

Xena cocked her head as if she'd never heard anyone say that, but she continued to growl.

"What does your card say?" Jasmine said again.

"It says, 'Fooey,'" Sequoia said. "But that can't be right."

"Fooey!" Jasmine said to Xena.

Something clicked in the dog's body and her entire demeanor changed. Her body relaxed and she wagged her tail.

Jasmine apparently pleased with herself, said, "Aw, you're pleased that someone is finally speaking your language, aren't you?"

But still, Xena didn't move, and Holly and Jasmine didn't attempt to go past her.

"Call her to you," Jasmine said.

Sequoia sighed. "Xena."

The dog wagged its tail, but remained focused on the visitors.

"Xena."

Nothing.

"Look at your card," Holly said.

"Xena. Here."

The dog whipped around and zoomed over to Sequoia. Sequoia felt a goofy grin spreading across her face, and kept her head down so her sisters wouldn't see it. Xena stood with the side of her head pressed against Sequoia's leg, her tail wagging at a million miles per hour.

"I see you smiling," Jasmine said as she and Holly walked into the living room. "Don't try to hide it."

The girls sat down on Sequoia's couch.

"Beautiful dog," Holly said. "Oh, and it's now Summer Fields. Auburn Sunset was too bright."

Jasmine gave Sequoia a stern look and said to, "Why didn't you use the commands?"

"I thought Mack was playing a trick on me," Sequoia said. "I mean, I saw it on the card, but it seemed like a made-up command. I pictured myself yelling, 'Fooey!' in the middle of the office and everyone laughing at me, just like they did on my first encounter with this dog."

"What was your first encounter with that dog?" Holly said, and Jasmine said, "I think you can move now. She'll probably just follow you."

"I don't want her to follow me," Sequoia said. "And I don't want to talk about the first encounter."

Holly and Jasmine exchanged a look, and Sequoia added, "It was embarrassing. Humiliating. And I don't want to relive it."

Still, as she walked into the kitchen to start dinner (and Xena followed her), she told them the story, and of course, they found it funny.

Every time Sequoia moved, she bumped into the dog. She opened the refrigerator and accidentally hit Xena with the door. She backed up to close the refrigerator and stepped on Xena's foot. Xena jumped back with a little yelp, and Sequoia found herself muttering, "Sorry," out of reflex. She hoped her sisters hadn't heard her, because they wouldn't let her live it down. Not after all the times she'd made fun of Jasmine for talking to Roxy or Remy or whatever her dog's name was.

"Hey, Sequoia," Jasmine called. Here it came. "Remember when you used to make fun of me for talking to Ruby?"

Ruby! That was it. Sequoia didn't answer.

"It's okay," Jasmine said. "You don't have to answer. I know you remember. Is it just me, or did I hear you apologize to that dog just now?"

"It's not just you," Holly said. "I heard it, too."

Sequoia had the insane urge to make eye contact with Xena and roll her eyes, but instead, she started assembling the salad.

The dog, apparently worn out from her guard duty, flopped onto the floor behind Sequoia, her back resting against Sequoia's heels.

"Well, this is annoying," Sequoia said. "I can't even move my feet."

The dog yawned, loudly, almost as if it were exaggerating the sound on purpose, and then closed its eyes.

"Great," Sequoia said.

While she finished chopping vegetables and tossing dressing into the salad, she kept her feet planted in place.

"Dinner's ready," she said to her sisters a few minutes later.

They walked in as she stepped over Xena, and they exchanged another look.

"Why do you guys keep looking at each other?"

"I never thought I'd see you step over a dog," Jasmine said. "You always nudge Ruby out of the way."

"She's so tiny I can push her out of the way with one foot," Sequoia said. "This beast isn't going anywhere."

"It's my next headline," Jasmine said. "'Sequoia Carr steps over a sleeping dog.' Or, wait. Maybe it should be, 'Sequoia Carr lets sleeping dogs lie.'"

"Clever," Sequoia said. "Why don't you set the table and tell us about your paint colors or fabric choices or whatever?"

Holly giggled and retrieved wine glasses. Xena remained in her spot, snoring on the kitchen floor, while they ate dinner. Sequoia figured she should enjoy it while it lasted. This was probably her last moment of peace, since training was scheduled to begin the next day.

CHAPTER TEN

Whereas most people would feel hopeful and optimistic upon waking to bright sunshine and chirping birds, Sequoia felt cranky Monday morning. She preferred going to work after sundown, and sleeping through the harsh light of the day. Her mood was only worsened by lack of sleep.

Sunday night, after Jasmine and Holly left the house, Xena spent several hours pacing around the house, obviously looking for Mack or some other sign of home. Sequoia tried to comfort the dog with her stuffed pig, but it didn't work. The dog dropped the pig in her crate and continued to pace.

Despite herself, Sequoia felt sorry enough for Xena that she called her over and let her put her head on the couch for petting. But Xena grew restless after a few seconds, probably because she could sense Sequoia really didn't like her. She took up pacing again, wearing a track fit for Nascar in the carpet.

She went into her crate easily enough, turned around about six times, and flopped down with her head on her paws, looking up at Sequoia as if asking for pity.

"Good dog," Sequoia said. Xena's tail thumped once and Sequoia walked away.

The house was silent for thirty minutes or so, but then Xena must have realized she was stuck in the crate long-term, and she began to whine. The high-pitched sound grated on Sequoia's nerves, but even a self-proclaimed anti-dog person knew the whining was a result of stress. So she put in some ear plugs and laid down in bed.

Then the yipping started. It penetrated the ear plugs. Sequoia put the pillow over her head. Then Xena started scratching at the metal on the crate.

Scratch, scratch, yip. Scratch, yip, yip. Yip, scratch, scratch.

Sequoia groaned, and Xena stilled, silent for just a moment. Then she started up again. *Scratch, whine, yip.*

Maybe if she brought the crate into her bedroom, so Xena wouldn't be lonely?

Of course, seeing Sequoia was beyond exciting to Xena, who charged out of her crate the moment Sequoia opened it, and ran laps around the living room, her muscular body bunching and lengthening at breakneck speed. At any other moment, Sequoia would have found this behavior funny. Didn't admitting that make her the bigger person? Bigger than what, she didn't know. She folded the crate down flat and dragged it through her bedroom door.

When Sequoia bought her house a couple of years ago, she chose a cozy place just big enough for one person, and maybe a guest. Needless to say, her bedroom, despite being the master, didn't feature much extra space for a dog crate. The only spot to put it was in the corner between Sequoia's bed and the wall.

"Ugh. I'm going to hear you breathing all night long, dog," she said to Xena, even though she could hear Xena, still running laps in the living room.

She finally got the crate reassembled and the bed inside it, and she called Xena to her. Xena slunk back into the crate and laid down, this time without turning around.

Sequoia should have known the lack of turns meant Xena didn't plan on sleeping. Still slightly out of breath from lugging the crate around, Sequoia got back into bed and turned off her bedside lamp.

The whining started immediately.

Sequoia whipped her blankets back and retrieved her phone from its spot on the kitchen counter.

It was late by normal standards—well after eleven p.m.—but she texted Mack, anyway: *Does this damned dog sleep in your bed with you, or what? I thought that was against the rules.*

Mack responded right away (he'd probably been waiting all evening for her to text with questions or a reassurance that the dog was still alive): *Of course not. But she's probably freaked out because she's in a new space. Try cuddling with her or something.*

Sequoia wrote back: *Cuddling? Are you kidding me?*

Mack: *Just get down on the floor with her for a bit.*

Sequoia didn't respond. She stalked back into the bedroom, got back in bed, and turned the lamp off again. Whining.

"Fooey," she said, softly at first. Even she could hear the uncertainty in her voice. Xena barked. "Fooey," Sequoia said, with a bit more force.

The dog gave one last whine and was quiet. Sequoia couldn't resist the urge to shine her flashlight on the crate just to see what was happening. Xena had put her head down between her paws, and was looking up at Sequoia.

Sequoia clicked the flashlight off and rolled onto her back. She closed her eyes and the whining started again. She'd heard her girlfriends talk about letting their babies "cry it out" when they wouldn't sleep through the night. Maybe she'd have to take a similar tactic with this canine. Her girlfriends worried their babies would suffer psychological damage if they were left alone to cry until they fell asleep, but this was a dog. Whining and yipping all night certainly wouldn't damage it permanently. It would probably fall asleep within a couple of hours and forget about this whole thing by tomorrow morning.

Unfortunately, things didn't work out quite that way. Xena whined and yipped and scratched. All. Night. Long.

This dog was going to make Sequoia homicidal. She'd kill the first person she saw in the morning.

Of course, that person was Elijah Sawyer, getting off his shift—*her* shift—walking out to his car.

"First night!" Elijah said. "How did it go?"

"Wow," Sequoia said. She'd just gotten out of the car, and had Xena on a leash to walk her into the office. "You're way too cheerful for your own good. I swore last night that I'd kill the first person I saw this morning. Congratulations. That's you."

"That bad, huh?"

Xena, Warrior Princess turned into Xena, Eager to Please when she saw Elijah, and pushed her nose into his palm over and over until he stroked the top of her head.

"Of course, she's all calm and collected for you. She was a night-mare for me last night."

"The ladies turn to putty in my hands, Sequoia," he said, and she shivered at his use of her first name.

"I believe it," she said, hoping her voice was as infused with sarcasm as she'd intended.

He chuckled, but became serious almost right away. "Hey," he said, touching her shoulder with one hand. "It's going to be fine. Good luck today, okay?"

Sequoia felt tears spring to her eyes. She inhaled and nodded. "Okay," she said. "Thanks. I think I'm going to need it."

"It's all sunny skies from here, Carr," he said in a louder voice.

He walked to his car and she walked into the office, Xena trotting along beside her like she hadn't been up all night spreading her suffering.

As promised, Mack was waiting for her in the office. He grinned like a maniac when he saw Xena, and the dog ran up to him like they were long lost lovers. Sequoia, arm hanging limp at her side after having the leash yanked out of her hand, rolled her eyes.

"She missed you last night," she said.

Mack winced. "Sorry, Carr. She's a bit of a baby. Did you cuddle with her?"

"Do you think I cuddled with her?"

Now Xena was leaning against Mack, who was stroking her side. The dog glared at Sequoia as if to say, "See? This is how you treat a Warrior Princess."

"Nah, I'm sure you didn't," Mack said. "But you're causing more misery for yourself. Cuddle with her for five minutes and get a full night's sleep."

"I'll save cuddling as a last resort. Why don't you teach me how to boss her around? I think if we establish the right kind of relationship, she'll shut up when I tell her to."

Mack shrugged. "All right. Let's go, Xena girl."

He strode through the office and out the back door. Xena trotted along beside him, perky as can be. Sequoia followed them, feeling conspicuous as the third wheel. Mack endured some cat calls from the other guys in the office: "Aw, Mackie, you got your old girlfriend back," and "Mackie and Xena, sitting in a tree ...."

Mack's ears were bright red by the time they all walked out into the sun.

So I'm not the only one who gets embarrassed.

For the first time, Sequoia felt a little camaraderie with Mack, even if he had put her through that stupid little test to see if she was smart enough to feed the dog. He'd done that only because he loved Xena, and Sequoia couldn't fault him for that. Beth Hardwick had said Mack wanted to go to investigations, but maybe she'd uprooted him just as she had Sequoia and that was the real reason he was retiring.

"Jerks," Sequoia said. She was referring to the other guys, and to Beth Hardwick, too.

Mack turned around and winked at her.

She shook her head.

"What?" he said.

"Nothing," Sequoia said. "I feel like we just turned over a new leaf. I'm looking forward to this, that's all."

"Huh," Mack said. She thought his cheeks flushed, just a bit. He cleared his throat. "Okay. So the first thing you need to know is that these dogs have a really high play drive. Everything is a game. So you want to start every training session by getting her excited. First, I put her harness on. It's like a signal that we're getting started. Did you bring it?"

Sequoia held up the harness, and Mack put it on the dog.

When he spoke to Xena again, his voice transformed. He cooed at her like a grandma would coo at a little baby. "Right, Xena? We've got to get you excited! Right? Ready to work? Ready to work?"

The dog's tail wagged so fast and hard Sequoia thought she might take off and fly.

"You've got to use keywords. Xena's are, obviously, 'Ready to work,' so I always say that when we're starting a session or when we're out on a call and I need to run her. I've already set up some hides, you know, stashes of drugs, around the training area. You have to set them up ahead of time. So always give yourself time for that. They have to sit for at least fifteen minutes. Thirty is even better."

Sequoia nodded. This was a lot to remember.

"It's a lot to remember, right?" Mack said. "Don't worry. I've got a manual. I forgot to give it to you yesterday. But really the best thing is just working with her, watching the other guys with their dogs. I promise, once you get the hang of it, it won't all feel so overwhelming. Just takes practice."

Sequoia nodded. "I'm sure you're right. I just feel like all of you guys have a knack for it. You actually like dogs. You know? And I'm not even starting from scratch. I'm starting out way behind."

Mack nodded. "I know. I have no idea why Hardwick is putting you in this unit. We all know how you feel about humans. And we all know how you feel about dogs."

His words stung—did everyone really know how she felt about humans?—but Sequoia shrugged it off. "Preaching to the choir, Mack."

"Look, Carr," he said. "The best thing I can think to do is just excel at this. You know? Just blow it out of the water. Give Hardwick a run for her money. I have a feeling she thinks she can beat you down, get you to make a mistake, demote you, maybe even fire you. But I think she's gonna be surprised when she sees how good you are. I've seen your other work, and I know you can excel at this just like you did with writing warrants and the Drug Recognition Expert stuff. Don't sell yourself short."

Speechless, Sequoia found a wobbly smile. "Thanks, Mack," she said. "Really."

There was a pause.

"No prob," Mack said. "Okay, let's get started. So to get her to hunt for drugs, you tell her, 'Search,'" and you lead her forward like this."

He leaned down and made kind of a sweeping motion with his arm. Xena put her nose to the ground, and, like a Hoover, ran forward.

"Watch her, now," Mack said. "There's a hide right here. She's going to alert. But sometimes, she can tell it's there and doesn't alert right away. You've got to watch for her signs and then bring her back and present an area again if you can tell she's picked up on something. Okay? So watch."

Sure enough, the dog stopped next to the tire of one of the cars in the training area. With her nose still on the ground, she backed up. Mack didn't say anything out loud, but he held up a finger.

Suddenly, Xena started scratching at the tire as if she were digging, her front paws scraping it with alarming speed. Sequoia couldn't help but laugh. Mack reached around to the inside of the tire and pulled out a metal box. As soon as he had it in hand, he praised Xena in that same high-pitched voice. He pulled a toy out of his waistband and Xena grabbed it with a ferocity that scared Sequoia.

"So the reward is praise," Mack said, his voice strained from wrestling with the dog, "but more importantly, the toy. It's always the toy. It's always the toy, isn't it, Xena?"

He gave Xena a couple of commands and she released the toy and sat down. "Good Xena," he said. "Good girl."

Mack showed Sequoia how to run Xena through the area, covering as much surface as possible, and the dog's work was all flying colors. Sequoia started to feel optimistic. She'd just rely on Xena's expertise.

Then Mack suggested Sequoia run the dog, herself.

"Now let's have you give it a try. Just this once, I'm going to tell you where the hide is, so you can lead her there. But usually one guy sets it and the other guys—uh, or gals, in this case—don't know where it is."

"Just hold the leash real lightly," he said, handing it to her. "She can sense if you're stressed or frustrated, so just try to stay relaxed. Remember, tell her, 'Search,' and then let her take the lead. Be confident, though. Don't let her pull you around."

Sequoia caught herself twisting the end of the leash in her hands. She took a deep breath and noticed Mack's eyes held a half-and-half mix of sympathy and humor.

"It'll be fine. It's your first time. Even if you mess up, it can't be worse than my first time."

"Okay, you've got me hooked. Spill it. What happened your first time?"

Mack grinned. Xena flopped down at Sequoia's feet like an exasperated teenager bored of hearing yet another rendition of her dad's heyday story.

"So, I was running that old dog of Tyson's, remember? Jerome? He was this crazy Lab named after some crazy little town in Arizona. Anyway, the guys thought it'd be real funny to have me run him without any hides placed. They didn't tell me there were no hides. They made this big deal of how his alert was a very gentle brush of the foot on whatever he thought the hide was in. I ran that dog, over and over again, watching that right front paw for any sign of a brush. Jerome, that damned dog, wasn't brushing his foot on anything. He wasn't even sniffing the ground, really. The guys kept saying, 'Run him again.'"

Sequoia pictured poor Mack, a young, overly enthusiastic, cop who'd undoubtedly been the butt of many jokes, running the dog over and over, with no results. She felt even more empathy. Empathy was not something she was used to.

"Jerks," she said.

Mack shrugged, and Sequoia marveled at how easygoing he was. Unlike Holly. A light bulb clicked on: Mack would be perfect for Holly.

"It was no big deal," he said, bringing her train of thought to a halt. "It was just their way of hazing me, I guess. They all had a good laugh."

"At your expense."

"Seriously. It sucked. But here we are, and you can be grateful I'm taking a different approach with you. I think it's easiest if you know where the hides are, your first time, so you can just get the feel for how she responds when she gets close, or when she's noticing it for the first time. Okay? Let's do it."

That tiny bit of human interaction made Sequoia feel considerably more relaxed, and the fact that it did made her feel quite strange.

She took a deep breath, and said, "Search."

Xena kicked into gear, her nose along the ground and her tail straight up in the air. It was actually kind of cute, Sequoia thought, but only kind of. And only until the stupid dog stopped in its tracks and sat down, facing Sequoia with one paw raised.

"Search," she said again, gesturing to the area in front of them.

Xena wagged her tail.

Sequoia turned around, and saw that Mack was doubled over, hands on his knees, tears leaking out of the corners of his eyes. He emitted little "heh, heh" noises that grated on her nerves.

"What's so funny?" she said.

"She's done," he said, choking the words out between chuckles. "She thinks she found them all, and she wants her toy."

"But I'm telling her to search."

"Tell her again."

Sequoia did, and Xena flopped onto her back, her tail wagging hard, a doggie version of a snow angel.

Mack approached the dog and, in a stern voice, told her to search. Xena hopped up and started searching again. Mack praised her in that annoying cooing voice.

"So it's just me," Sequoia said.

"Could be," Mack said. He walked the dog back over to where Sequoia stood. "Not you, personally, but just that the two of you haven't bonded yet. Plus, she can probably sense your uncertainty. Try again." He handed her the leash and she told Xena to search.

Xena sat down, ears perked, and stared at Sequoia.

"Try petting her," Mack suggested.

Sequoia patted the dog on the head.

"No, not like that. Pet her like you mean it. Like you love her."

"I have no idea how to pet a dog like I love it."

"Oh, geez," Mack said. "Maybe you have more to learn than either of us realized."

CHAPTER ELEVEN

"How'd training go? I see you survived."

Elijah approached Sequoia's desk and automatically reached down to pet Xena's head. How was it automatic for people to pet animals like that?

"I survived," Sequoia said. "But it was rough. I don't really do so well with dogs."

"Just like you don't do well with men?"

He really was handsome, all clean-shaven and muscular. Sequoia shook her head to clear it of wayward thoughts.

"Exactly," she said. "What are you still doing here, anyway? Your shift ended more than an hour ago."

"Maybe she can tell you don't like dogs."

Evasive, Sequoia thought. *Curious.*

"She can. I'm sure of it. But I don't know how to change my aura, or my energy, or my vibe, or whatever. Maybe I should go to one of my sister's stupid yoga classes."

"Have you ever realized how often you describe something as stupid?" He stood there, starting at her, arms crossed.

"Now you're getting on my nerves. Are you just hanging around here to irritate me, or what?"

"Nah, I was just leaving. Don't worry about Xena. It'll get better.

Hey, tonight's my first night off. Want me to come over after you get off shift and work with the two of you?"

"Wait. What do you know about dogs?"

"You'd be surprised," he said.

"Why are you offering to help me?"

"You need it. Plainly."

She sighed, and although she was tempted to turn him down—she didn't want help he wasn't obligated to give—she thought about what Mack had said about nailing this, about becoming great at it. She made a decision, and nodded. "Yes, I do need it. And I'll take you up on it. Just this once. Because Mack made a really good point today, and he's right. Which means I need all the help I can get, as soon as I can get it."

Elijah knocked on Sequoia's front door a few hours later, and as she led him and Xena into her backyard, he said, "So what did Mack say today?"

"He said I need to establish a bond with her. Which requires petting. And cooing at her like grandmothers coo at babies. He actually wanted me to cuddle with her. On the floor."

Xena sat down next to Sequoia's left leg, which Sequoia knew was supposed to be her default position.

Elijah nodded as if cuddling with a dog (a working dog!) wasn't the most ridiculous thing he'd ever heard. "What else?"

"She can sense my frustration."

He nodded again. "Were you frustrated?"

"At first, I wasn't," Sequoia said. "I was just nervous. But when she sat there looking at me, wagging her tail like she was so pleased with herself, I started to get frustrated. I know, I know, she'd already found the hides Mack found, but she wasn't listening to me. So yes, then I got frustrated."

Xena bumped Sequoia's palm with her nose and Sequoia let her hand rest on Xena's head.

"Okay," Elijah said. "I know they didn't give you much time to bond with her, and I think that's the most important thing to do at this point. For right now, you just need to play some games with her. Play fetch, praise the heck out of her when she brings the toy back, coo at her, rub her. Know what I mean? Like she's the. Best. Dog. In. The. World."

"But she doesn't like me. I'm the only one she's not begging for hugs or whatever. Doggie hugs. You know what I mean."

The dog nudged Sequoia's hand.

"She can probably tell you don't like her."

"Why does everyone keep saying that?" Sequoia said. "Are dogs mind-readers or something?"

"It's an energy thing," Elijah said. "You, being a native of Seabreeze, should understand that. I mean, you're practically buzzing with energy right now."

Sexual energy. The thought leapt into her head and it was all she could do to keep her expression neutral. Elijah cocked his head, and she shook hers.

"So what do I do?" she said.

"Throw the toy for her."

As soon as Sequoia took the tennis ball out of her pocket, Xena stood up and started twirling.

"Wait," Elijah said. "Make her sit again. Then throw it."

For once, Xena obeyed when Sequoia told her to sit. When she threw the ball, Xena's head whipped from the direction the ball had gone and back to Sequoia's face, again and again.

"Get it," Sequoia said, and to her almost-delight, the dog took off after the ball, charging fast, her movements powerful.

As soon as she ran it down, she picked it up and trotted back to Sequoia. But when Sequoia went to get the ball out of Xena's mouth, Xena wouldn't let go of it.

"Isn't there a command for letting it go?" Elijah said.

Sequoia took her cheat sheet out of her pocket, found the command, and was—again—surprised and almost-delighted when Xena released the slobbery ball into her palm.

She had to resist the urge to do some kind of victory dance, and instead, threw the ball again before wiping her hand on her jeans.

"If I wasn't covered in slobber I'd give you a hug right now," she said as Xena tore away after the ball.

"You could give me a hug, anyway," Elijah said.

"Hey, you never told me how you know so much about dogs," she said.

"Wow, that was an obvious subject change."

Sequoia shrugged. "So? Tell me."

"My uncle is a dog breeder and trainer," Elijah said. "He sells dogs for law enforcement and personal protection. It's my dad's brother, Uncle Jimmy. He lives in Colorado. When I was a kid, we always switched off traveling for holidays. Whenever we went there, we'd stay for a week at a time, and he always let me tag along with him when he worked with the dogs. I loved it."

Sequoia threw the ball again.

"So why didn't you go into K-9s yourself?" Sequoia said.

Elijah shrugged. Xena came tearing back, the ball between her teeth, her tongue hanging out to one side. This time, he took the ball from her and threw it again.

"I don't know. I just never felt like it was right for me. I like regular patrol. I've thought about maybe buying a breeding pair or two from my uncle when I retire and starting my own business. But that's a few years off."

In a a strange flash of imagination, Sequoia pictured herself on the floor of future-Elijah's house, playing with a few puppies. She shook her head. While she'd originally planned to invite him to stay for dinner, she now thought better of it. Escape was the best option. She felt like a jet pilot. She had to eject now, before she morphed into a completely useless, needy woman. She pressed the button.

"I guess I'd better go on in and get dinner started," she said. "Thank you so much for coming over."

His expression showed genuine surprise at the abrupt end of their training session and conversation, and she felt a little guilty. But when he pulled away from the curb after petting Xena one more time and congratulating her on a game of fetch well played, Sequoia felt the parachute open, and she drifted down to the safety and security of solitude.

Solitude wasn't quite the same with a canine roommate. At first, Sequoia tried to continue their game of fetch. But between her own crazy train of thought and the dog's selective hearing, it didn't go well.

Each time Sequoia threw the ball, she pictured Elijah's hand on it, the fluid motion of his body as he threw it across the yard. Once or twice, she even imagined his hands on the bare skin of her torso.

It was at that moment that she called in quits, in part because she was about to have full-blown imaginary sex with Elijah Sawyer in her own backyard and in part because the stubborn dog refused to retrieve the ball. She just sat there and looked at Sequoia, then watched her walk across the yard to get the ball and throw it again.

When they went inside, Xena followed her everywhere. She sat by her side in the kitchen, flopped down at her feet when she sat down to eat dinner, stretched out on the floor in front of the couch later in the evening.

Between the dog's snuffly breathing and the overzealous licking and chewing of her hindquarters, Sequoia yearned for the peace and quiet she so enjoyed.

She yearned for it even more when her phone dinged with a text from Elijah just before she went to bed that evening: *I'm going in early, which means I'll get off early - want to go for a run before your shift?*

She thought, I go for a run every day.

But she knew that wasn't what he was asking. He was asking if she wanted to run with him. Which, of course, she didn't.

And that wasn't because she didn't want to go for a run with him, per se, but because she was afraid of the way her mind was responding to him. All that nonsense about his hands on her skin was just unacceptable. It had been a long time since a man got to her that way, and when that particular situation crumbled around her, she'd promised herself she wouldn't let it happen again.

Well, she hadn't thought she'd run into this problem again, either. When Walt Walters had correctly convinced her that she was incapable of being a good partner, she'd shut down the hands-on-skin section of her brain.

Yes, she knew enough about human urges and needs to know she'd eventually have responsible sex with no-strings partners like Alex Light and George Harrison, but she never got emotionally attached. When she did think of sex with them, it wasn't their hands on her skin she pictured, but the simplicity of a good release.

Sex with them could be sex with anyone, really. They were replaceable.

So the repeated, specific image of Elijah's hands on her skin was disturbing.

But.

There was always a "but," wasn't there? It was just temporary. Yes, there was something about him, but she didn't have to change her principles. They had something in common now. Actually, two things. She felt her mouth twisting into a wry smile. They had both the Marvins and Xena in common.

They could be professional acquaintances and nothing more, couldn't they?

Even while one side of her brain answered, *Yeah, right,* the other side of her brain directed her fingers to respond to Elijah's text.

See you at 7 a.m.

Then, in the rare moments of sleep she stole between Xena's whining jaunts and crate-scratching episodes, Sequoia dreamed of Elijah Sawyer, his lithe body moving fluidly above hers.

CHAPTER TWELVE

"You're a glutton for punishment, aren't you?" Sequoia said as she approached Elijah the next morning.

So what if she'd chosen the running pants Holly said made her look like a gazelle? So what if she'd worn the headband Jasmine said "made her eyes pop"? (Which Sequoia knew was a compliment but also sounded like a science project gone bad.)

Elijah's eyes widened in appreciation when he saw her, and she felt her skin tingle with satisfaction.

"I wouldn't call this punishment," he said. "Where's Xena?"

"I'm not bringing that beast running. She'll kill me," Sequoia said. "I left her in the kennel out back. Ready?"

They started out at a slow jog, and as always, Sequoia stopped after about a quarter-mile to stretch. She thought about angling her rear end towards him as she did her hamstring stretches, but decided he'd know it was contrived.

Without speaking, she started jogging again, and after a little lag, Elijah caught up to her quickly.

Sequoia saw the curiosity in Julie's eyes when she approached with a running companion.

"How's the job?" Sequoia said.

"It's great," Julie said, and her enthusiasm had Sequoia slowing to talk to her. Elijah slowed down, too, and put his hands on top of this head, fingers laced.

"Are they treating you well?" Sequoia said.

"The best," Julie said. "I mean, it's mindless work, but I'll be getting my first paycheck next week. Can't beat that."

"I'm so happy for you," Sequoia said, and then she nodded and jogged away because she had yet another strange urge: the urge to invite Julie out for coffee. Sequoia rarely shared meals with anyone other than her sisters or her co-workers. While coffee wasn't exactly a meal, it was the gateway to a meal. And a meal was the gateway to a real relationship.

Elijah was right on her heels this time, and, of course, he continued the line of questioning he'd started at breakfast the day he found out she brought Julie food every day.

"She got a job, huh?"

"Yeah, she did. At that bookstore, Turn the Page. She's doing stocking and stuff. Nothing big, but she can move up to cashier and maybe management. And she likes reading. So it's a good fit, I think. Should be enough to get her an apartment."

"That's great. Hopefully she doesn't go to Peaceful Breeze."

"I know. I've given her a list of places she can afford and there are a couple that are slightly better than that. But she'll need more of a work history, I think. She can keep staying at the shelter until then, I guess."

They jogged for a few more minutes, coming down to the harbor, where Sequoia turned right to run towards the open ocean. The ice plant, thick green and dotted with white, yellow, and orange flowers, cascaded down the slope between the running path and the water. Sequoia inhaled through her nose, and concentrated on the warmth of the sun on her face.

"Beautiful day," she said, not remembering she wasn't alone until Elijah spoke.

"So, I've been thinking," he said. "I want to try an experiment."

Conversations that started this way never ended well, Sequoia thought. She wished, hard, that she'd declined his invitation to run together. This is why running alone always worked out so nicely. But maybe she was reading too much into it. Maybe this had something to do with Beth Hardwick or the Marvins or Xena.

Sequoia took a deep breath and said, "Hit me with it."

"You know how you told me you're not cut out for relationships?"

He made air quotes around "not cut out," and she cringed. She'd imagined the worst, and it was coming true. He wanted to try an experiment, which undoubtedly would revolve around her (tried-and-true) assertion that she wasn't relationship material. Could it get any worse?

"Yes. I do know how I told you that," she said.

"Now, now, don't go getting all prickly on me, Sequoia."

When she found herself loving the sound of him saying her name, she bit down, hard, on her bottom lip. "I'm not prickly."

"Okay."

They ran along the coast, and Sequoia focused on the greenish-blue water, sparkling in the sunlight. She waited for Elijah to speak.

"So. The experiment," he said.

She sighed, loudly.

"I hear your disdain," he said. "Noted. But just hear me out."

"Fine."

"I want you to give me the chance to convince you that you could, you know, *do* a relationship."

Alarms blared.

Was this Elijah's excuse, or made-up story, for getting her in bed with him? Was this his idea of a joke? Was it the equivalent of that day so long ago when Mack sicced Xena on her in the office and all her co-workers had a week's worth of entertainment at her expense?

No wonder she'd been prickly.

"Do you have a bet with someone?" she asked. "Or are you just on a personal mission to add another notch to your bedpost?"

Elijah snorted. "You're so jaded."

"Aren't we all?"

"Maybe when it comes to Boy Scout leaders and priests," he said.

Yes, they'd all read that book on the psychology of law enforcement officers that referenced these two groups of people. "But not when it comes to relationships. I think that if you give yourself—and me—a chance, you'll see that you really are relationship material."

She shook her head.

"This is a terrible idea."

"Is it?"

"I've known for years that I'm meant to be alone. A spinster. I mean, not even a cat lady. I can't even maintain a friendship with a cat, let alone many cats. You come along now, after having known me for a few short weeks, and you want to change something that's been set in stone for years? I don't think so. I mean, why do you think you're the one who can convince me that my reality is different from what I'm living?"

Even as she spoke, she wondered why she'd even let the conversation open up. She should have just shut him down right away.

"Excellent question," he said, holding up a finger.

She couldn't help but smile, and he went on, "I think I see you differently than other people see you. Other people see you as aloof, snobby, stuck up and hard-nosed."

When she grimaced, he laid a hand on her arm. "Sorry, but we both know it's true. Anyway, I see you as a funny, sharp, kind woman who could bring a lot to someone's life. And who, if you'd let it happen, could enjoy what someone else brought to your life."

Elijah's words shocked Sequoia speechless for a moment. She'd been called lots of things, but never kind or funny. They ran along the cliff, close enough to the edge that she could feel the sea spray when the waves hit the rocks. It felt so refreshing. She wanted to jump off the cliff and into the water, and swim to some remote island where she could sip umbrella drinks and enjoy her own company. Forever.

After a long pause in the conversation, Elijah said, "Well?"

Sequoia said, "Well, that was quite a speech, Casanova."

"Just tellin' it like it is."

They ran along for a few more minutes, turning right and then right again to head back to the office. When they passed the coffee shop, Elijah broke the silence.

"So? What do you say?"

"About what?"

"Shut up. About the experiment. Will you take me up on it?"

She shook her head. "Um, no," she said. "Of course not. I don't want to be an experiment to you or to anybody else. I've done the experiment already, actually, and it failed. So."

He shrugged. She did her best to get a look at him out of the corner of his eye, and she couldn't really read his expression.

"Okay," he said. His tone was light, and she was disappointed that he wasn't disappointed. "Your choice. But the offer's open."

They completed their run without talking anymore. By the time they got back to the office, Sequoia wished she could head home. But her shift started soon. Rather than giving Elijah any kind of proper farewell, she walked past him and into the locker room.

Good ideas always came to Sequoia in the shower, and despite the lukewarm water in the locker room, Sequoia still managed to do some serious thinking under the spray.

She had to admit that she wouldn't mind getting between the sheets with Elijah. As the water coursed down her torso, she thought it wouldn't be so bad to get into the shower with him, either. Undoubtedly he'd be a great lover. He'd already proven himself to be considerate.

He had to be skilled, she thought as she tipped her head back to wet her hair. How could anyone that good-looking not be? He struck her as one of those athletic types, who'd thrown perfect spiral passes at age seven and run five-minute miles in high school, all without trying too hard.

But how did she feel about the whole relationship being some kind of weird experiment in his secret relationship lab?

The payoff—great sex—was definitely there ... but was she willing to resort to analysis and examination as part of Elijah's experimentation? Why had he even brought this up, anyway?

Knowing the male psyche, it was probably because he wanted to prove to himself that he could bring Sequoia Carr down. He could be the one to break through her walls, melt her icy heart, and whatever other manly clichés she wasn't thinking of now.

She poured shampoo into her palm and began scrubbing her

scalp. What would it be like to have Elijah in the shower behind her, rubbing her hair into a lather, right now? Of course, she shivered.

Even while her lady parts warmed at the prospect of Elijah Sawyer naked behind her in the shower, the rational three-quarters of her brain began to feel more than a little indignant.

How dare Elijah Sawyer suggest such an operation?

Didn't he think she knew herself well enough to know she wasn't good as one half of a pair? Didn't he think she'd be in a relationship if she wanted to? Didn't he think she was capable of determining, for herself, whether she could make it work with anyone else?

Obviously not.

Self-righteousness made her face hot.

He probably just wanted to be able to brag to his friends that he'd conquered the unconquerable Sequoia Carr.

Well, that wasn't going to happen. Sequoia Carr wasn't anybody's project. Still, she thought as she toweled off, if she did have a pretend, experimental relationship with a man, Elijah would be a pretty good specimen. A little voice from somewhere behind her right ear told her she should concede, give it a go, but she ignored it. Dating someone, even experimentally, could mean nothing but disaster. Anyway, Elijah hadn't seemed too upset when she'd turned him down cold. He'd probably already dismissed the idea.

AT THIS POINT, no one expected Sequoia to make any actual work-related appearances with Xena. So she decided to take an office day, and let the dog follow her inside, where she curled up under the desk and made herself completely forgettable.

"This is the most I've liked you since we met," Sequoia muttered.

Then she looked around to see if anyone had noticed her talking to the dog. No, no one was even in the office.

"Good," Sequoia said. "Because that would be embarrassing."

Sequoia's phone dinged. The text message was from Elijah: *Have you reconsidered?*

Hmm. So he hadn't already discarded the idea.

She wrote back: *Not yet,* and tapped Send before she realized she should have left it at *No.*

"Shit," she whispered. "That was my subconscious talking, Xena."

He sent her an emoticon with a red face with devil's horns. She wished she could roll her eyes at him, but she found herself smiling as she set her phone down. How could she respond to that?

Once she'd caught up on her reports and emails, she decided to head out and patrol for a while. She stationed herself at her favorite spot along the highway, although she wondered how lucrative it would be on day shift.

Before she even saw a single speeder, her phone signaled another text. Sequoia kicked herself for hoping it was from Elijah, and she kicked herself again for feeling elated, jubilant even, that it was.

He'd typed: *How about now?*

She could ignore him. In fact, she probably should ignore him. And she did. For a few minutes.

But then she couldn't help herself. Her fingers flew, almost compulsively, over the keyboard: *Leave me alone, man. I'm a lone wolf.*

She tried to find a wolf emoticon, but no luck. So she deleted the text and put her phone on the passenger seat without responding.

Finally, someone sped by in a little black roadster, and Sequoia flicked on her lights and sirens, hoping for a distraction. Unfortunately, the stop took less than five minutes, because as soon as Sequoia found out the driver was a man on his way to the hospital where his wife was in labor, she wished him luck gave him an escort.

Her phone dinged again as she pulled away from the hospital.

What, no witty comeback?

She surprised herself again by grinning at the phone. This time, she responded: *I don't even know what to say to you.*

He wrote back immediately: *Say yes. You won't be sorry.*

I'm not sure your 'experiment' is a good idea, she wrote.

But are you sure it's a bad idea?

"No," she said aloud. Again, though, she put her phone on the passenger seat without sending a response.

Her shift would have passed slowly if Elijah hadn't continued texting her.

At one point, he wrote: *I think it's a good idea.*

When she didn't respond, he wrote: *Come on. I know you do, too.*

Finally, she responded: *I gave you my answer.*

He wrote back: *Was your answer no?*

When Sequoia laughed out loud, Xena stuck her head through the pass-through window and tried to lick Sequoia's face. Sequoia cringed and pushed the dog's head away.

I can't even remember, she wrote.

Hmm. I don't think it was. I think it was something kind of deflective, like "I'm not relationship material."

I don't even know what to say to you right now.

Say you'll try it.

Should she? Not for the first time, she pictured Elijah filling various roles in her life. What would it be like for him to stand next to her at the kitchen counter, chopping vegetables for salad? What would it be like for him to sit at her counter, drinking a beer while she fried chicken, or for her to see him grilling steaks on her barbecue while she sipped wine?

What the hell was she thinking?

I need some space, she wrote.

Okay, he responded.

He didn't write again for the rest of her shift. She kept checking her phone, checking to see how many bars she had for reception, wondering whether he'd texted, but it hadn't come through. It was only when she finally checked off and drove home—to her empty house—that she realized she was actually missing the witty banter.

And it was then that she knew she wanted to take him up on the experiment. Not because she was convinced that he could prove to her that she was relationship material, but because she wanted to spend more time with Elijah Sawyer.

CHAPTER THIRTEEN

EVEN THOUGH SHE'D DECIDED SHE WANTED TO TRY THE EXPERIMENT, Sequoia didn't want to tell Elijah right away.

The night he made the proposal, she went through her routine picturing him by her side at every stage of it. Would he sit on the couch with her and read? Would he wear his socks to bed?

And, she wondered, shivering with anticipation, what would it be like to make love to him all over the house?

Still, the stubborn side of her waited until the following morning to let him know she was game. When she woke up, and after she'd had some coffee, she texted him: *Fine.*

That was it. She wondered how he'd respond when he saw it. Would he throw his head back and laugh? Would he grin, but not say anything? Would he whisper, "I told you so," or, "You're on"?

She had no idea.

And she had even less of an idea because he didn't respond for quite some time.

She went for a run, showered and put on her uniform, and got Xena into the car, all while checking her phone over and over again. Still no answer. But, she thought, only two hours had passed. He would just be coming off shift. He shouldn't be sleeping or anything. So he really should be able to answer.

Maybe she'd see him when she got to the office.

An aggressive driver derailed her, though, and she had to pull him over and write him a ticket before she actually made it to the office. Elijah was long gone by then, and he still hadn't answered.

For the second day in a row, as she went through the motions, she spent every spare moment thinking about Elijah and what he was doing. Maybe he was meeting up with another woman.

If slapping herself was an effective form of preventing stupidity, she would have done so, then. What did it matter if Elijah was meeting up with someone else? What did it matter, for goodness's sake, if he was having sex with that someone else at this very moment? She had no claim over him.

And then a huge sense of relief filled her veins when her phone alerted a text had come in.

Only, it wasn't from Elijah, it was from Jasmine, who was confirming their dinner plans for that evening.

"Shit," Sequoia said.

Xena, looking steadily out the patrol car window, seemed unconcerned. Sequoia heard her tail wagging, swishing against the smooth surface of her doggie compartment.

Hours passed and still no word from Elijah. Finally, it was time to head to training with the other K-9 officers, so Sequoia moved out of her hiding spot and headed toward the office. She hated that she was still thinking about Elijah.

She'd expected him to jump on her acceptance, to begin laying plans for the experiment right away, but nothing. It was humiliating. How stupid. She should never have accepted his challenge.

Because ultimately, wasn't that what it was? A challenge?

He was challenging her to a relationship of which she already knew she wasn't capable.

And she'd accepted.

So shouldn't he say something?

She marched into training with Xena at her side, praying her new K-9 partner couldn't sense the flurry of emotions running through her body.

After an hour of intense training, during which Xena did almost nothing Sequoia commanded her to do (other than sit there and wag her tail), the phone made its friendly dinging noise and let her know Elijah had responded to her.

He wrote: *Let me take you out to dinner. Clouds Café, 5 p.m. This Saturday? I'll pick you up at 4:45.*

Without warning, Sequoia's body simply lit up. Her heart beat faster, her skin tingled, her ears buzzed. She was vibrating. Her cheeks ached.

"This is ridiculous," she said to Xena. "I'm reacting like a twelve-year-old."

Xena looked at her as if to say, "So what?" and Sequoia drove home without looking at the dog again.

This was it. Should she go on a date with Elijah? Was this the point of no return? Maybe it was. And if she turned him down, she'd be sorry. But would she be even sorrier if she went out with him?

It was unlikely—beyond unlikely—that he'd want to spend much time with her after a couple of dates. She'd proven that before (several times over).

Elijah was a smart man. He'd discover the truth on his own, soon enough.

But what if she could enjoy his company until then? Living in the moment, and all that. It wasn't much of a stretch, actually. They seemed to have several things in common. He seemed to enjoy her company, her stories.

But Sequoia knew from experience that a man liking her company and stories didn't mean he'd like dating her, long-term. But just one dinner? What could dinner hurt?

Finally, after over-thinking how her acceptance should read, she wrote back, *Yes, I'll go to dinner with you. See you Saturday.*

She had a date with Elijah Sawyer, this Saturday.

"Shit," she said to Xena. "I'd better figure out what to wear."

"SO I DON'T WANT to look slutty, and I don't want to look like an old woman. In other words, don't put me in fishnet stockings and hooker boots, and don't put me in a cardigan."

Holly had just arrived at Sequoia's house, and Sequoia was mixing her a drink while they waited for Jasmine to show up. Xena paced back and forth between Sequoia and Holly, alternately licking their hands until Sequoia finally banished her to her crate.

"Wait. I still can't believe you have a date," Holly said. "Like, a real, live, actual date."

"Well, I do," Sequoia said. "Accept that reality, and let's move on."

"Just wear dark jeans and a nice top," Holly said. She twirled the olive jar on the counter. "I can't believe Sequoia the Queen is asking for clothing advice."

"It's not clothing advice. It's dating advice. There's a difference."

She slid Holly's martini across the counter, and Holly picked it up and took a sip before answering. Sequoia could tell she was suppressing a smile.

"Of course," Holly said. "I guess I didn't even realize you dated. You don't, do you? That's why you're asking for clothing-slash-dating advice. Who is the mystery guy, anyway?"

Sequoia shook her head. She didn't know exactly why, but she wasn't quite ready to tell Holly the mystery guy was Elijah. Maybe because Jasmine had spotted him first and suggested that Sequoia date him. So instead of answering, Sequoia said, "How's your dating life going? Still seeing that one guy?"

She tired of Xena's whining and released her from the crate. Of course, the dog was exuberant, and started up with the hand-nudging and -licking again.

"Why can you never remember the names of guys I date?"

"There have been too many?" Sequoia said. She was only half-joking. Holly did move from guy to guy like she was the creator of her own speed dating event. But it seemed like she'd been with the same one—Jeremy? Jimmy? Something with a J—for a while now.

"Anyway," Holly said. "We're here to talk about you. What finally got you to agree to go on an actual date with someone? A date where you actually care what you're going to wear?"

"That story is going to have to wait until Jasmine gets here. I'm only telling it once."

"Ooh, there's a story?" Holly's eyes lit up over the rim of her glass. "I love stories. Especially Sequoia stories. We never get to hear those."

When Sequoia didn't respond, Holly said, "Just give me a teaser. Like, a trailer. You know, like a movie trailer?"

"Um, no," Sequoia said. "Not going to happen. How is your personal training stuff going?"

Holly sighed. "It's going fine, Sequoia. I'm almost done. I should have my certification within a month."

"A month? Really?"

"Really," Holly said. "Just because you haven't noticed me working hard doesn't mean I'm not working hard."

Sequoia knew they were both remembering the time in high school when Holly labored and labored over this biology presentation. She kept it in her bedroom, and no one saw it until it was completely done. Sequoia had made such a big deal of being surprised at how well-done it was that Holly had finally told her to shut up.

"Sorry," Sequoia said now. "I've been a little preoccupied, that's all. That's great you're almost done."

Jasmine, always the peace keeper whether she knew it or not, came through the front door at that moment, saving Sequoia from causing further damage. Xena acted completely jubilant, prancing in place while wagging her entire body.

"Sorry I'm late," she said, bending down to pet the dog, who licked her face with a ferocity that made Sequoia cringe. "Stuck at work. And that's something I need to—"

"Sequoia has a story," Holly announced, emphasizing the word "story."

Jasmine glanced at Sequoia and then looked back at Holly. Why did she look so guilty?

"Let me make you a drink, Jas," Sequoia said, grabbing the bottle of gin.

But just as she began to twist off the lid, Jasmine held up a hand.

"No, it's okay," she said. "I can't stay long, anyway. Let's call this meeting of The Garden Club to order. To the closet."

Sequoia looked at Holly, who was looking back at her with an expression Sequoia knew mirrored her own. They both shrugged, and Sequoia led the way to her bedroom. Xena, of course, brought up the rear.

Because Jasmine's strange behavior was setting off alarm bells in her mind, though, she decided to keep her story to herself. This was not the time to admit she was the subject of Elijah Sawyer's experiment.

Come to think of it, why had she considered sharing that with her sisters, anyway? It was embarrassing, for one, and two, they'd be disappointed when they learned that the two of them were dating only in the name of science … not because of any real connection.

So when Holly sat down on Sequoia's bed and looked up at her expectantly, Sequoia shrugged a shoulder in an effort to seem nonchalant.

"Okay, it's not really that much of a story. I was just building up the excitement. It's just that Elijah Sawyer asked me out a week ago, and I turned him down. But then I changed my mind."

"Wow. That is not much of a story," Holly said.

Now, Jasmine looked at Sequoia as if *she* were the one behaving strangely.

"Well, let's choose an outfit," Sequoia said.

Holly went through Sequoia's closet with laser precision and cunning efficiency, and laid three outfits on the bed. Jasmine nixed two of the shirts immediately because they showed too much cleavage ("I know you've never worn these, Sequoia Jean. You should just get rid of them.").

Holly paired the third top with a pair of dark skinny jeans and high heels.

"So your running pants have got nothing on this outfit," she said. "He's gonna flip when he sees you in heels. Seriously. I can't wait to hear about his reaction. When's your date, again?"

"Saturday."

"That's tomorrow," Holly said.

Sequoia nodded.

After a beat of silence, Jasmine said, "Look, I've gotta go."

Before Sequoia or Holly could ask her where she had to go to, she practically disappeared.

"That was weird," Sequoia said.

"Like a ghost," Holly said.

From her spot on the floor at the foot of the bed, Xena whined, her head cocked to one side like she, too, wanted to know what was going on with Jasmine.

CHAPTER FOURTEEN

It wasn't like this was a real date, Sequoia kept telling herself. So why in the world was she experiencing symptoms of nervousness, like sweaty palms and a sensitive stomach? Why had she planned her date preparation down to the minute?

To make things worse, it was almost as if Xena could sense her anxiety. The dog sat as close as possible to her, following her every move. Even when Sequoia moved from the bathroom sink to the shower, the dog relocated, and then sat back on her haunches, looking quite watchful.

Right now, at precisely one hour and twenty-seven minutes before she was set to leave, she was turning on the shower. She'd give the water two minutes to heat up, and then she'd get in. When she got out fifteen minutes later (allowing for time to shave her legs —what was she thinking?), she would put on unscented lotion. She'd then have thirty minutes to mess with her hair, because she knew her go-to hairstyles (a bun, a French braid tucked in, and a French twist) weren't going to cut it for tonight. Even if she wore her hair down, she'd need time to dry it.

Was she being so organized because she wanted to give Elijah's experiment the best possible chances of uncovering an accurate answer? Or was it because she wanted to look her best so she could prove to him that nothing—not even high heels and extra mascara (six minutes: double the usual amount of time she allotted)—could make a man fall in love with her?

Or, Heaven forbid, was it because she actually wanted to impress him?

She stepped into the shower, cranked the heat up even more, and let the scalding water beat down on her head. Preparing for a man was such a different task than preparing for work.

Preparing for romance was so much more difficult than preparing for life-and-death situations. Which is exactly why being a cop suited her so well.

Xena was now leaning against the shower door. Sequoia could see her fur against the glass. "Weird dog," she said.

The sudsy soap felt so silky against her skin that she started envisioning Elijah and a bottle of massage oil. This sped up her shower time considerably, and she emerged after twelve minutes instead of fifteen.

Great. She hated being ready too early and being forced to wait around. It only made the nerves worse. She toweled off and stepped over Xena, whose head swiveled so she could watch Sequoia's every move.

Maybe if she spent a little longer on the lotion.

She texted Holly and Jasmine: *Should I wear perfume?*

Holly texted back: *Yes. But just 2 sprays.*

Jasmine texted back: *Sure.*

Jasmine's shorter-than-usual text reminded Sequoia of her strange behavior the night before. Although Sequoia wasn't one to analyze and over-analyze the behavior of people in her personal circle, she did find herself curious.

Not curious enough to ask, though, at this point. She had clothes and perfume to put on, and hair to style. Finally, *finally*, the clock meandered its way to forty minutes after four, and Sequoia was ready.

She took one last look at herself in the mirror—long, dark hair flowing over her shoulders, thin legs encased in tight jeans, calves rounded above spiky heels. Her eyes looked quite nice, if she did say so, herself. The mascara made them look lighter than usual—almost amber. And she smelled good, too.

When Elijah's experiment failed, at least she'd go down looking drop-dead gorgeous.

Xena followed her into the living room, where they both sat facing the front door. Sequoia was surprised when she realized she was stroking the dog's head, and stopped immediately. Xena turned around to glare at her.

Elijah knocked on the door.

Xena barked, and Sequoia stood up. She put a hand on the dog's head. The barking stopped.

"Let the experiment begin," she said.

Yes, Sequoia Carr felt a surge of satisfaction when Elijah saw her and his mouth dropped open. Did that make her vain? She didn't care if it did.

"Wow," he said. "You look … normal."

"Wow," she said. "You're great at compliments."

He looked down at his feet, one of which scuffed at something on the ground. Was he *embarrassed?* Xena, who had until that point observed from Sequoia's side, now ran up to nudge Elijah's hand.

"Hi, Xena," Elijah said, squatting down so they were face to face. "I can't believe I just said she looked *normal.*"

Xena licked Elijah's nose. He stood up, wiping his nose with one hand.

"And to think I called you Casanova on our run the other day," Sequoia said. "Let me just put her in her crate, and we can go."

She shook her head as she walked Xena to the bedroom. She wasn't really shaking her head about calling Elijah Casanova. She was shaking her head because she'd referred to the run as "their" run. Double possessive.

That was weird.

As soon as you started sharing possessions, you were practically a couple.

"No rush," Elijah called. "Our reservation's not until quarter after. They couldn't get us in right at five."

"There's that word again," Sequoia muttered to Xena. "'Our'

reservation. Next thing I know he's going to be talking about 'our' experiment, and before I know it, 'our' bedroom. This whole thing smells like disaster. Or maybe that's just the stink of your dog bed."

Xena walked into her crate, turned around six times, and laid down.

"I'll see you in a few hours," Sequoia said.

When she came back into the living room, Elijah was standing in the same spot she'd left him and the low afternoon sun silhouetted his lean body like he was some sexy cowboy in a Western romance novel. Instead of inviting him to remove his shirt, though, she grinned.

He looked uncertain, then, like he didn't know what she was thinking, and therefore, wasn't sure how to act. He walked toward her, and something in the air changed. The scene felt charged somehow, with electricity or lust or maybe just nerves. She'd never stopped to consider that he was nervous, too, but he confirmed it when he stood before her and took her hands in his.

"I'm sorry I said you look normal," he said. She saw a hint of humor in his eyes, but his expression remained serious. "I'm just not used to seeing you in street clothes. You know? It's either a uniform or those damned sexy, skintight running pants you wear. But this? This is even better. You look great, Sequoia, is what I should have said. You look delicious. And it's probably a good thing this is our first date. Because if it wasn't, we would definitely miss our reservation."

Sequoia felt *her* mouth drop open and a jolt of heat drop to her lady parts.

"Why, thank you, Elijah," she said when she found her voice. "I do believe you've just given me an actual compliment."

He shook his head again, then dropped one of her hands but held the other as he led her out of the house.

"You've gone and made me hungry," he said. "Let's get dinner."

When they reached the car, he pulled her back when she automatically reached for the passenger door handle.

"Let me get that for you," he said. "My experiment, my rules."

At least he wasn't referring to it as their experiment, Sequoia thought. She hid her pleased expression as she slid into the seat.

Clouds Café was the swankiest offering in Seabreeze. High ceilings and sparkling glass light fixtures made it feel modern, while a corner fireplace, white linen tablecloths and candles at every table made it cozy.

The management hired only experienced staff members, so it was unlikely that Elijah and Sequoia would come across any of the people they'd arrested in the past (an uncomfortable situation that occurred way to often at restaurants of a lower grade).

The hostess led them to a corner booth, and they were immediately faced with an uncomfortable situation Sequoia hadn't anticipated, as if this whole experiment thing wasn't uncomfortable enough on its own: both of them wanted to face the door when they sat down.

The only satisfactory option was to sit next to each other on one side of the booth, which they managed with minimal shuffling.

"Well, this is cozy," Elijah said.

The hostess handed them menus, and when Elijah pointed out the lemon butter scallops, Sequoia leaned across him to look at his menu.

"Mmm, you smell good," Elijah said. "Really good."

His voice had taken on a guttural quality, which made Sequoia suddenly and extremely uneasy. So the perfume had been a good idea. She'd have to remember to tell Holly. She considered switching to the other side of the booth but thought that would be giving up too easily.

It wasn't like he had the same reaction to her that she did to him, she reminded herself. This was more of a challenge to him, simply to see if he could convince her that she could do relationships. Not a relationship, with him, specifically. So moving would give him more power than she was willing to give him at this point.

Instead, she straightened up and closed her menu.

She said, "I'll have the peppercorn steak."

Elijah ordered a bottle of wine, and as soon as the server walked away after pouring each of them a glass, he lifted his in a toast.

"To the experiment," he said. "Cheers."

"Cheers," Sequoia said, although his mention of the experiment created a fluttery feeling in her stomach and chest.

"So, I wanted to lay this out," he said, his expression businesslike. "You know, the parts of the experiment? So, I think, obviously, the question is, 'Is Sequoia Carr capable of a healthy romantic relationship?'"

"Shouldn't you be writing this down?" she said, half-joking.

He felt his shirt pocket. "I don't have a pen on me."

"I do," she said. "If there's one thing I've learned from Jasmine, it's to always keep a pen and notepad handy."

She handed him the pen and notepad she removed from her purse. He wrote *The Sequoia Experiment* at the top of a blank page, and then listed out the headings: *Question, Background Research, Hypothesis, Testing, Analysis and Conclusion.*

"This is actually humiliating," Sequoia said. "I mean, you're writing this down."

"It's an experiment, not a romantic relationship," he said.

That shut her up.

"So," he said, turning slightly toward her in the booth, pen poised, "We know the question."

He wrote it down. "Background research, completed by the subject herself, Sequoia Carr, shows that she is incapable of a romantic relationship. The scientist, Elijah Sawyer, suspects that said research was flawed by some kind of traumatic relationship experience. The scientist, Elijah Sawyer, has conducted his own background research by spending time with the subject. Thus, the hypothesis: Sequoia Carr is, in fact, very sexy."

She gave him a stern look. He pretended to cross something out, and said, "Er, I mean, Sequoia Carr is, in fact, capable of a healthy romantic relationship."

Sequoia put her head in her hands. Then she sat up and took a sip of her wine.

Elijah continued. "Testing will now commence. During testing, scientist Elijah Sawyer will court subject Sequoia Carr."

"Court? Is that old-fashioned?"

"Yes. But I think traditional courting will provide the most scientific data, in this case."

"But I'm not old-fashioned."

"You're old-fashioned in terms of the qualities I believe make you relationship material, which are kindness and compassion. I know you're independent, too, but I think certain men respect that spirit in a woman."

"Certain men?"

Elijah broke eye contact and smoothed the napkin on his lap.

"Shouldn't you describe the process of said testing?" Sequoia said.

"I will," Elijah said. He tapped his temple. "In here. But I'm keeping it under wraps so as not to taint the testing process. Although, I will say I have a feeling you're going to enjoy it."

Sequoia was surprised when the server returned to fill her wine glass and she noticed Elijah had barely touched his. She wondered if wine was an element of the testing process, and she vowed to slow down, lest her judgment should become impaired.

"I would like to conduct a little more background research, though," Elijah said. "And as my subject, you're obligated to answer all my questions."

She wondered if he could feel her squirming.

"I can practically feel you squirming."

"Hm."

The server saved her from any immediate questioning when he brought their food. Again, Sequoia debated moving to the other side of the booth. She liked her own space. But again, she forced herself to remain in place so Elijah wouldn't think he was making her squeamish.

He took a bite of his food and a sip of his wine, and then set his silverware down. "Tell me why you believe you're destined for singledom."

She chewed her steak for way longer than necessary. "Do I have to?" she finally said.

He shrugged one shoulder. "Yeah."

"Fine." She began to tell him the story of Walt Walters and his bimbo of a girlfriend. As she spoke, she felt a great tension unfurling, like a sail being let out to catch the wind. She'd never told anyone the whole story before, mostly because she knew she was the party at fault. She shared with Elijah the way she'd felt when Walt blamed her for their relationship's demise—slightly hurt but mostly, vindicated. It was as if Walt's comments simply verified what she'd known all along. Her sisters, the people closest to her, often chided her for being too honest, too intense, too serious. And Walt echoed their sentiments. So it must be true.

The truth, she discovered, was that she would end up alienating anyone with whom she tried to create a long-term relationship. She'd belittle that person, make him feel inadequate, and generally just wear him down. It's what she'd done to Walt, and he only sought other companionship (slutty, long-legged companionship) because Sequoia had driven him to it.

"So there you go," she said. "How is that for background research?"

When she finished, Elijah let out a long, low whistle.

Then he apparently remembered they were in a swanky restaurant, and looked around to see if anyone had noticed the whistle.

"That Walt guy really did a number on you, didn't he?"

Sequoia hated that she saw something close to pity—even if it was just empathy—in his eyes.

She shrugged as if to brush it off. "I mean, he was right. I was cold. I was unavailable, emotionally and otherwise. I'm not as intense at work as I used to be, but at that time, I never turned down a call or an overtime detail. I loved it. I was crazed about being out there on patrol. So it's no wonder he needed more than I could give. Or would give."

"Did you ever think you didn't give more to him because he's a jerk?"

"Have you met Walt?"

"No," Elijah said. "But you've told me enough. He blamed you for his own bad behavior. Haven't you seen that enough in our occupation? You should have known not to take what he said at face value, yet you were about to ruin your own chances of ever finding love. Until me."

His grin showed that he'd meant that last part as a joke, and she relaxed.

"Not very scientific, Sawyer," she said.

He said, "Just you wait."

When Elijah pulled his car up in front of Sequoia's house after dinner, he said, "Now you sit tight. I'm going to come around and open your door for you. That's what a gentleman does while courting, and it's what you deserve."

Before she could answer, he was out of the car and at her side, offering a hand to help her to her feet. They both knew she didn't need a hand, and he had to know how difficult it was for her to allow this kind of courtesy. Again, he kept his hand wrapped around hers while they walked, and he stopped to face her when they reached the door.

"I had a really nice time tonight," Elijah said. "Surprisingly so."

She felt an indignant expression cross her face, and he amended, "I mean, I figured we'd have a nice time. Obviously. But I was pleasantly surprised at how nice you were to me. Considering."

He dropped her hands and then tucked a strand of hair behind her ear.

"You're really beautiful, you know," he said.

Her breath caught. When he leaned forward, she felt like she should back away. Feelings, actual emotions, swirled through her being. Was this really just an experiment to see whether he could talk her into bed, and if so, how fast?

But then he whispered in her ear, "Goodnight, Sequoia," and walked back to his car before she could even find the words to return the pleasantries.

Sequoia's phone rang just as she let Xena out of her crate. She barely heard the ringing over the dog's frantic, slobbery greetings, but managed to answer it and open the sliding glass door for Xena at the same time.

"Hey, Holly," she said. "You couldn't wait for me to call you, right? How'd you know I'd be home so early?"

"Sequoia."

Of course, hearing the serious tone of Holly's voice put Sequoia on alert. Was something wrong? Why wasn't she throwing out a million date-related questions? Had someone kidnapped her? Had her car broken down and stranded her on the side of the road, vulnerable? Knowing Holly, some kind of disaster had transpired. Out of reflex, Sequoia started looking for her keys, ready to go out to her own car and rush to Holly's side.

"Holly. You're freaking me out. What's wrong?"

A high and breathy laugh came through the earpiece, and relief flooded in.

"Have you seen today's paper?"

"Not yet. Why?"

"Remember how strange Jasmine was acting last night when we were helping you choose an outfit for your date? And then she left early?"

"Yeesss," Sequoia said.

"Well, I think I know why. Go grab the paper, read the front page, and call me back."

Holly disconnected.

With a growing sense of dread, Sequoia followed her sister's instructions. The newspaper lay on the driveway, rolled so tightly she couldn't see much more than a strip of black and white text and a color photo. She tucked her phone under her arm, picked up the paper, and unrolled it.

She picked out Jasmine's byline automatically, as she had since her sister began working at the *Daily Trumpet* years ago.

She saw the headline next, and that sense of dread grew stronger, permeating every part of her body, right down to her fingertips.

CHAPTER FIFTEEN

Sequoia couldn't avoid work forever. She couldn't even avoid it for a single shift. Plus, she'd never been one to shrink away from a challenge. But Beth Hardwick was one challenge she wouldn't mind hiding from. Forever.

Xena didn't seem to mind Beth Hardwick. Of course, the traitor dog trotted right up to the woman like she was her new BFF.

"In my office," Beth said to Sequoia.

Sequoia felt like she was eight years old again, following the school principal, Mr. Pearson, to the office after throwing wood chips in the toilet. That was two-and-a-half decades ago. She'd hung her head in shame then, but she held her chin high now.

They sat down, and Beth leaned forward to put her elbows on her desk, hands folded. "I'm sure you saw that article in the *Daily Trumpet* Saturday. Your sister's article."

Sequoia nodded. "I did."

"What did you think of it?"

The headline, splashed across the top of the page, just below the banner, screamed, *City of Seabreeze Prosecutor Plans to File Embezzlement Charges Against Seabreeze PD Lieutenant.*

Beth Hardwick was being accused of embezzlement, and there, below that bold announcement, stood Jasmine Carr's byline.

"I can't really say," Sequoia said after a long pause.

"You can't say, or you won't say?" Beth said.

"I don't even know what to think. Innocent until proven guilty, right? So I don't have an opinion at this point."

"Well, you should. Your sister wrote the article."

"My sister is a professional, just like I am. She undoubtedly wrote the story based on public information and facts. I read the story, and it's very fair. She reported the facts. Just like I do at work, I'm remaining objective."

"Yeah?" Beth said. Her pretty, pouty lips twisted into a sneer.

"Yeah," Sequoia said.

"Well, I'm *not* remaining objective. If you don't get your sister under control, you're going down, too."

That same feeling of dread that had planted itself in Sequoia's gut when she first saw Jasmine's headline was growing into a tall, nasty vine. It wound itself upward, tendrils looping around her esophagus, threatening to choke her. She swallowed.

"For what?"

"It doesn't matter. For your sister pulling me down. I won't go down easily, and I won't go down alone."

"Why didn't you take Earl Little down with you instead of having him killed?" Sequoia said.

Beth was smart enough not to react, but Sequoia didn't miss the quick flash of recognition in her eyes, almost an affirmation. Cops had found Earl's dead body in his apartment a few weeks back, and rumors circulated implicating Beth's involvement. Maybe the rumors were true. Maybe she was worried he'd give too much away when it came to the department's missing money.

"I have no idea what you're talking about. Earl was in the wrong place at the wrong time."

"Because you made sure he was."

Xena was on alert, her pointy nose turning alternately toward Beth and Sequoia as they spoke. Sequoia was no detective, but Beth Hardwick was practically walking herself into a confession right now. She hadn't once outright denied involvement in Earl's death.

And again, her eyes registered acknowledgement of what Sequoia said.

"Look, Carr," Beth said. "You'd better find a way to convince your sister to stop writing stories on this particular topic. Understand?"

"Oh, I understand," Sequoia said. "I got it. Here's what you might not understand, though. My sister is an adult. Just like it's my job to enforce the laws, it's her job to report the news. She doesn't control what the news is any more than I control which crimes people commit on any given day. If you don't want her reporting the news, don't create it."

Beth gestured to her office door. "I think we're done here."

As Sequoia put her hand on the knob, Beth said, "And Carr? This conversation never happened. As far as I'm concerned, you were in here complaining about that dog."

Once again, Sequoia was surprised to see Elijah still at the office even though his shift had ended an hour ago. As she walked out of Beth Hardwick's office and noticed him standing near her desk, she made a conscious effort to smooth the scowl off her face.

"Morning," he said.

"Ugh," she said.

"Wow. That is not the way to greet a nice guy who treated you to a very nice dinner and a bottle of wine not two nights ago. Also, if I'm courting you, I expect more positive responses to my greetings."

"You're right," she said. "I'm sorry. How are you?"

"I'm fine. But I'm guessing your mood has something to do with Jasmine's story in Saturday's paper. Which we both missed because we were so excited about the beginning of our experiment."

Sequoia rolled her eyes, but felt herself smiling at the same time.

"You know," she said. "I could use some help with Xena this morning. Want to join me?"

"Got nothing better to do," he said. She took the comment at face value until he said, "Come on, Carr. You can't let guys talk to you like that when they're courting you. My research is revealing that you don't set high enough expectations. It's a privilege to spend time with you. I should be jumping on the opportunity. Which I am. Let's go."

"I have no idea what to make of this," Sequoia said.

As they walked past Beth Hardwick's office, Sequoia could see her glaring at them through the window. Just then, she closed the blinds with a quick tug.

"What's happening there?" Elijah asked.

"Since the conversation never happened," Sequoia said, "I'll have to fill you in later."

As soon as Elijah opened the door to the training yard, Xena burst through it and tore around the place like her tail was on fire.

"Wow, somebody's excited about training," Elijah said. "Have you been working with her?"

"Yeah, but she doesn't do what she's supposed to when we're working together. The other guys can get her to do anything. They got her up on the hood of a car yesterday, and she was all pleased with herself. I can barely make her sit."

"Is she still whining in her crate at night?" he said.

"I know, it's because I'm not cuddling with her."

"Don't get defensive. See, Sequoia, this is where men think you're cold and bristly. I asked a simple question and you're shutting me down because you believe I'm going to say you should cuddle with her and you think it's ridiculous. In fact, you probably wouldn't admit it even if you did cuddle with her. Don't get prickly just because I asked you a question."

How did he already know her so well?

"Fine. Yes. She is still whining and scratching in her crate at night. And no, I have not cuddled with her."

Xena had returned, and Elijah threw a ball for her. She watched it fly, her ears perked and her eyes focused, and then she charged after it, following it bounce for bounce until she snapped it up in her jaws. Her precision was actually impressive.

"You need more bonding," Elijah said.

"Are we still talking about dog training?"

A wicked gleam came into Elijah's eyes, and Sequoia blushed.

"Why, yes, we are still talking about dog training. Although bonding is a subject about which I'm pretty passionate. In fact, it might be part of my research during this experiment."

In what had become typical during a training session, Xena did everything Elijah commanded her to do.

"She's on it today," he said at one point, delighted with her antics as she alerted on a hide he'd made particularly difficult.

Sequoia felt a tiny stirring of pride at the dog's performance.

"She is," she said. "But it's so frustrating that she turns into a regular house dog whenever I try to get her to do something. I tell her to look for drugs and she spins around, waiting for me to throw the ball. I tell her to sit and she spins around again, like she has no idea what I want her to do."

"Just give her time," he said. "She doesn't quite know you guys are a team."

Sequoia groaned. "You're probably right," she said. "But why does she think you're her teammate?"

"I like dogs. It's a vibe, sweetheart."

"Whatever. Just don't try to tell me cuddling is the way to her heart."

"Maybe it is," Elijah said.

Satisfied with Xena's work, Elijah took off her harness. He followed Sequoia as she walked toward the building.

When they came to the door, Elijah reached up as if he were going to open it. Instead of grabbing the knob, though, he placed his palm flat on the door and leaned forward so the front of his body was just a breath away from the back of hers.

"By the way, Carr," he said, his breath warm in her ear, "you make those uniform pants look really sexy."

Before she could respond, he opened the door and followed her in. All morning long, Sequoia wondered what it was about Elijah that always left her speechless.

"SOMETHING STRANGE IS HAPPENING, HERE," Sequoia said to Xena several hours later. "First of all, I'm talking to a dog. So it's clear that I've lost my mind. Second of all, I actually miss Elijah Sawyer."

She'd never admit it to anyone, especially not to the man himself. But Xena wouldn't tell.

If talking to the dog weren't strange enough, Sequoia had—and then gave into—the urge to invite Elijah to lunch. Before she even realized what she was doing, she'd picked up her phone and sent him a message: *Can I take you out to lunch to thank you for your help with Xena today?*

It was a cover, and he'd know it. She wanted to spend time with him and it felt so needy. But it wasn't like she was texting him and asking him for a booty call. In some ways, inviting him to lunch felt even more scandalous, because it had nothing to do with sex. Well, almost nothing. She couldn't stop thinking about the feeling of his breath on her skin and the tone of his voice when he said she looked sexy in her uniform pants.

He didn't respond right away, and Sequoia felt grateful for the calls that came out, distracting her from checking her phone every five seconds.

Someone called in a family fight at the Peaceful Breeze, and Sequoia arrived to see a disheveled man come flying out the front door, followed closely by a heavy-looking soup pot. The man's wife screamed at him from inside, something about him having picked up the wrong kind of tomato sauce at the store. Once Sequoia got that argument settled, she responded to a fender bender just near the mall, where a texting teenager missed a red light and rear-ended an old lady.

Every time her brain had a spare moment to think, she second-guessed her decision to invite Elijah to lunch. What if he was sleeping? What if he had plans already? What if he was having lunch with someone else?

When she finally got back into her patrol car after scooping a drunk guy off the bar at the bowling alley, Elijah had responded to her text.

The drunk guy, who Sequoia had poured into her backseat to

take him to the drunk tank, groaned at her to, "Step on it, lady!" and she told him to shut up while she read her text message.

Are you asking me out?

So he was going to make her spell it out. He couldn't just accept or deny the invitation. She didn't even know how to answer. Should she say that yes, she was asking him out? She was still on the clock, though, so she could reasonably say that she wasn't. It wasn't really a date, after all. Or was it?

"Are we going, or aren't we?" the drunk guy slurred from behind her.

Xena barked at him, a single short yip.

"You tell him, sister," she said.

Sequoia put the car in gear and drove to the jail. Just as she pulled up, she received another text.

Just kidding. I can tell from your lack of response that you're either busy or don't know how to answer. Which is an interesting addition to my research. I don't want to put you on the spot, so, sure, I'd like to have lunch with you.

"Funny guy," Sequoia said.

She wrote back, *Taco Don's, 2 p.m.*

Then she half-carried, half-dragged her passenger into the jail.

LUIS, the owner of Taco Don's, opened his arms, palms up, when Sequoia walked in.

"Hola, amiga! How are you today? We have a special, just for you. Two fish tacos with beans and rice for five dollars."

Sequoia heard the jingle of the bells above the door, and could sense Elijah behind her a few seconds later. When he walked right up next to her and said to Luis, "I'll have whatever she's having," Luis's eyes lit up.

"Ah, the two of you?" He pointed at Sequoia, then Elijah, and then Sequoia again. "You are an item now?"

When they looked at each other, Elijah grinning and Sequoia

grimacing, Luis clapped his hands together. "How wonderful! Lunch is on the house today. Two fish taco specials, coming up."

"So you missed me, huh?" Elijah said when they settled at a corner table.

Sequoia chose that particular table so they could both sit facing the door without squeezing into a booth like they had the other night. She played with her straw wrapper, folding it into a set of stairs.

"Your silence affirms my suspicions," he said.

"You're pretty jovial, mister."

She finally made eye contact with him. His gaze was intense, and again held that thoughtful expression that both intrigued her and made her uncomfortable.

"How's your day going?" he said.

Small talk. She could do this. She ran through the calls she'd taken that morning. He shook his head when he told her about the soup-pot-throwing wife.

"That's love, right there," he said. "I promise never to bring you the wrong tomato sauce."

"Tomato sauce is tomato sauce," Sequoia said.

Luis walked out of the kitchen, carrying a tray. Both Sequoia and Elijah, accustomed to retrieving their orders off the counter, got to their feet to take the tray, but Luis said, "No, no, sit, please. I insist. Special delivery, for a special couple."

No one had ever complimented Sequoia's social niceties, but, for once, she kept her mouth shut and refrained from correcting Luis. As he arranged their plates and set out white paper napkins, she thought about what it would be like to be one-half of a real couple, in which Elijah was the other half.

To make lunch at Taco Don's a regular thing, to share work stories over meals all the time. Not that she wanted anything like that, but a girl could be curious.

"We should do this more often," Elijah said.

Sequoia's face must have looked panicked, because his eyes held understanding. "Don't worry. I'm not trying to convert you. I've just never seen Luis make a special delivery before."

When Sequoia's shoulders relaxed, Elijah added, "And also I enjoy your company. Don't freak out. That's something I'm supposed to say to you, as a man who is courting you. Yes, even if the courting is purely experimental."

He could read her so well.

"Careful," she said. "You don't want to taint your research by being nicer to me than most men are."

"It's most men who are the problem," Elijah said.

CHAPTER SIXTEEN

THE PROBLEM OF JASMINE'S NEWS STORY, AND THE POTENTIAL FOR future stories, weighed on Sequoia's mind throughout the days following the conversation that never happened with Beth Hardwick.

When Sequoia looked at the situation objectively, the timing of her sister's transformation from fluff writer to serious reporter was unfortunate, but Jasmine was just doing her job. And she was good at it.

Because the police department's money was taxpayer money, it was the newspaper's obligation to report on it. Beth Hardwick probably was embezzling money. She'd all but admitted it.

So, Beth Hardwick would just have to stuff it.

As Sequoia had anticipated, Jasmine—probably terrified that Sequoia would be mad at her about the story—tried to cancel The Garden Club's regularly scheduled weekly dinner, feigning "possibly a head cold or maybe allergies."

Sequoia didn't blame her. Normally, she would be mad.

But something had changed over the past week or two. Maybe it was lack of sleep due to dog noises. Or maybe it was newfound maturity.

Or maybe, said a tiny voice, *it's all the time you've been spending with*

Elijah Sawyer. He's painting your entire life with a special coat of happiness.

Sequoia silenced that voice immediately. She and Holly had arrived at Jasmine's house a few minutes before, at the usual time, and let themselves in. Jasmine hadn't looked the least bit surprised to see them.

"I see you've already set out our wine glasses," Sequoia said. "And you've set our places at the table."

"I was expecting someone else," Jasmine said.

"I thought you had possibly a head cold or maybe allergies," Holly said.

"I lied so I wouldn't have to see Sequoia," Jasmine said, her words running together. "I'm scared."

Sequoia poured the wine and savored the way Jasmine's mouth dropped open in surprise when she said, "Oh, your story? Don't be scared. It was well-written. You did your research. How does that saying go? 'Sisters before bosses'?"

"I think it's sisters before misters," Holly said.

"Something like that," Sequoia said. "Anyway, Jas, it's fine. Seriously. Off the record, Beth Hardwick threatened to take me down with her." Sequoia made finger quotes on, "take me down." "But to tell you the truth," she said, "I'm not worried about it. And that food smells really good. Chicken again?"

She led the way to the table.

"It's chicken, yes," Jasmine said. She pulled it out of the oven. "What has gotten into you, anyway? I thought you were going to kill me right here in my living room tonight after you saw that story."

"Over one story? No. Besides, if I was going to kill you, I would have killed you over that haircut you gave me my junior year. I can't believe I let you talk me into a pixie cut. Not just a pixie cut, but a pixie cut by you with a pair of Mom's sewing scissors."

"My hair-cutting skills were, admittedly, not very strong," Jasmine said as the three of them dished up. "But that was the day I knew I needed to reshape my dreams of becoming a hairstylist."

"And you became a journalist, so you could ruin my life again,"

Sequoia said. She'd meant it as a joke, but Jasmine blanched. "I'm totally kidding. Geez, don't take everything so seriously."

"You looked so hideous with that haircut," Holly said. "And on another note, why are you so cheerful?"

"Am I?" Sequoia said.

"Ooh! I know!" Jasmine said. "Luis told me you came into Taco Don's with a special someone. He said you sat at a table together."

Sequoia felt her face burning right away. Luis. That traitor. Gossip. He was like a little lady hen. Sequoia put her wine glass to her lips, tilted her head back, and drained that thing.

"She's blushing," Holly said.

"Working lunch," Sequoia said.

"It was Elijah Sawyer, wasn't it?" Jasmine said. "I knew it. I knew from the moment I saw him that you'd think he's hot. He is hot. So are you guys, like, an item, or what?"

"No," Sequoia said. They now treaded on dangerous ground. She could never admit that Elijah had convinced her to take part in this experiment. "Really. It was a working lunch. He's been helping me with Xena. I took him to lunch to thank him."

"Wait," Jasmine said. "You took him to lunch?"

"Have you ever taken anyone to lunch?" Holly said.

"Give me a break, you guys," Sequoia said. "It was just lunch."

"If it was just lunch, you wouldn't have gulped that wine down like a camel storing up for a drunken summer in the Sahara. Anyway, what's the big deal? You're dating someone. So what?"

If Sequoia were the researcher rather than the subject, she'd be taking note of her own feelings and behavior at this very moment. It had to mean something.

"It wasn't a date," she said, and then, because the wine hit her, she blurted out, "The other night at Clouds, now *that* was a date. I mean, we drank a whole bottle of wine. I've never done that at a restaurant. You know, the server comes over and refills your glass almost like magic."

She realized her mistake too late. Jasmine and Holly stared at her, eyes wide.

"Wait, what?" Jasmine said. "A date at Clouds? That is, like, *upscale*, my sister."

Sequoia nodded. Why was she spilling her guts like this?

"Dish," Holly said.

"Remember when we were kids and Jasmine kissed that guy, what was his name? It was her first kiss. Remember?"

Now Jasmine blushed. "Noah Thomas."

"Yes!" Sequoia said. "And we grilled you on it for days. I mean, it was really only minutes, but I'm sure you felt like it was days. You were so irritated with us."

"You guys were all up in my business," Jasmine said.

"Like you guys are all up in mine, right now," Sequoia said.

Jasmine and Holly exchanged a look.

Jasmine nodded. "We're all up in your business, but we're not asking you things about how he moved his tongue or whether his lips were soft or firm."

"Not yet," Sequoia said. "But isn't that where it all goes from here?"

"Nonsense," Jasmine said. "But have you kissed him? Tell me you kissed him, after Clouds. I mean, that's the height of romance."

Holly nodded, her eyes bright with anticipation.

Sequoia couldn't explain to her sisters that the romance bordered on contrived, since it was part of an experiment. She decided not to try.

"It was really nice," she said. "Elijah's really nice. We enjoyed each other's company. Then, this week, he helped me with Xena. So, I thanked him by taking him to lunch. I was in uniform. It was Taco Don's, not anywhere like Clouds. So it wasn't a date."

Sequoia also couldn't explain to her sisters that the lunch at Taco Don's had felt almost as romantic as the dinner at Clouds. Minus the uniform and that gossip Luis.

"Tell yourself whatever you need to," Holly said. "But I think you're pretty smitten."

"Twitterpated," Jasmine said. It had become her go-to word, when, several months before, her high school boyfriend, Parker

Abbott called her to reconnect after nearly two decades and Jasmine's editor saw her reaction to that phone call.

In the end, Jasmine had chosen Hudson Stover over Parker Abbott, but she'd stuck with the word, twitterpated, ever since.

Of course, Elijah chose that moment to text Sequoia, and as she read his message, she found herself becoming twitterpated.

This is your friendly reminder that we have a date in the morning with Xena. Wear those purple running tights.

The Carr sisters had never had proper boundaries, and Holly was already leaning over Sequoia's shoulder, reading the text.

"He said, 'Wear those purple running tights,'" she said. "Ooh, Sequoia, I can practically feel the chemistry."

"It's just a reminder text," she said.

"It would have been," Jasmine said, talking with her mouth full, "if he hadn't mentioned the tights. The mention of the tights changes everything."

"Stop talking with your mouth full. It's gross."

To Jasmine, Holly said, "Don't you agree?"

"Most certainly," Jasmine said.

They were right, she knew. She did feel chemistry. But the running tights comment could simply be part of the experiment, part of Elijah's typical courting process. So she wasn't going to get all twitterpated over it.

Besides, Elijah's comment wasn't necessarily a compliment. It was a request. And a reasonable one: she looked great in those running tights.

Still, as Sequoia pulled on her purple running tights the next morning, she couldn't help but notice a little anticipatory thrill at the thought of Elijah checking out how she looked in them.

The magazines she and her sisters read as teenagers talked about men undressing women with their eyes, which Sequoia had always found disturbing and perverted.

Now she realized those magazines were written by women. Women like her grown-up self. And the thought of Elijah Sawyer undressing her with his eyes made her skin tingle. The thought of

Elijah Sawyer undressing her with his hands made other places tingle.

You've lost it, Carr.

Elijah had suggested they meet at six a.m. at the Banana Slug Trailhead in Redwood National Park. The trail wouldn't be busy that early, and it would give them plenty of space to run with Xena.

The area was really beautiful, Sequoia thought as she drove through the forest to the parking lot. Tall, fuzzy redwood trees jutted into the air, their flat green leaves creating sheaths of sunlight and speckled shadows.

And when Sequoia had the flash of a thought that the scene looked almost magical, she kicked herself.

When she got out of her car and saw Elijah's reaction to seeing her, she wasn't disappointed. Then he whistled, a long, low catcall from across the parking lot. Sequoia had the foreign urge to walk up and hug him.

"Looking good, Carr," he said.

She resisted the impulse to say, "I know," and instead reached out and squeezed his upper arm. "Thanks, Sawyer. You're not looking so bad, yourself."

He wore black athletic pants and a fitted black workout shirt that clung to his biceps. She could practically see his six-pack, too.

"Ready?" he said.

For a moment, she'd forgotten they were meeting up for a run. "I'm totally ready," she said. Then she wondered if he read the double entendre.

"Great. Don't forget the dog."

Nope. He hadn't read the double entendre. Or maybe he had and was ignoring it.

Sequoia pressed the button on her uniform to open Xena's door, and the dog bounded out of her crate to greet Elijah with slobbery kisses. Once Sequoia clipped the leash onto Xena's collar, Xena spun in circles, tangling herself up, prancing around, nudging Sequoia's hand with her cold nose.

"See?" Sequoia said. "She's spastic. I have no idea how you expect me to run in a straight line, side by side with her."

He held out a hand. "Let me try it for a minute. Just for the warm-up. And then I'll show you what to do."

Of course, as soon as Elijah took the leash, Xena whipped into shape, sitting at his left side like she'd been sitting there all her life. When they started jogging, Xena pranced along, her front feet lifting off the ground like she was a merry-go-round animal.

The trail wound down into a creek bed and over a little wood-and-steel bridge, then back up and through a meadow.

"It's so beautiful," Sequoia said to Elijah.

He looked at her, grinning widely. "It is."

They stopped to stretch. Xena laid down, her tongue hanging out of her wide open mouth.

"See?" Elijah said. "She's already getting tired. This is perfect. We'll spend some of that energy now, and hopefully she'll sleep through the night. It's good for bonding, too. See how she's looking at you?"

"She's not. She's looking at you."

"Well, I am something to look at, that's for sure."

"Ha. You are. Definitely. So are you going to show me how to get that dumb dog to run alongside me without killing me?"

She wouldn't have brought it up if she'd known the lesson would involve Elijah walking beside her, his hands moving from her hands to her waist to her shoulders as he guided her in how to hold Xena's leash, and then steered her in one direction and another so Xena could practice staying on her left side.

Not because she didn't like him touching her, but because she thought she might like it too much. She was hyperaware of the way his hands skimmed over her skin. She almost wished she'd worn a long-sleeved shirt instead of a tank top. Again, not because she didn't want to feel his skin on hers, but because she didn't want him to see her goosebumps.

"This is nice," she said. He looked sideways at her, and she added, "I mean, how Xena's walking so nicely. This has never happened before. Usually I have to pull on her leash like she's a sled dog, you know? But right now, she's walking right next to me. You have the magic touch."

"You haven't even seen it yet." He winked at her. "All right, let's start running again."

They started out slowly, and Xena stayed right beside Sequoia. Every several steps, she nosed Sequoia's hand, but other than that, she acted like she knew what she was supposed to be doing.

"It's working," Sequoia said, keeping her voice at a near-whisper.

"I can see how happy you are," he said. "You know, happiness is an aphrodisiac."

"It is, is it?"

"Definitely."

"Wait," Sequoia said. "Is this part of your research?"

"Wouldn't you like to know?"

Happiness may or may not be an aphrodisiac, Sequoia thought as they ran along, mostly without talking. She could hear Elijah's breath, sense his energy beside her. There was something special and melodic about the sound of their footfalls hitting the hard-packed trail in unison. Something symbolic, too, Sequoia thought.

Two pairs of feet, two sets of breath. She could get used to this. How would it sound when their breath mingled during sex?

Sequoia picked up her pace and made a conscious effort to think about something else. Of course, "something else," really could be anything. It could be football, if she watched it. It could be the weather or work.

"Why the big sigh?" Elijah said.

"Oh, just thinking," Sequoia said. "Nothing big."

"Huh."

Despite her best efforts, Sequoia spent the rest of the run with sexually-charged images of Elijah (and herself) playing out in her mind. Elijah in his tight workout shirt and a pair of boxer briefs (not that she knew if he wore boxer briefs). Her own body laying on top of his, her hair tumbling down over his face before she leaned down to kiss him. What would sweaty, post-run sex with Elijah Sawyer be like?

She sneaked a glance at him, at his strong profile and the determined set of his jaw.

It would be amazing.

Her skin would just glide over his. He would taste salty. His hands would feel rough on her stomach and her breasts. His mouth would be hot. And his—well, that would be firm and warm and big inside of her.

Without warning, Xena crossed in front of Sequoia, and Sequoia tripped over the leash. She went down, hard, and landed on her hands and knees on the trail, her breath coming fast but not because of the fall.

Of course, being the gentleman he was, Elijah was at her side right away. For just a split second before he helped her to her feet, he stood right behind her and she felt the stirrings of arousal.

What was she, a teenage boy?

He must have sensed the tension. When he pulled her to her feet, they stood facing each other, almost touching, for a few solid seconds before he asked whether she was okay and stepped back.

For her part, Xena actually seemed worried about Sequoia. That is, if Sequoia were ever to personify the dog's behavior. The whole time Sequoia was on the ground, Xena licked her face and sniffed her ear, and as soon as she stood up, the dog sat down and leaned against her leg.

After Elijah disengaged from the sexually charged moment, he rubbed Xena behind the ears.

"She's worried about you," he said.

"If I were a dog person, I'd think that was cute," Sequoia said. "Shall we finish our run?"

They started jogging again, and Elijah said, "Admit it. You do think it's cute. Even though you're not a dog person."

In response, Sequoia picked up her pace again. At this speed, Elijah wouldn't have the breath to talk to her. When they arrived back at the trailhead, he managed, "I know what you were doing."

He walked around for a few minutes with his fingers interlaced on top of his head while she stretched her legs. Xena crawled under the back of Sequoia's car to lay down in the shade.

When Sequoia stood up from stretching her hamstrings, Elijah was standing right in front of her. He put his hands on her hips, backed her up against her car, and then leaned towards her so their bodies were touching.

"I enjoyed our run this morning," he said.

He reached up and tugged on her ponytail, then tilted her head back and kissed her in a way that hovered somewhere between sweet and dangerous, that made her want to wrap her legs around his waist and take him right there in the trailhead parking lot.

When he ended the kiss, she felt like saying, "Now I'm the one who's out of breath," but instead, she smirked at him, hoping she looked seductive and inviting rather than schoolgirl-excited.

She must have, because he kissed her again, and this time it was full-on dangerous, making her tremble in a way she thought happened only in romance novels.

"Invite me home with you," he said, his lips still against hers.

"Come home with me."

CHAPTER SEVENTEEN

Sequoia's seven-minute drive home from the Banana Slug Trailhead gave her just enough time to develop cold feet. What was she thinking?

She glanced in her rearview mirror at Elijah's car and wondered if he was experiencing the same change of heart she was. Probably. This was just an experiment, after all, not a real relationship. Although, she thought, maybe that made it more reasonable to have no-strings, no-obligations sex.

But was it?

Xena sat in the backseat, facing backwards, her ears pointed straight up as if she was watching Sequoia's back, and Elijah was the enemy. Or like she was making sure he was following them.

"Never count on me to read a canine mind," Sequoia said.

Xena's tail thumped on the seat at the sound of Sequoia's voice.

She'd just tell Elijah she'd changed her mind. She'd tell him she was caught up in a moment, after a shared trauma. Falling on her face wasn't exactly traumatic, but it would pass. He would understand. He knew she wasn't good at this relationship crap.

She pulled up at the curb in front of her house. He pulled up behind her and she smiled at the irony.

They got out of their cars. She noticed right away that he looked wary as he approached. She let Xena out, and the dog bounded to the front door.

Just as Sequoia began to speak, Elijah held up a hand. "Wait. I already know what you're going to say. And I'm not going to beg, although I admit that I'm not above it with you, for some reason. The only reason I won't beg is because I think it would embarrass you. Anyway, I just wanted to say one thing. Just imagine saying yes."

"Elijah, I—"

"Wait. You didn't even take a second to imagine it. And if you did take the time to imagine it, then I'm afraid your expectations of me fall quite short. I'd like to think it would take longer than that."

The tension decreased, just a little.

"Seriously," he said. "Go ahead. Imagine it."

Xena trotted back to Sequoia's side, tired of waiting to be let in the front door. As Sequoia put a hand on Xena's head, she thought, *Why not? I'll go ahead and imagine it. Just to humor him.*

"Okay," she said. "But only in the name of science."

"Close your eyes," he said.

She obeyed, and let her imagination take over.

They'd walk together to the front door, and he would open it for her. She would have to fight the urge to make a comment about feminism, but she would swallow it down and walk in ahead of him. As soon as they were inside, he'd shut the door and turn her around to face him. They would kiss, and he would begin removing her clothes. First he'd take off her shirt. He might insist that she remain in her running pants for the time being.

"See?" Elijah said, breaking into her mental movie reel. "You're smiling. You like the idea of inviting me in, don't you?"

"Leave me alone. I'm visualizing."

They were both sweaty. Would they shower, or just have sweaty sex? Probably better to shower the first time. She would lead him into the bathroom, where she would turn the water on to nearly scalding. Then he'd lick the sweat off her neck, her collarbone, and her breast.

She shivered.

The real, solid Elijah, the one who was standing in front of her, took both of her hands in his.

"Open your eyes," he said. When she did, he said, "I want to make love to you. Whether it's in the name of science or experimentation or chemistry or the fact that I really, really like you. It just feels right. And I think it feels right to you, too."

He looked so sincere, his eyebrows drawn together and his eyes looking directly into hers. And she thought, *Why the hell not?*

Without speaking, she led him to the front door, still holding onto one of his hands.

It was everything she'd imagined, and yet completely different from what she'd imagined.

He opened the door for her, and she didn't even consider a feminist remark. For once, she enjoyed the sense that he wanted to do something nice for her, without pointing out to him that she could open the door herself. He followed her inside, but instead of turning her around and kissing her, he said, "Can I get you a drink?"

"This is my house," she said, feeling awestruck by the humorous tone she heard in her own voice. "Why don't I offer you a drink?"

"Why don't you?"

"Can I get you a drink? All I've got is water and wine."

He chose wine, and all she had was a sparkling white, something the label promised was fruity and refreshing. Then, of all the things he could have chosen to do, he sat on her couch, then patted the cushion next to him. Sequoia followed his lead.

"You're like a man," he said, and when she glared at him, he amended, "I can tell you're just hankering to go in the bedroom and get it over with. Quick and dirty."

When she continued to glare at him, feeling unsure of what to say, he chuckled. "It's not a bad thing, Sequoia. You're not like a man on the outside, I promise you that. But let's sit and chat for a little while. I knew that drive home would let the idea of sex together percolate in that complicated mind of yours. And I knew you'd come to one of two conclusions. Either A, you would be unable to resist me the moment we pulled up outside your house, or B, your feet would have frozen. I knew it'd be B. Which is why we're sitting here now. So you can readjust to the idea of sex with me, and become unable to resist me. Cheers."

Amused, she clinked her glass to his and took a sip of her wine. It bubbled on her tongue. Even though it was just one tiny sip, the fizzy sensation and her proximity to Elijah's body made her feel relaxed and pliable.

"You don't usually do this, do you?" he said.

"No, it's usually sex first, talking later. If any. Sometimes it's a, 'wham, bam, thank you, ma'am' situation. And I like it that way."

"I can't believe you just admitted that," he said.

She shrugged. "Well, since this is all just an experiment, I feel that I should be completely honest with you. For research purposes."

"I think we should proceed with our research now."

The way his gaze penetrated hers made Sequoia's entire body heat up with anticipation.

"All right, Mister Scientist. Tell me what this research entails."

"Step one. Take off your shirt."

"It's my natural inclination to remind you that I'm sweaty. And probably smelly."

"And completely sexy," Elijah said. That prickly, tingly feeling expanded throughout her body. "Take it off."

She set her wine glass on the coffee table and pulled off her shirt, the thrill thrumming through her now.

"Lay back," he said.

She did, and her heart beat faster.

"Now, hold still," he said.

She tried, but she could feel herself vibrating. Elijah held his glass several inches above her sternum, and then titled it just slightly. The moment the cold liquid hit, she had to fight not to move. He spilled just enough that it pooled near her belly button, and then he set his own glass on the table and leaned over her to lick it off her skin.

"This couldn't possibly be scientific," she said.

"Shhh," he said. "I'm researching, here."

He tucked one arm around her waist, lifting her body closer to his mouth. She arched against him and felt her blood running hot.

She wanted him to travel downward and upward, removing her pants and taking her mouth at the same time.

Just when Sequoia felt like she might explode from desire, Elijah sat up and said, "Maybe we should take off our shoes."

She groaned in response.

Shoes? They were the last item of clothing she was thinking about removing.

"What?" he said.

Sequoia removed her shoes and kicked them across the living room. Elijah took off his, too, and ran a hand from her knee to her thigh. He stopped when his palm spanned her upper thigh and his thumb rested just a centimeter from her lady parts.

"Want a refill?" he said.

She groaned again. "You have to be kidding me."

"What?"

"Don't feign innocence," she said. "Don't forget I'm a professional behavior analyzer. I know what you're doing."

Elijah stood up and took both of their glasses to the kitchen. Sequoia listened to the sounds of him in her home, setting the glasses on the counter, opening the fridge, pulling the cork, pouring the wine.

How strange to have a man moving about her house as if he belonged there. The men who came to her house always carried Styrofoam containers and rarely stayed long enough for a refill.

"This is nice," she said, without meaning to.

"Yes," he said. "See? You like having me here, which I believe is evidence that you are, in fact, cut out for a relationship."

"Huh."

Because her eyes were closed, she went by sound, and she heard him chuckle as he walked towards her. He set their wine on the table, and pulled her up to sitting.

"Finish your wine, and let's shower."

If she'd been standing, she would have swooned at that. A shower with Elijah Sawyer would be like all the holidays combined. Easter, Christmas, Thanksgiving, Halloween.

"I won't argue," she said.

"You can't."

Before Sequoia knew it, the two of them were in her bathroom. She cranked the shower to its hottest setting, just as she'd imagined she would, and while she waited for the water to heat, she approached Elijah and put her arms around his waist.

He put his arms around her shoulders and held her against him. He smelled so good, like sweat and the forest and wine.

"You're surprisingly good at this, for a self-diagnosed relationship loser."

She tilted her head back and he took her mouth with his. There was no trace of the gentle Elijah. This kiss meant business, and as his tongue explored her mouth, she felt her body tingling yet again as it responded.

Through his sweatpants, she could feel him pressing against her. She didn't bother resisting the urge to pull the pants down. They dropped to his knees, and she used a foot to push them down the rest of the way.

Then she dragged his shirt over his head, dropped it on the floor, and ran her hands down his bare back.

She'd had sex with men since Walt Walters broke things off with her, obviously, but she'd never anticipated it in this same way. She felt like a junkie about to get her next fix. Nothing seemed quite real with Elijah. He was so ... so tasty, in so many ways. He was solid yet agile, gentle yet demanding. And the more he touched her, the more she wanted him to touch her.

"I love you in those running pants, but it's time for them to come off," he said.

One tiny part of her panicked. These running pants were tight by design. Pulling them on or off required quite a bit of wiggling. Such wiggling may be embarrassing in front of this solid, agile, gentle, demanding man.

Before she could think too long about it, though, he pulled them off in one quick motion that left her breathless.

"That's better," he said as she stepped out of the pants. "You look even better naked than I expected."

She couldn't say why the remark pleased her as much as it did. In fact, she felt kind of stupid for feeling all giddy and wanting to crack open one of those teenager magazines she and her sisters had read twenty years ago. Surely they could explain what all of this *meant*.

"I think the shower's hot, now," he said.

He even opens the shower door for me, she thought. The shower seemed unusually luxurious, the water massaging her scalp and her skin in a way that made her think Elijah's presence was unnecessary.

But then he hoisted her up so her legs went around his waist. He pressed her back against the shower wall, and leaned into her body with his, kissing her with a new, unexpected urgency.

She kissed him back, matching his tone with her own sense of urgency. His mouth trailed down her neck, and over her collarbone, and he took her nipple between his teeth.

Immediately, she wanted to arch back, take him inside her, and make wild and crazy love to him right here, right now. But of course, Elijah maintained his composure, and murmured against her mouth, "We should probably wash up and get out."

How long could one man drag things out? She wanted him, and she wanted him right now. This very instant.

Then he took the bar of soap and lathered it up in one palm before sliding his slippery hands all over her body. He rubbed her back, her neck, her butt, and her stomach before lifting her once more.

Without warning, he slid her down onto him, and she gasped with surprise and the kind of arousal she hadn't experienced in so long she couldn't remember.

Maybe it's because you've never experienced it.

He lifted her hips and let them slide down, slow motion, several times before lifting her off him. By this time, Sequoia wanted nothing more than to ride him fast and hard, to pump that smug look right off his face.

But he seemed to have ideas of his own. Instead of taking her from start to finish as quickly as possible, he seemed to want to enjoy the scenery. Not that she could fault him. Most of the guys she dated —and herself, for that matter—didn't care for the warm and fuzzy nonsense.

It was a nice change of pace to operate with the knowledge that your sexual partner enjoyed pleasuring you. He lathered up some more soap in his hands, and massaged her shoulders and neck before moving down to the muscles around her shoulder blades.

Sequoia hadn't even realized how tense she was, but as his thumbs made slow circles, she felt the stress dissolve. Several times within the first few minutes, she began to turn around so she could face him.

"Don't rush me," Elijah said each time. "You're supposed to enjoy this."

Sequoia chuckled, and was surprised when she didn't have to force herself not to think about the hot water they were wasting. Yes, the thought entered her mind, but she was able to push it away without too much effort.

When he did turn her around, after so much massaging that she was warm and malleable like wax, she ran her fingers up his arms.

"You're so sexy," she said to him.

He pretended to stumble. "Whoa. You've gone and made me swoon from surprise."

After rinsing the soap off her body, Elijah shampooed her hair. He stood in front of her, and she felt at once vulnerable and completed.

Somewhere in the distant recesses of her reasonable mind, she thought that she should stop this train before it got going too fast. It was headed right for heartbreak. In fact, the tracks ended there, on the edge of a cliff, and the train would shoot straight over that edge, leaving her smashed and broken on the hard, unforgiving, rocky ground below.

Another, less reasonable part of her mind argued that this was fun and enjoyable and, yes, strangely fulfilling, and she should just go with it until it ended. She could jump off the train before it ran off that cliff.

So she shut down her reasonable mind and let Elijah lead her out of the shower, dry her off, and walk with her to the bed, where he laid down beside her and entered her without any fanfare.

He moved inside her, slowly, while looking into her eyes with that now-familiar intense expression that said she was a complicated puzzle he was determined to solve. For some reason, the sense that he was getting to know her while turning her inside out aroused her even more, and she slid over the edge within seconds. He followed, and they fell asleep, all tangled up.

***

SEQUOIA NEVER FELL asleep with a man beside her. She just didn't. She couldn't. All those breathing noises and all that rustling around made it impossible for her to relax. So when she woke up and saw Elijah grinning at her from across the pillow, she wasn't sure what to make of it.

Her initial thought was that she couldn't believe she'd fallen asleep so easily with him there in her bed. Her second thought was that he was so sexy she wanted to take him back inside her at that very moment.

Of course, she couldn't let him know that, so she said, in a demanding tone, "Why are you grinning like that?"

He reached up and tucked a piece of hair behind her ear. "I don't know," he said. "I guess because I'm surprised at how nice it is to wake up here, like this."

She'd never admit she'd been experiencing similar thoughts. So she didn't say anything.

"For research purposes," he said, "how often do you do this? Fall asleep with a man in your bed?"

Wait. How had he known he should even ask that question?

"This is creepy," she said.

"I'm sorry. I was totally joking. You just don't seem like the type to let anyone sleep in your bed, that's all. I was just surprised you relaxed enough for both of us to drift off."

"No, no, it's not creepy that you asked," she said, waving him off. "If anyone understands the need to ask questions, it's me. It's creepy that I feel like you can read my mind. And don't look so smug about it."

He laughed, a deep, sleepy rumble, and pulled her close to him.

"I'm not smug about that," he said. "I'm smug about my mad skills."

She barely had time to respond before he was kissing her again, leading her down a path she had forgotten existed.

An hour later, the two of them stood in Sequoia's kitchen, making quesadillas for lunch.

"Oh, I almost forgot to tell you," Elijah said. "I have big news."

"Must not have been that big if you almost forgot to tell me," Sequoia said.

She immediately put her hand over her mouth. Comments like those always hurt Holly's feelings. But Elijah simply continued: "Beth Hardwick moved me to your shift. Starting tomorrow."

"That sucks," Sequoia said.

Elijah set down the cheese and the grater, and turned towards her. She could tell he wasn't sure how to respond. He was waiting to formulate a reaction until he got a better read on her.

"I just meant that the day shift is really boring," she said. "I hate it. I just meant it sucks for you."

He shook his head. "You definitely have a way with words. A really bad way."

"So I've been told."

"I thought it would be fun to work together," he said. "We had a couple of good night shifts together, didn't we?"

"Yes," Sequoia said. "We did. It was fun, and I'm sure it will be fun to work day shift together. As fun as day shift can be."

Still, she cringed at the thought of spending all that time with him. Being on the same shift meant being off at the same time, too, which meant they'd have a bunch of time to spend together. Now he'd probably want to grab dinner together, or breakfast. He'd probably want to suck up all of her alone time, like a sponge.

"Wow, you are totally panicking right now," Elijah said. "I can see your little wheels turning, faster and faster. You're freaking out. You're thinking I'm going to want to be with you, all the time. I can read you like a book, Carr."

Sequoia felt her mouth drop open. He saved her from responding when he said, "Don't worry. I'm not that needy. In fact, I am a very busy person. I promise not to be at your house, giving you multiple orgasms every day."

Now she found that she wanted to laugh, and when she did, she couldn't stop. It was ridiculous of her to assume that Elijah would want to spend every waking moment with her. And even if he did, she couldn't say their time together hadn't been entertaining and yes, *productive,* if she thought about the time in the shower and between the sheets in that way.

"You're right," she said. "I'm sorry. That was very presumptuous of me."

Shaking his head, he went back to grating cheese. She went back to shredding chicken.

He slept over.

In the morning, as they maneuvered around each other in her bathroom and bedroom, getting ready for the day, she said, "This is all very domestic."

She'd never dated—*or, correction, slept with*—another cop before. The logistics were kind of interesting, with two sets of gear laid out in the living room and two pairs of boots next to the front door.

If she thought too hard about it, she felt her airways constricting, threatening to suffocate her.

"I'm jumping in the shower," she said, desperate for a moment alone.

Not that she felt uncomfortable around him. In fact, the opposite was true. It seemed almost too normal to see his toothbrush next to her sink, his sweatshirt hanging on the back of her dining room chair. And that was the problem.

If she became too accustomed to his beers next to hers in the fridge, to setting the table for two, to his feet on the coffee table, he'd break her heart when he left.

Because no matter how hard the teeny, tiny, previously quarantined part of her mind that believed in long-term love tried to convince her otherwise, she absolutely wasn't cut out for love. They'd all leave her at some point, Elijah included.

Which was very unfortunate.

She turned off the water, toweled off, and stepped out of the shower to find Elijah had left a cup of coffee for her on the counter. Emotion welled up inside her chest, and for a moment, she thought she might cry. It wasn't the sweetest or most romantic gesture anyone had ever made. It was just coffee. Doctored up exactly as she liked it. So why was she reacting this way?

"Thanks for the coffee," she called out, unsure of where Elijah had ended up while she'd been showering.

He came around the corner, then, and kissed her on the temple. "You're welcome."

And that was it. He got into the shower and she went into the bedroom to get dressed, and that emotion continued to swell inside her torso like a balloon inflating. As she pulled on her pants, she was ashamed to see an actual tear plop onto her comforter.

"Get a grip, Carr."

The truth, though, was that she was overcome with gratitude for the small things like coffee on the counter. Even more, she was overcome with sadness that this was all an experiment and Elijah Sawyer would be walking out of her life in a few weeks' time.

Sequoia resolved to put her focus where it belonged—where it would always belong: work.

Placing her focus on work might prove to be a bad idea, Sequoia realized when her shift began. Things there seemed destined to go downhill, too. There were no happy endings in sight.

Sequoia and Elijah drove to work separately, but, of course, since they shared starting and ending points, they arrived at the same time and walked in together. Elijah held the office door for her, then made some crack about how unflattering her uniform pants were.

She was still smiling as they came through the door, but the withering look she received from Beth Hardwick put an end to her amusement like a cement wall would stop a train.

"Carr. Sawyer," she said, giving them a quick, cool nod. "In my office."

If they'd been in junior high, she would have elbowed Elijah and made a face at him behind Beth's back. Instead, she avoided eye contact, and jumped when she felt Elijah's hand cupping her ass. She could have sworn she heard him stifle a laugh, but she couldn't look at his face for fear of letting that dam open up.

Beth held the door for them, and closed it behind them.

"I would offer you seats," she said, "but you're not going to be here long."

Elijah took the stance Sequoia now recognized as his, "Don't b.s. me," pose: feet wide, arms crossed, chin slightly tucked, gaze direct.

What did Beth Hardwick think of that pose? Probably that he was pissed off. Probably that he was ready for a fight. So, in an effort to keep Beth from getting defensive before they even started, Sequoia decided to try to counter Elijah's attitude with one of relaxation by putting her hands on her hips and smiling.

Of course, it backfired.

"Stop looking so combative, Sawyer," Beth said. "And Carr, for Heaven's sake, wipe that insolent look off your face."

They both shrugged and changed positions. Beth rolled her eyes.

"Listen," she said. "I saw the way you both walked in here. All kissy-kissy, flirting your way through the door. I put you on the same shift, not because I want to watch reruns of The Dating Game, but because I want to see which one of you fails first. One of you has got to go. And soon. Which one's it going to be?"

This time, Sequoia couldn't help it. She looked right at Elijah, and when he shrugged at her, she shrugged back.

"Is that all?" he said.

Beth's eyes widened in surprise, but she nodded. Her chest rose as she inhaled. She wanted to say something else, Sequoia thought, but stopped herself.

"We're done, here," she said.

CHAPTER EIGHTEEN

More than any other type of call, domestic dispute calls carried a dangerous energy, a buzzing of sadness and fear and anger. People who needed the police to break up their family fights were usually beyond reason, their eyes flashing with that disconnect between the present moment and whatever hurt they were suffering. They did crazy things.

So when dispatch notified Sequoia that she was the closest available unit to a family fight in the neighborhood adjoining Seacliff State Beach, she experienced the familiar jolt of nerves that preceded an adrenaline rush.

Sequoia went into pursuit mode, her foot pressing the accelerator, her hand reaching for the switches to turn on her lights and sirens. It was all automatic as she listened to the notes the dispatcher rattled off: a neighbor called nine-one-one because she heard yelling and pounding. The neighbor said she'd been hearing similar noises for an entire week, but this time the yelling had escalated into screaming.

Sequoia arrived at the tiny house near the beach without the ability to recall how she'd gotten there.

She heard the screaming—well, it was more like wailing—from

the street. She could tell from the pitiful tone that colored it that something had gone terribly wrong here.

She didn't want to walk into this house. On a deep breath, she got out of the car and took stock as she approached.

The place sat off the street, a tiny, gray bungalow with a sagging roof and a dilapidated porch and peeling paint. The grass grew in a half-dead patch between the sidewalk and the house.

The late-morning sun burned through the fog, giving the whole scene an eerie house of horrors look.

For a split second, Sequoia imagined the property well-kept, with a watered lawn and a few flowering shrubs, maybe even a fresh coat of paint. Then another mewling scream brought her back to reality. With a hand on the butt of her gun, she walked up the walkway, her sixth sense on high alert.

She called out, "Seabreeze PD, come on out," but, of course, no one responded.

Through the open front door came the sound of something heavy hitting a wall, and then more crying. Sequoia walked closer. All her senses were hyper-focused on the scene before her. Her ears listened hard for any threats, and her eyes scanned the front of the house for any changes or movements. Mostly, she heard her own breath coming fast, her own heart beating hard.

As she approached the porch, she called out again. No one responded. She shouldn't be surprised.

Not for the first time in her career, Sequoia wished for a free pass on this call. She wished she was a bystander, or the neighbor who'd called the police. She wished she could call nine-one-one right now and get somebody else to come out here. But right now, it was only her. She was the police. She took a breath to steady herself, but still, she felt shaky.

Suddenly, like someone flipped a switch, everything went silent. The screaming stopped. Everything went still.

"Seabreeze PD," she called again. "Come on out of the house."

Now she drew her gun, because that sixth sense told her someone was watching her. Her colleagues had shared stories of similar situations, where an angry, drunken person stopped a rampage to shoot at cops through open windows. None of these windows were open, but it didn't matter. Someone could open the front door or come around the side of the house in less than a second.

Sequoia could almost feel the air pulsing.

The screaming started again and the piercing sound cutting through that terrible silence rattled Sequoia's nerves.

The front door of the house flew open and a woman stood there, silhouetted in the doorway. Her hands were empty at her sides, and her whole upper body expanded and contracted with her breath. She might appear to be unarmed, but Sequoia knew from experience that she could very well have a weapon in the waistband of her holey sweatpants.

"Seabreeze PD," she said, forcing calm into her voice. "Walk towards me, slowly, please. Keep your hands where I can see them."

The woman obeyed, moving as if she were walking through molasses. Sequoia kept her eyes focused on the thin, wiry frame, goosebumps rising on her skin as if this was a real-life ghost story.

"What's your name?"

The woman shook her head.

"Is anyone else in the house?"

This time, the woman didn't respond at all. Sequoia repeated herself, and still, the woman didn't answer.

Sequoia had never been patient. When she and her sisters were kids, she'd rush them through telling their stories, whispering or groaning, "Get to the point," as they meandered along with description and exposition, putting off action as long as possible.

Even now, she had to make a conscious effort not to rush people through their stories on calls. "Don't tell me why you were headed to the store," she'd said countless times, "Just tell me how you ended up hitting this poor old lady's car."

If she were being honest with herself, she had to admit that sometimes hearing all the details could help break a case wide open, get to the root of what actually happened.

Sometimes people changed their stories on each telling. Other times, they added more and more detail until a coherent plot opened up. So she'd been forced to learn patience over time.

But right now, with this apparition of a woman walking toward her, Sequoia's patience ran thin. Sequoia shook her head even while performing her initial assessment. White female, early twenties, one hundred fifteen pounds, blonde hair.

"Is anyone else in the house? I need you to answer me."

The woman continued to walk.

"I need you to turn around and kneel down, please," Sequoia said. "Get on your knees and put your hands on top of your head."

The woman obeyed, her movements stiff and jerky as if she were made of wood. Sequoia heard a car pull up along the street, and managed to spare a quick look at it. A police cruiser. Thank goodness.

As far as she knew, there was someone else inside the house, so she hurried to holster her gun and handcuff the woman. She pulled her to standing and led her over to the base of a massive oak tree at the edge of the property.

When she got her first glimpse of the woman's eyes, Sequoia startled. In addition to being totally glazed over and ringed by mascara, one of them was bruised a deep, angry purple and swollen halfway shut.

"Sit here a minute," she said.

Then she walked back toward the front door of the house, drawing her gun again.

She'd been in this business long enough that nothing should surprise her.

Yet, when the person who emerged through the front door was another woman, tall and scraggly and as troll-faced and ugly as anyone Sequoia had ever seen, she froze, just long enough to process the difference between the villain she'd imagined (an overweight, middle-aged man in a tank top and ripped pajama pants with greasy hair and a seven o'clock shadow) and the one who stood in front of her now, and that was just long enough to give that villain the advantage.

The girl under the oak tree finally spoke up, yelling, "Mamma!"

and in the space of yet another split second distraction, the woman in the front door charged Sequoia.

She was unarmed, as far as Sequoia could tell. *But even unarmed people can beat the crap out of you,* said that voice of reason. Sequoia holstered her weapon.

Just as Sequoia prepared to step out of the way, leaving the woman to tumble onto the sidewalk, the woman pulled a gun out of the back of her waistband and leveled it at Sequoia's face. The daughter started screaming again, from her spot under the oak tree.

A million thoughts ran through her mind, fragment-style, even as her mouth managed to form the words, "Drop the gun": *Why did I think she was unarmed? So much for the benefit of the doubt. Now I'm going to die. Stupid. Even if I don't die, it's months in the hospital. Maybe they'll let me get rid of the dog.*

That final thought triggered one desperate action as the woman's finger wrapped around the trigger. It probably wouldn't work, she thought, considering how Xena felt about her. Or, rather, how she didn't feel about her. Still, it was worth a try. Some poor jerk had trained the damn dog. Even while the woman's finger began to tighten on the trigger, Sequoia reached up and pressed the button on her shoulder.

She heard the door of her patrol car whoosh open, and she heard Xena bark. Although she couldn't see the dog, she imagined Xena charging forward, sleek and strong, ready to take down this crazed woman.

Then Sequoia heard the gunshot.

At the same time as she felt herself go down, Sequoia watched the blood spread across the woman's chest, blooming outward from her shoulder. She'd heard that when you suffered a serious injury, everything happened in slow motion.

But she experienced this moment as if it were on fast-forward. The woman fell forward, her blood rushing out across the sidewalk in stark contrast to the gray concrete. Xena was there, alternately barking and growling at the woman and licking Sequoia's face, her tongue moving from chin to cheek to eye to mouth, her nose making snuffling noises that would have bordered on comical if Sequoia weren't dying.

Then some force was jerking her to her feet. It felt as if someone had grabbed ahold of her shirt from behind and lifted her right up. If this was what it felt like to leave this earth for Heaven, then maybe she didn't want to do that, after all.

Although, maybe she was going to Hell. She'd failed enough people in her life that she may not be Heaven-bound, after all. But wasn't Hell beneath her? Shouldn't her spirit be sinking down into the patchy grass?

The woman under the tree was screaming again.

Was this an out of body experience? She landed on her feet. The ground felt solid beneath them. Suddenly, that same force spun her around, and she found herself face to face with Elijah Sawyer.

Oh, geez. Of course she'd see his image when she was about to die.

The world spun around her, and everything went black.

IT FELT like a second later when Sequoia heard groaning sounds. That damn woman under the tree. Sequoia wished she'd shut the hell up.

The sound of coherent voices entered her consciousness next.

"She's coming around," someone said.

Someone else said, "She's opening her eyes."

Then Elijah said, "Sequoia? Carr?"

The groaning stopped and she realized the sound had been coming from her own body. This realization made her want to groan again. She suppressed that urge and tried to sit up.

Well, she wasn't in Hell. Or if she was, it looked a lot like the inside of the back of an ambulance.

"It can't be Hell," she said. Her voice sounded slurred to her own ears. "I'm surrounded by good-looking men."

She saw Elijah and the paramedic exchange a glance, and her

heart made a funny fluttering movement in her chest when she saw how relieved Elijah looked.

"What happened?" she said.

"You passed out."

"I thought I was dead."

"You looked dead," Elijah said.

"The lady?"

"She'd dead. Most definitely."

"Shit," Sequoia said. She dropped her head into her hand. "How'd she get dead?"

"I shot her," Elijah said.

When Sequoia didn't respond, he said, "I heard the call come out on the radio and I was just a couple of blocks away, so I decided to head over and back up whoever took the call. Of course, you took it, and when I got here, I saw you'd just put the screamer under the oak tree and were heading towards the screamer's mother. I knew you were giving her the benefit of the doubt, and then I saw her pull out that gun. So I shot her, just about the time you released Xena from the car."

Sequoia nodded.

"You should have seen that dog," Elijah said. "She freaked. After she made sure you were okay, she went after the lady. She grabbed onto her arm and started yanking it from side to side. It took me forever to get her to let go."

Sequoia found herself smiling and blamed it on whatever drugs the paramedic had probably given her. "So she does love me."

"I guess she does."

"I wonder what Beth Hardwick's going to say about this one," Sequoia said.

"Well, you don't have to wait to find out." The voice belonged to Beth Hardwick, herself. The Lieutenant had appeared at the back of the ambulance, her head just level with the stretcher mattress. "Brief me on what happened."

Beth Hardwick barely batted an eye when Sequoia described the incident from start to finish. At the end, though, she said, "Well, let's hope the two of you didn't mess things up. I'd hate for one or both of you to get fired. As you know, there's going to be an investigation. It'll all come out in the wash, I guess. You two take the rest of the day off, okay? I'm assuming we'll have to put you on leave. I'll call you later."

After she left, the paramedic cleared Sequoia to go home. Elijah followed her back to the station, and then insisted on driving her home in her car.

"You okay?" he said, more than a million times.

"Are *you* okay?" she finally asked when they pulled up in front of her house. "I mean, I'm fine. I didn't do anything. I gave that she-troll the benefit of the doubt and almost got myself killed. You were on top of things, at least. But you had to shoot her, and that's my fault."

"It's not your fault," he said. "You were giving her the benefit of the doubt. You're a good cop. You wanted to talk her down."

"I made a mistake."

"You did."

Sequoia was grateful Elijah was driving. She closed her eyes. "I could have gotten us both killed," she said. "I didn't even know you were there. I saw you pull up, but I didn't realize it was you. I just glanced at the car long enough to make sure it wasn't another member of that nuthouse family, but I didn't take my eyes off that woman for any longer than that. And then I holstered my gun."

"That was a dumbshit move. Good thing I showed up to save your fine ass." Elijah put the car in park and opened his door. "Wait there."

He came around and opened her door, then helped her stand and pulled her body against his.

"You scared the shit out of me, Carr," he said.

Then he kissed her on the head and led her inside.

ELIJAH SAWYER HAD COME to Sequoia's rescue. She turned this thought over in her mind as they walked to her front door, Xena trotting along before them. He'd come to back her up, and then he'd saved her life.

Then, as if that weren't enough, he sat with her in the ambulance and drove her home. He opened her car door, helped her out, and was now opening the front door.

He guided her into the house, his hand on her lower back, and then helped her out of her duty belt and heavy boots. Sequoia felt so taken care of that another round of tears threatened to leak from her eyes.

"Do you have any tea?" Elijah said.

He was in the kitchen, opening and closing cabinets.

"I might," Sequoia said. "You know I love my coffee. But Holly has given me tea so many times I can't count. There might be some in there that I haven't thrown out."

Just the sight of him rummaging through her kitchen cabinets sent those tears falling. Sequoia rushed into the bathroom to wipe them off, and, really, to hide.

"I found some," he called. "Is chamomile okay?"

"It's fine," she said. "I'll be out in a minute."

Elijah Sawyer. He'd invited her to breakfast. He'd helped with the dog. He'd taken her to dinner. He'd set his gun belt out next to hers. He was making her tea.

Oh, yeah, and he'd saved her life.

Somehow, during the past couple of weeks, Elijah Sawyer had worked his way in, slowly, gradually, one tiny move at a time.

A realization had dawned on Sequoia within the past few days, but she'd carefully tucked it away. Now, though, it was staring her in the face.

She loved Elijah Sawyer.

She was in love with him.

"What the hell am I going to do?" she said to her reflection.

The answer was clear. He was dating her out of curiosity, out of a need to prove that he could break her. But he didn't love her.

Sure, he had a professional duty to back her up, and he probably respected her, professionally, but he didn't love her. He couldn't. That man could have any woman of his choosing, which was why conquering the unconquerable Sequoia Carr was no more than a game for him.

"You're going to have to get over it, Carr," Sequoia said to herself.

"Tea's ready," Elijah called.

Sequoia used some folded toilet paper to wipe the mascara from underneath her eyes. Then she took a deep breath and headed back out to the kitchen to drink tea in the comfort of the man she loved, while simultaneously reminding herself all of this was only temporary.

———

CHAPTER NINETEEN

"How's the tea?"

She couldn't believe he was asking about the tea. Why wasn't he asking about her big epiphany? Why wasn't he asking her research questions about what he'd done to make her fall in love with him, or when, exactly, she'd known? It would be kind of awkward to admit she'd made this realization in the bathroom, but still. There had to be some kind of scientific formula.

"It's good."

Elijah sat Sequoia down at the kitchen counter and was now pulling food out of her refrigerator and pantry. He was still in his uniform pants and undershirt, and she could see the muscles moving in his back, chest, and forearms as he worked. She kept her hands wrapped around her mug and watched her mistake on repeat.

"You've taken one sip in the past twenty minutes."

"Okay," Sequoia said. "I hate tea. Holly always buys it for me because she says I'm wound too tight and tea will relax me. But I hate it. It's pointless. Even if you get a flavor that's supposed to taste good, it always has that weird, yucky, underlying tea taste."

He chuckled.

"You know, I feel the same way. I guess I've fallen into Holly's notion that it would relax you. But screw it. I'll make you some coffee."

He set down the knife he'd been using to chop carrots (how had carrots ended up in the fridge?) and began brewing coffee. He went back to chopping while she watched.

Although she'd thought his blocky hands were kind of barbaric-looking at first, now that she knew what he could do with them, they were so sexy. She imagined them framing her face.

The coffeemaker gurgled.

"I feel guilty that you're the one taking care of me, when you're the one who got in a shooting today," Sequoia said. "I should be taking care of you."

He'd turned away from her to make her coffee, but she could hear the amusement in his voice. "You letting me do this *is* taking care of me," he said. He turned around and set her coffee on the counter in front of her. "You've given me a purpose for today. Aside from talking to your sister."

"My sister?"

"Yeah, your sister. Jasmine? You know her? Looks exactly like a blonde version of you?"

"I know her. But I didn't know the two of you talked."

"She texted me."

"She texted you?"

"Is your hearing okay?"

"I just didn't know she had your number."

"I was the public information officer for a while, remember?" he said. "Anyway, she said she's been trying to reach you all day. She heard that call come out on the scanner."

"Oh." Sequoia felt the heat rising to her face. Why had she been so inconsiderate? She should have texted Jasmine back.

"I texted her back, told her you're fine, uninjured, rescued by a hero, all that stuff."

When she rolled her eyes at him, he said, "No, really. I told her you're fine and that I'm with you. She said she'd stop bugging you but she'd really like to hear from you."

Before he could go back to chopping vegetables, Sequoia reached across the counter and grabbed his hand.

"I'm so glad you're here."

Then, embarrassed at the emotion that clogged her throat, she put her own hands to use lifting her coffee cup to her face. Before she knew what was happening, he was at her side, pulling her to her feet.

He framed her face with his hands, exactly as she'd just imagined, and he kissed her so gently and with so much tenderness that the tears prickled at the backs of her eyes for the second time in as many minutes.

His hands slid down to her shoulders and then down her arms to her hands, and his kissing became a little less gentle.

"I want to make love to you," he said.

It was almost a whisper, almost a growl, and it turned her on so much she wanted to strip down right there. Still pulling his body against hers, Sequoia began walking backwards, towards the bedroom.

They were both undressed by the time they made it to the doorway, and they tumbled onto her bed. They skipped the foreplay, and she came the instant he plunged into her.

She could feel him smiling as he rode with her through the aftershocks, and when she was finished, he said, "Let's try that again, a little more slowly this time."

He took his time, then, exploring her body with his mouth, his fingers trailing over every part of her, leaving trails of energy behind them. The second time he entered her, she was shaking.

Within moments, he emptied himself into her and they lay side by side on their backs, breathing hard.

"Wow," he said.

She nodded. "Wow."

"Now I'm hungry. I'm going to go finish making dinner."

"How'd you come up with carrots, anyway?" she said.

"I stocked your fridge. I'm making my famous chicken soup. It's very healing."

He kissed her on the nose, pulled on the jeans he'd left on the chair next to her bed, and disappeared, leaving her alone with her jumbled thoughts.

All along, she'd known this was just an experiment.

But she hadn't known she would fall for Elijah Sawyer. In fact, she had assumed she wouldn't fall for him, that the two of them would enjoy each other's company for a short time, he would deem her undateable, and they would move on.

Which was why her all-consuming feelings for him surprised her. Every time something happened during her day, she thought about Elijah, and what he'd say about it. She couldn't wait to tell him when Xena did something right (which was rare) or when she made an interesting stop, like the one where a couple of guys had concealed a bong under the backseat of their car and invented a contraption that allowed them to smoke weed while driving.

Even when she was dating Walt Walters, she'd never felt so needy over a man. Which was why she had to disengage from Elijah Sawyer. Immediately.

THE NEXT MORNING, after suffering through an interminable, restless night, Sequoia sneaked out of the house with Xena. She had no idea how Elijah managed to sleep so hard he didn't even hear her get up, pull on her running tights, and get out the door.

As always, running let the tension dissolve, flow out of her body so it stopped buzzing around in her brain. Xena seemed to sense that today would be a good day to mind her manners, and she ran along next to Sequoia as if she'd been doing it all her life.

A couple of times, she bumped Sequoia's hand with her nose, which Sequoia found endearing.

Even though going to visit Julie Sandusky would mean running a total of more than nine miles, or perhaps *because* it would, Sequoia ran all the way from her house to the Seabreeze Transit station. By the time she remembered to think about whether Xena was in shape for such a long distance, she was already four miles in and almost to Julie's normal spot.

So she kept going. Xena didn't seem to mind. She held her ears straight up, facing forward, and her eyes, alert, scanned the scenery in front of them.

Sequoia stopped short when she realized Julie wasn't there.

Reason stepped in with a calm reassurance. Maybe Julie was working. But, irrationality argued, bookstores don't stock their shelves during the day. Maybe she finally got a real apartment, reason said. Irrationality argued that she hadn't really had time to save up for a security deposit.

She could ask around, but that would arouse suspicion and draw attention to Julie, and Sequoia didn't want her to have to deal with that when she did get back. She wasn't in uniform, but all the regulars knew she was a cop. So she turned Xena around, and they ran back home.

Without Xena, the run would have taken Sequoia about an hour and twenty minutes. But because Xena wasn't in shape, she slowed down for the second half of the run and it was almost two hours before they got home.

Hopefully, Elijah would have woken up to an empty bed and an empty house, taken the hint, and left.

When she opened the front door and smelled the scent of bacon frying and pancakes cooking, she couldn't decide whether she was relieved or disappointed.

"Nice run?"

He was so good-natured. If he'd been the one to take off for two hours after amazing sex and a wonderful dinner, she would have been hurt, and she would have hightailed it out of there.

"It was good," she said. "Thanks. Breakfast smells delicious."

"It's going to taste delicious, too," he said. "How did Xena do?"

"Great. Kind of tired for the second half. I would have been back sooner."

"Long run."

She felt wary. "Yeah."

"Come eat," he said.

After she fed and watered Xena, Sequoia came to the table, which, she noticed, held two place settings. Elijah delivered her coffee. She wanted to tell him about Julie, but this didn't seem like an appropriate time.

Once he was seated, he said, "I know what you're doing. And you're messing up my experiment."

This wasn't what she'd expected.

"What?"

"You heard me. I'm not saying I know what our future holds, or exactly how you feel about me. But what I do know is that there's something between us. It's freaking you out. And you're pulling away."

Because she had taken a bite of the breakfast burrito, she didn't answer right away. Instead, she shrugged a shoulder.

"Go ahead and shrug your shoulder," he said, and she was relieved to see a bit of humor in his eyes. "But you pulled the disappearing act this morning. You did that only because you felt vulnerable."

When she raised an eyebrow at him, he held out his hands, palms facing her. "Research. I've done my research. I'm a scientist, remember?"

She finally swallowed. "You're just saying there's something between us as part of your experiment. The researcher can't get emotionally invested."

Now he raised an eyebrow at her.

"I think you might be insane," he said. "But I'm glad you had a good run. And it'll do Xena a lot of good to get some exercise. Anyway. I'll take off after breakfast, give you your space. Okay?"

She nodded.

They went through the rest of breakfast without speaking, and true to his word, Elijah packed up and left, but only after washing all the dishes and giving her a hot, steamy kiss—one that put her lady parts in a tizzy—on his way out.

I NEED to call an emergency meeting of The Garden Club.

Sequoia sent the text before her front door had even shut behind

Elijah's sexy backside, and her sisters responded before he'd gotten down the walkway and into his car.

Jasmine: *Oh, thank goodness. I've been waiting to hear from you. I'm relieved you're still alive. Or is this someone else pretending to be Sequoia?*

Sequoia rolled her eyes. Even though she thought Jasmine was being ridiculous, she responded with the password they'd come up with as teenagers, which they swore they'd always use to verify each other's identity: *Jardin.*

Jasmine wrote: *Okay, proceed. When would you like to meet?*

Holly: *Is everything ok?*

Sequoia responded: *How about this evening? And yes, of course. Isn't it always?*

Jasmine: *See you at 6.*

Holly: *I'll bring wine.*

JASMINE AND HOLLY ARRIVED, together, at precisely six o'clock. A look through the peephole revealed that Holly had an oversized bottle of wine tucked under one arm, and Jasmine clutched a pink bakery box. They both looked nervous, their mouths drawn in matching frowns and the twin line between their eyebrows furrowed deep.

When Sequoia opened the door, they plastered smiles onto their faces and held out their offerings.

"Come on in," Sequoia said, infusing her voice with as much cheer as she could muster.

It wasn't that she was unhappy, she reminded herself. It was just that she was uncertain. She was uncertain of her feelings for Elijah. She was uncertain of his feelings for her.

The one thing of which she was certain, however, was that she needed to break things off, as soon as possible.

But uncertainty struck again: she was uncertain about her own reaction to breaking things off with him. It made her unhappy. Which was probably why she felt so unhappy now, even though she hadn't yet ended the relationship—or, rather, the experiment. And *that* was even more reason to end things.

Holly walked right into the kitchen and took down wine glasses, pouring each of them a serving so generous she struggled to hand out the glasses without spilling them.

Sequoia took a few big gulps of hers and watched, amused, as Jasmine and Holly did the same.

"I had a big epiphany yesterday," Sequoia said.

"Was it that call?" Jasmine said, her forehead wrinkling with concern. "Because you can get counseling, you know. Three free visits, I think it is."

Holly nodded, all sympathy.

They were understanding now, Sequoia thought. But they'd change their tune when she revealed the real epiphany.

"No," Sequoia said. "Although it has something to do with that, indirectly."

Her sisters looked at each other, and Sequoia could practically hear the unspoken conversation: they thought she'd lost it. They thought she was crazy. If that call, missing death by a hair's breadth, didn't upset her, what possibly could?

They looked at her again.

"Do go on," Jasmine said, her tone as gentle as a bomb diffuser's touch.

"It's Elijah," she said.

"Elijah Sawyer?" Jasmine and Holly said at the same time.

"One and the same."

Before she realized what was happening, Sequoia was acting like her teenage self again, running through every single detail of her quasi-relationship with Elijah.

She told them about the first couple of times they'd crossed paths, about how they'd had breakfast together, and about how she'd let him talk her into participating in his stupid experiment.

She told them about the steamy sex and the running and the dog training. She told them about the breakfast burritos and the perfectly prepared coffee and the way he opened doors for her.

"I can't believe I let myself fall for him," she said, her voice coming out in a humiliating moan. "I can't believe it."

"You're so stupid," both of her sisters said.

"Thanks, but you don't have to give it to me in stereo," Sequoia said. "Bitches."

Jasmine and Holly giggled, in stereo, and Jasmine said, "Sequoia, he only proposed the experiment because he knew you'd never date him, otherwise. He started this whole thing because he has feelings for you, too."

"It's so obvious, it's almost funny," Holly said. "It would be, anyway, if you weren't glaring at me like you want to kill me right now."

"It's not funny," Sequoia said, "and it's not true. Elijah Sawyer doesn't need a mess like me any more than he needs a hole in the head. He could have anybody he wants."

Jasmine nodded. "He's definitely a catch, but so are you! You're selling yourself short."

"And number two," Holly said, holding up two fingers, "He has insecurities, too. As evidenced by his proposal to treat this like an experiment."

"How could he possibly have insecurities?" Sequoia said. "I mean, he's good at everything."

"Because you're intimidating, Sequoia," Holly said.

"Ah, I see," Sequoia said. "So it does all come back around to me. I'm unfit for relationships and this is proof. I'm so intimidating that when I do meet a normal man, he is too scared to ask me out on a regular date."

"You're impossible," Jasmine and Holly said.

Holly refilled Sequoia's wine glass. Jasmine took down three plates and put a slice of chocolate cake on each one.

"Have some cake with your wine," Jasmine said. She thrust a plate at Sequoia. "It'll make you feel better."

"Look," Holly said. "The bottom line is that you do mess up your relationships. But it's not because you're not capable. It's because you go around looking for reasons they're going to be messed up. Why don't you just enjoy the ride, for once?"

"Even if it ends in disaster," Jasmine said, "you will have gotten to enjoy the ride."

"I suppose that sounds fairly reasonable," Sequoia said.

It might sound reasonable, she thought as they finished their cake and Holly chattered about a new marketing plan for her personal training business (which sounded way too detailed to be real). But if Elijah Sawyer had wanted a date, he would have asked for one. This whole situation called for some more research—on her part.

CHAPTER TWENTY

She'd call it The Elijah Project.

No, that was stupid. The Elijah Experiment?

Yes, that had a nice ring to it. The Elijah Experiment would commence immediately, Sequoia thought. Because she hadn't been the one to fire her weapon at the call with the screaming daughter and the crazed mother, she went back to work after one more day off.

Elijah was on administrative leave, probably for another week or so, which meant Sequoia could think about him without suffering from the effects of the chemistry that swirled between them.

She'd need a list. A place to record all the things he'd done and said that would indicate whether he had real feelings for her. This was an embarrassing throwback to her teenage years. She and her sisters had made innumerable lists: the pros and cons of dating a particular boy, or the best and worst things about a certain girlfriend. They'd listed out their favorite bands and movies and teenage movie stars, their favorite books and candy bars, their least favorite teachers.

It had been years since she'd made anything other than a grocery list or a to-do list.

Now, as a full-fledged adult, a professional woman, an officer of the law, for goodness' sake, she was going to make herself a list of Elijah Sawyer's loves-me and loves-me-not behaviors. Ridiculous.

Obviously, she couldn't work on any kind of physical list at the office. But she could begin preparing it in her mind and set aside a fresh notebook to bring with her in the car.

As she checked her email, scanning subject lines with all the interest she'd taken in her middle school pre-Algebra tests (which wasn't much), she thought about how Elijah had treated her these past few weeks.

He'd proposed the experiment, which obviously fell into the loves-me-not column. He'd helped her with Xena. This item's placement was questionable. He'd done it out of professionalism and friendship, not romance. She'd have to stick it in the loves-me-not column. She knew she had plenty of items for the loves-me column: he'd made her tea after the shooting, he'd texted Jasmine back when Sequoia ignored her, and he stuck around when she ditched him and went for an unreasonably long run.

This was difficult.

Nothing stood out in her inbox, so Sequoia gathered her new notebook and headed for her patrol car. As soon as she got in, she opened the notebook and made two headings, abbreviating them so that if the notebook fell into the wrong hands, no one would know she was acting so childish: *LM, LMN.*

What about saving her life?

Again, it was a matter of professionalism. He'd backed her up because he knew domestic disputes were dangerous. And same with the Marvins episode. He showed up there to give her backup.

But he'd never given her backup before ... so maybe these things belonged in the *LM* column after all.

She pulled out of the driveway and felt herself unwinding.

This was where she belonged: alone on the road. She was a lone wolf. With a dog, presently, but that situation was only temporary.

What was she thinking, even making this list, even considering a relationship with Elijah Sawyer a prospect? Assuming the *LM* column was longer than the *LMN* column, obviously.

Her phone signaled a text, and she glanced at it when she pulled up to a stop light.

It was from Elijah: *Good morning. Just checking in to see if you're still trying to avoid me. If so, no biggie. I'll wait you out. Did I ever tell you the story of Davey Roberts?*

Sequoia hadn't even realized she was smiling, and she had to make a conscious effort to stop.

The light turned green and she didn't have a chance to respond right away.

He texted again before she even got to the next intersection: *So did I?*

She used voice-to-text: "You're so not patient. I'm driving. No, you never told me that story."

As an afterthought, she added: "And good morning to you."

This whole conversation was definitely going in the *LM* column.

When she got to the next intersection and stopped for another red light, she read Elijah's next message: *He was our next-door neighbor when I was a kid. One day I invited him over to play. He always said he'd be on his way and ended up taking an hour to get there. Which, as a kid, is a long time, right? Anyway. I decided I'd ambush him with water balloons the next time he came over. So I made a bunch of water balloons and put them in a bucket. Then I called and invited him over. I knew it'd be a while. I hid behind this shrub near our house. My plan was, when he came around the corner, I'd jump up and start tossing balloons.*

Sequoia wrote back: *Is this a cliffhanger? Or is that the whole story?*

Elijah responded: *Sorry. Long text, I know. But it's a good story.*

She texted: *Carry on.*

He did: *Only, Davey never came. I'd told my mom I was going outside to play with him, so she didn't check on me. I sat out there, behind that shrub, for like, hours. I mean, it was dark by the time I went inside and called him again, and his mom answered. She was like, 'Oh, sorry, Elijah, Davey's sick. He threw up just as he was leaving for your house. I thought he was going to call you.' I must have sat out there all day.*

"Shit," Sequoia said. "This is definitely going in the loves-me column."

She responded: *I'm at once impressed and intimidated.*

You should be. Invite me to run with you tomorrow.

Another item for the *LM* column.

She wrote: *Fine. See you at the station at 6:30.*

The next morning, while Sequoia waited for Elijah to show up, she realized she actually had butterflies in her stomach. Which hadn't happened since junior high school.

"Come on, Carr," she said to herself. "Get a grip."

Still, for some reason, the anticipation of seeing Elijah was making her nervous. Xena seemed to sense it, because she couldn't quite sit still. She'd sit, and then hop up and turn around and sit again. Sequoia didn't bother chastising the dog. It didn't have the brain power to cope with anxiety.

When Elijah pulled his car into the parking lot, Sequoia's heart gave an involuntary palpitation. She groaned.

"Why are you grimacing at me?" he said as he approached her.

He kissed her, hard, before she could respond, and she just shook her head.

"Ready?" she said.

"Are you?"

Wait. What are we talking about, here?

"I'm ready," she said. "Let's do this."

"I've been waiting for you to say that," he said.

"Have you?" she said.

They started jogging, and she was surprised how easily they fell into unison.

"How far do you want to go?" he said.

She thought about answering, "All the way," but she refrained, and instead said, "Six miles?"

Out of the corner of her eye, she saw him nod.

"Poor Xena needs a shorter day," she said.

"I think that's the first time I've heard you call her by name," he said.

She didn't answer. When they arrived at her typical stretching spot, she gave Xena the commands for lay down and stay, and miraculously, she obeyed. Elijah and Sequoia stretched their legs, and

Xena remained statue-like, except for her head, which moved every time she heard a new sound.

"Did you bring a sandwich for your friend?" Elijah said.

"I did, but she wasn't here the last time," Sequoia said. "I'm sure it's nothing to worry about. Maybe she already got her apartment."

"Want me to put my feelers out?" he said. "It might be weird if you started asking around, but I could do it from another angle."

Another item for the *LM* column. Although maybe this was just his cop instincts kicking in. But he wouldn't have offered if he didn't care about her.

"That'd be great," she said.

"I'll let you know what I find out."

"I hope she's okay," Sequoia said.

"Me, too," Elijah said. "Maybe she'll be there today. Let's find out."

They took off, then, Xena running alongside them, her tongue lolling out of one side of her mouth. A few drivers raised hands in greeting, which never happened when she was alone. Sequoia wondered what the three of them looked like to an outsider.

They looked like a normal couple, out for a jog with their dog. How strange. And yet, how satisfying.

Again, Julie's spot was empty. Elijah and Sequoia shared an unspoken acknowledgement of her absence, and finished the run in silence.

Sequoia's mind wouldn't stay quiet, though. Where was Julie? It's not like Julie would have contacted Sequoia to tell her she'd gotten an apartment. They weren't actual friends. But she had to know Sequoia would be worried about her, or at least wonder about her.

Actually, Sequoia realized, that wasn't necessarily true. Most people thought Sequoia didn't worry about anyone. Only her sisters knew differently.

"You're worried about her," Elijah said as they slowed to a walk at the station.

Sequoia nodded.

"I'm sure she's fine," he said. "I'll get a lead on her, okay?" Then he grinned. "I got connections, you know."

This made her feel slightly better, and took a deep breath as they began their cool-down.

Could she quantify that "made her feel better" ability and put it on her list?

"I'll miss you at work today," she told him. "It's boring without you there. I don't seem to get into any good stuff."

"You miss me," he said. He stopped walking, feigning shock. "I never thought I'd hear you say something like that."

"Wait," Sequoia said. "Are you saying you actually thought about what you'd hear me say?"

He cocked his head to one side. "Maybe."

"Huh."

"I know. I agree."

Was he acknowledging that he thought about her more than he expected? Was this a sign that he had developed real feelings for her? Or was she reading too much into those four words? This over-thinking was embarrassing.

"Well," Elijah said. "You'd better get showered and get to work. I'd say I'd join you, but …."

She finished his sentence: "It would be kind of awkward for you to join me in the ladies' locker room."

"It would. Especially with what I'm imagining would transpire during that shower. I'll see you around, Carr."

Halfway through Sequoia's shift, Jasmine texted, requesting another meeting of The Garden Club. Now that Sequoia was on day shift, her sisters were getting carried away when it came to spending time with her.

They'd always met up once, maybe twice each week, but now it seemed like her sister wanted to see her all the time. Between them and Elijah, her social schedule felt overwhelming, really.

Still, she agreed to meet later that evening.

"I brought Xena so she could play with Ruby," she said when Jasmine opened the door.

Jasmine looked completely shocked for a moment. Her mouth

opened and her eyes widened, but within a half-second, she tried to cover it up by wringing her hands together.

"Why do you look surprised?" Sequoia said, her tone more demanding than she'd meant it to be.

"What?" Jasmine said.

"You're trying to hide it, now, but I saw it. Don't lie, I'm a master at reading human behavior."

"You remembered Ruby's name."

"Damn dog."

"You never get her name right on the first try," Jasmine said. "That is, if you even try at all."

"So?"

"Are you coming around? Is Xena transforming you into a dog person, or is it love?"

"Shut up. Why did you call this meeting?"

"Ooh," Jasmine said. "Sensitive, are we?"

Sequoia gave her a look, and she said, "Fine. I called the meeting to give you an update on Hudson's place. I wanted to tell you about the window coverings I picked out."

Jasmine was lying. Sequoia picked up on her tell—her eyes shifting down and to the left, her front teeth catching on her lower lip.

"Liar," Sequoia said. "Why are you really here?"

Jasmine tittered, which made Sequoia bristle.

"Fine," Jasmine said. "I wanted to see how things are going with Elijah."

"Couldn't you just have asked me?"

"You wouldn't have been honest," Jasmine said. "But here we are, in person. Now you have to tell us. But wait for Holly."

While they waited, they took the dogs outside to play. Ruby, a tiny mutt who barely registered on a scale, seemed to enjoy taunting Xena, running this way and that, using her size and agility as a weapon against the larger and much clumsier Xena. For her part, Xena seemed to enjoy the chase.

"Whoa," Jasmine said at one point. "You're actually smiling while watching the dogs play. You're like a whole new person, Sis."

"Shut up," Sequoia said again.

Finally, Holly arrived, her hair messy and her makeup smeared.

"Wow," Sequoia said. "You look like you just did the walk of shame. Remember that, in college? You'd be at a guy's dorm, you know, doing it, and then you'd have to walk out with messed up hair and makeup. Not that I ever did it, but I remember you guys talking about it."

"Shut up," Holly said.

"I sense a theme," Jasmine said. "Let's call this meeting to order, shall we?"

"Yes," Holly said. "Definitely. How's it going with Elijah? Did you guys agree to stop experimenting and start, you know, acting like normal people in a normal relationship?"

"Seriously?" Sequoia said. "This is why we're getting together tonight?"

"I can't think of a better reason," Jasmine said. "Your love life is of the utmost importance and interest to your doting sisters."

"You guys kill me. But I do have a list. Let me get it."

As she walked out to her car, Sequoia heard her sisters giggling. It only got worse when Sequoia returned and slid the notebook across the table toward her sisters, who leaned over it, instantly absorbed in this written documentation of their sister's love life.

"Wait. Did you really make a list with headings that stand for 'loves me' and 'loves me not'?" Jasmine said.

"My abbreviations aren't as mysterious as I'd planned, are they?" Sequoia said.

"Um, no," Holly said. "Not at all. I like your list, but why do you have so many question marks?"

Sequoia explained how some of the items may be considered professional courtesy. Jasmine and Holly pursed their lips, creating twin expressions of doubt.

"What?" Sequoia said. "Any cop would back up another cop. Any good cop, anyway."

"He's been running with you and Xena?" Jasmine said. "Any guy who will run with you and your dog definitely has the hots for you."

"She's not my dog, though," Sequoia said. "She's the department's dog. I'm just in charge of her. Hopefully temporarily."

"She really is clueless," Holly said to Jasmine.

"Yeah, no kidding," Jasmine said. She switched her focus to Sequoia. "He totally has the hots for you. If he didn't, he wouldn't stick around and cook breakfast after you pulled the disappearing act for two hours."

"This is a really detailed list, Sequoia," Holly said. "I'm impressed and a little freaked out. I mean, who would have thought you'd apply this kind of research to your love life? Most people just go off whether they're excited to see a guy. But you? You put every single move he makes into a comprehensive list with columns and question marks."

"Shut up," Sequoia said.

"You shut up," Holly said. "I simply speak the truth."

"Anyway," Sequoia said. "I didn't list every single move."

"Take it easy on her, Holly," Jasmine said. "I think she really isn't sure whether he likes her. I know, I know," she said, before Holly could interject. "It seems crazy to us. But this is Sequoia we're talking about."

Here, she switched into a movie trailer voice and added, "The self-proclaimed Woman Incapable of Love."

Sequoia nodded. "Exactly."

"If he's not in love with you, yet," Jasmine said, "he's definitely about to tumble. Head over heels, ass over tea kettle, whatever you want to call it."

"Agreed," Holly said. After a pause, she added, "Now, don't go breaking his heart."

CHAPTER TWENTY-ONE

WHEN SEQUOIA RECEIVED ELIJAH'S TEXT FIRST THING MONDAY morning, her heart automatically picked up its pace.

I need to see you, it said.

Before she had a chance to figure out how to respond, he added, *Yes, that sounds kind of sexual. It's work-related. Although I wouldn't mind seeing you in a sexual way, either.*

Sequoia definitely felt some type of emotion, but she wasn't sure what it was. So she just wrote back, *Ok. Meet at Taco Don's in an hour?*

She arrived three minutes early, and Elijah was there, leaning against his car in the parking lot. Sequoia's body surprised her by having a visceral reaction to seeing him there, in his snug jeans and leather jacket. If they weren't in public, she'd throw her own car into Park, jump out, and attack Elijah Parker.

Where is this coming from? She shook her head, hoping that would get her desires under control.

When she climbed out of her car, automatically standing aside so Xena could hop out, too, she took one more steadying breath before approaching Elijah.

Of course, by the time Sequoia arrived at his side, he was already giving Xena a good scratch behind the ears.

"I admit, I'm a tiny bit jealous. I'd like that enthusiastic of a greeting."

When he looked up at her, she saw a definite glint in his eyes. He gave Xena the command to sit and stay, and then he wrapped one hand around the back of Sequoia's neck and tipped her back, kissing her thoroughly before standing her back up and grinning at her with all the smugness of a little kid who won a carnival game.

"Well. That was *exactly* what I was going for," she said, meanwhile thinking she'd have to add that to the *LM* column.

Then, as quickly as his grin had spread across his face, it faded. "All right. I'm cutting to the chase," he said. "I found out about your friend Julie."

Sequoia's stomach dropped and her heart pounded. Stress set in, even as she felt overwhelmed with gratitude. Sequoia swallowed the ball of nerves that had formed in her throat. "What did you hear?"

"One of my sources said he heard her old boyfriend came around again."

Dread started to claw its way into Sequoia's consciousness. "And?"

Elijah blew out a breath. "And he convinced her to move in with him, just until she gets an apartment."

Sequoia felt her hands curl into fists. "And that's it?"

If Julie Sandusky had moved back in with that loser Trenton Washington, the cohabitation wasn't how the story ended.

"So far," Elijah said, once again practically reading her thoughts.

"Do you know where he's staying?" Trenton Washington never really *lived* anywhere. He was a leech on society and moved around from free spot to free spot while all the taxpayers of Seabreeze supported him and his cocaine habit.

"The guy I talked to said he thinks Washington's staying over at The Riverside."

Sequoia groaned. The Riverside, a half-crumbling apartment building akin to the Peaceful Breeze, was a hotbed of drug activity and prostitution. A recovering alcoholic like Julie Sandusky had no place there. That is, unless that place was beside her convict ex-boyfriend.

"I could send someone in," Elijah said, "to talk to her, you know?"

"I don't know. I don't want Washington getting hinked up. I don't want him wondering why somebody's nosing around. He'd probably think she's an informant and kill her."

"Yeah," Elijah said. He crossed his arms and leaned back against his car. "You're right. Can you reach out to her at her new job at the bookstore?"

"Yeah," Sequoia said. "I suppose I could go over there one night, assuming she's stocking at night."

"Assuming Washington didn't convince her to quit her job," Elijah and Sequoia said at the same time.

"I know he's fed her that, 'I'll take care of you, baby,' line before," Sequoia said. "And she ate it right up."

"Let's start at Turn the Page tonight," Elijah said. "And then we'll go from there."

Sequoia nodded. She didn't know why, but she felt like crying again. For now, she'd chalk it up to worry over Julie. The other emotion, which felt suspiciously like a deep regard for Elijah Sawyer, could wait.

As Sequoia's unremarkable Monday shift ended hours later, she experienced increasing anxiety over what she and Elijah would find when they arrived at Turn the Page. Best case, they found Julie Sandusky, alive and in one piece. Worst case, they didn't find Julie Sandusky. Which meant that if she was still alive, she might not be in one piece.

In addition to the anxiety, though, Sequoia experienced a feeling that was somewhat foreign to her: she felt supportive and taken care of. Her sisters played that role in many aspects of her life, but not in the actionable way Elijah was doing. He planned to pick her up after work and drive her downtown. He'd used the words, "Let's" and "we'll" when making plans for finding Julie, and for some reason, these word choices really stood out to her.

Jasmine would be so proud of her for examining his word choices, and Holly would say she was overthinking them and that she should let her feelings guide her.

Sequoia drove home and changed into jeans and a sweatshirt. She fed Xena and put her in the crate (to a chorus of yips and whines). Just as she came back into the living room, Elijah knocked on the door.

"Are you ready for this?" he asked when she opened it.

"I'm not sure," she said. "I admit, I'm a little nervous about what we might find."

"Me, too," Elijah said.

Turn the Page was on the other side of town, and they made the drive in silence. Sequoia noticed the fall weather was cooling down. She could smell chimney smoke, which reminded her of Christmas. She wondered whether she'd have any holidays off this year—she never really checked until Holly or Jasmine brought it up.

Halloween was next week, and carved pumpkins sat on the front porches of most of the houses they drove past.

"I can't remember the last time I carved a pumpkin," Sequoia said. She didn't even realize she'd spoken aloud until Elijah responded.

"I haven't done it in years," he said. "I used to love it. We'd always make our parents carve these really intricate designs, you know, the ones you need the template for."

Sequoia and her sisters had loved carving their own. Jasmine's creations were usually cheerful, with big, gaping, toothy smiles. Sequoia's were often scary, with frowning eyebrows. And Holly never did faces. She carved flowers or trees or leaves into her pumpkins, year after year.

"I think the last time we did it all together was when I was seventeen, right before I left for college."

"Wow," Elijah said. "Decades ago."

"Very funny."

Finally, Elijah turned his car onto Beeker Street, one of the oldest in Seabreeze. The leaves on the tall, old trees that lined Beeker were starting to turn, creating a festive canopy of green and yellow that practically sparkled in the setting sun. The quaint storefronts lined up neatly underneath the trees, and potted mums sat next to doorways and in windows.

"Pretty," Elijah said.

Sequoia nodded. She didn't say so, but she felt like the fall leaves, accentuated by spindly black branches, were more ominous than anything else, death-like fingers reaching down toward the book store, looking for souls to steal.

"I hope she's here," Sequoia said.

"Me, too," Elijah said.

He reached across the console and squeezed her hand before pulling into a spot in front of the book store. The Closed sign hung in the window, but the lights were still on.

"That's a good sign," Sequoia said, again, speaking to herself before she remembered Elijah was there, too.

"It is," he said. "Let's check it out."

From the sidewalk, they could see most of the store's interior, but not into the storeroom, which was through a door at the back. That door stood open, but it opened directly into a hallway, which looked black and empty from where Sequoia and Elijah stood.

"Should we knock on the door?" Elijah said.

"We could," Sequoia said. "But I'll tell you, if I was in there alone, and especially if I were Julie Sandusky, I wouldn't come out here to answer it."

Elijah nodded. "I suppose Julie doesn't have a phone number?"

"Not that I know of," Sequoia said. "But we could try calling the store and see if anyone picks up."

"Maybe we should have come in uniform during a shift," Elijah said.

"I know," Sequoia said. "I thought about it, but I didn't want Beth Hardwick breathing down my neck about it if she found out I stopped by on a personal matter."

"You could send the guys in investigations down."

"I could," Sequoia said, "but I don't want to waste their time until we're reasonably sure there's a problem, you know?"

"Yeah. Let's just hang out here for a few minutes."

They stood there, side by side, looking through the window of the bookstore, waiting for Julie (or someone) to emerge from the storeroom.

"If somebody's stocking books, they'd have to come out and put them on the shelves at some point, right?" Sequoia said.

"Right," Elijah said. "Theoretically."

"What's your favorite book?" Sequoia said after a few more beats of silence.

"My favorite book of all time? 'Hitchhiker's Guide to the Galaxy,' for sure."

"I liked that one," Sequoia said. "But I think my favorite of all time was 'The Secret Garden.'"

"My mom made me read that one as a kid," Elijah said. "I liked it. But, you know, I liked adventure books better. I always loved a good adventure. Still do."

More silence passed.

"I'll knock," Sequoia said.

"Go ahead," Elijah said.

She knocked, three hard raps on the glass door. They waited. Nothing changed. The lights remained on, the storeroom door remained open, and the main part of the store remained empty.

Sequoia knocked again, and again, they waited. Nothing changed.

"Try opening the door," Elijah said.

"Locked," Sequoia said after giving it a push.

"Let's go around back," Elijah said. "And if we don't have any luck, we'll send investigations out this week."

Sequoia nodded. She knew the lack of an answer shouldn't make her too nervous. If someone was inside, she and Elijah would look like regular people off the street. And since the store was closed, there was no point in answering the knocks.

Still, wouldn't Julie at least look out the window to see who was there? Sequoia sighed as they walked down the narrow alley between the book store and the bakery next-door.

"Don't stress just yet," Elijah said. "We'll get this figured out."

After the same lack of response at the back of the store, Sequoia thought it didn't seem likely.

"Remember," he said, once again sensing her thoughts. "This was our first try. We haven't even begun to exhaust our resources. Come on. I'm taking you out to dinner."

Once they were back in the car and driving, Sequoia said, "I know this is a strange request from me, especially. But can we get takeout? I feel bad leaving Xena home alone all night."

Elijah raised his eyebrows. "Well, of course."

"Don't make that face," she said, taking note of the playful tone in her voice. "She hates the crate, but I know if I leave her out she'll destroy my furniture."

"I don't mind getting takeout," he said, "but I want to point out, Carr, that I think you're coming around."

"How about Chinese?"

He dropped her off at her car, then went to pick up the sesame chicken and Mongolian beef while she went home to let Xena out and set the table. When he got to the house, she was surprised to see that he'd also picked up a bottle of wine and flowers.

"Just to decrease your stress," he said as he held up the wine. "I'll open it. You put the flowers in water."

Touched, she said, "You're the most thoughtful man I've ever shared a relationship experiment with. These are really beautiful. Nice fall colors."

He didn't answer right away, and when she looked at him she saw some thought flit across his features. Then, he said, "Well, thank you. I think. You're the only woman I've ever shared a relationship experiment with."

"Touché," she said.

Even though she'd made the comment in jest, his demeanor changed slightly after that. He seemed quieter, and a bit closed off. Unless it was her imagination. She watched him as she served the food onto the plates, and wished she hadn't said anything.

Somehow talking about Julie again didn't seem like a good move, so she ate without speaking. Halfway through her sesame chicken, Elijah said, "I know you thought the wine and flowers were a surprise, but I have one more surprise for you in the car for after we eat."

"Is it dessert?" Sequoia said.

"Well, we could make dessert with it, but no. It's more like a craft."

"You brought pumpkins! Did you? Did you bring pumpkins?"

He nodded. "There goes any element of surprise. Yes, I did. I thought we could carve them and put them on the porch."

"I love it!" Sequoia said, and she was surprised to find that she really meant it. Carving pumpkins would be a good distraction from the Julie problem and the relationship experiment.

And all that knife-wielding and sawing would give her the chance to release some stress.

"I can see that glint in your eye," he said. "You can't wait to use your knife. Am I right?"

"You already know me so well."

Along with the pumpkins, Elijah had brought newspapers to spread on the floor, and carving kits with tiny, fancy knives and scoopers.

"Wow, you are really prepared," Sequoia said. "I'm impressed."

"I was going to bring pumpkin beer, too," he said, "but I thought that might be overkill with the wine, especially on a work night."

They used permanent markers to draw faces on their pumpkins.

"I don't want you to see mine," Elijah said, angling his pumpkin away from her.

"You're like Holly," she said. "Always keeping hers a secret. But that makes me want to hide mine from you, too."

When Sequoia was done drawing, Elijah handed her the biggest knife from the kit.

"Wow," she said. "You really do care about me."

"Yeah," Elijah said. "About that."

Warning signals started going off in Sequoia's brain. Buzzers, bells, flashing lights. Was he going to end things? Was he going to say this was their last night together? The experiment had proven him wrong, and it had proven Sequoia right: she couldn't do relationships.

If he planned to break things off, why did he bring pumpkins and newspapers? Why did he bring knives, for goodness' sake?

Probably because he felt sorry for her. Of course. That made perfect sense.

"It's okay," she said. "You don't have to explain."

"Yeah," he said. "I actually do have to explain."

She took a deep breath.

"Why do you look so nervous?" he said. "Hasn't anyone ever told you they're in love with you before?"

Sequoia heard the knife she was holding clatter to the floor. Her vision started to go blurry around the edges.

This was not what she'd expected. She might pass out. She remembered someone telling her once that you couldn't pass out if you were laying down, so she flopped onto her back and took some slow, deep breaths.

"Are you okay?" he said. He scrambled to his feet and crouched over her, peering down at her face, his forehead wrinkled with concern.

"I'm fine," she said. She closed her eyes. "You're not in love with me."

Before he could answer, she said, "And to answer your question, no. No one has ever told me they're in love with me."

"Sequoia," he said. "Open your eyes and sit up."

She licked her lips. He grabbed one of her hands and pulled her back into a sitting position.

He said her name again and she opened her eyes to look at him. He looked so sincere she could almost believe he had real feelings for her.

"Look," he said. "This started out as an experiment."

"And a challenge," she added.

"The truth is, I had feelings for you. I was curious about you. I wanted to get to know you. But I knew you'd never give me a chance if I asked you out for dinner or drinks."

Sequoia shrugged one shoulder. That's exactly what her sisters had said. "You're right about that."

"So I made it a question rather than a statement. I made it scientific research because I knew you'd at least give me a chance. You'd at least give us a chance."

"Right," she said, sitting up. "And I did. But first of all, you can't actually know if you love me or not, because our relationship has evolved in your laboratory setting. And second and most importantly, even if you do truly believe you have feelings for me, you don't understand what you're getting yourself into. I haven't been the real me during this experiment. I've been nicer and more open to trying things because I knew it was just an experiment. So you don't even realize that you're headed straight for disappointment."

He picked up her knife and handed it to her.

"Keep carving. It's therapeutic to have something to do with your hands while we're talking."

"You're insane."

"Maybe."

He went back to carving his own pumpkin.

"So," he said. "Anyway."

"Anyway," she said.

"I want to be with you. I want to carve pumpkins with you tonight and next year, too. I want to go running with you and Xena. I want to set my duty belt next to yours every night."

"You might think that's what you want," Sequoia said, "but—"

"Stop telling me how I feel," Elijah said. "You're irritating me."

"I'm just going to disappoint you," she said again. "You don't know what you're getting into."

"I know exactly what I'm getting into," he said. "And I think you do, too. I have a feeling you feel the same way about me as I do about you. If not, you would have kicked me out the other night instead of letting me stay over. You would have turned me down when I invited myself along on your run. You would have spent the night after the shooting alone. Anyway, the experiment isn't over. So you're not off the hook just yet."

She didn't know what to say, so she didn't answer. Instead, she turned her finished creation around to show him.

"Dracula?" he said. When she nodded, he said, "I like it."

"Dracula sucks the life out of people," she reminded him. He turned his pumpkin around, then, to show her a sun, its rays shooting out from the center.

"I'll let you figure out the symbolism on your own," he said.

Later, as they stood admiring their side-by-side jack-o-lanterns on her front porch, she wasn't sure what to make of the symbolism. Either the sun killed Dracula, burning him to a crisp, or she was Elijah's sun, and it had nothing to do with Dracula.

Then she remembered they'd kept their drawings secret … which meant he hadn't even known she was carving Dracula.

If Elijah Sawyer believed Sequoia Carr was anything like the sun, he was sorely mistaken. There was only one way to fix this.

They made love that night, slow and tender in Sequoia's bed, the edges softened by the bottle of wine and, undoubtedly, by Elijah's admission.

He didn't know she was saying good-bye as she traced the lines of his face with her fingertips and kissed the stubble on his chin. He didn't know she was memorizing the way his body moved against hers, the way his hands felt as they trailed down her stomach, the way his body moved over hers.

When they lay together afterward, he fell asleep almost instantly, and she remained awake, pretending for one last night that they could really be together. She ran her fingers through his hair, trailing her fingertips over his bare back and down his spine, listening to his breath, feeling it against her chest.

If, she thought. If she could be with anyone, she'd choose Elijah Sawyer.

And that was exactly the reason she had to let him go.

The night passed quickly, and her alarm signaled the end of their time together and the beginning of her existence alone.

"You're being dramatic, Carr," she whispered to herself. "You already had a solitary existence."

Of course, the alarm and the whispering woke Elijah, and he nuzzled her neck. "Can we fit in one more round before work?" he asked.

"You know we don't have time," she said.

"I can be fast," he said.

She chuckled, and he moved up as if to enter her.

How could she break things off with him now?

Her body responded to him, and she let him in, joined him in the sleepy movements. Usually, she'd be calculating, readjusting her schedule to ensure she could still fit in her shower and coffee and run. But this morning, because it was the last time she'd ever make love to him, she enjoyed the feel of his skin sliding over hers.

And even after showering and drinking coffee, she couldn't bring herself to tell him it was over. So she took her dog and went to work, leaving the man she loved sleeping in her bed.

CHAPTER TWENTY-TWO

"Wait," Jasmine said.

"Yeah," Holly said. "I'm still trying to wrap my head around this."

"So you're thirty-two years old and you broke up with the man you clearly love, by text?" Jasmine said. "By *text*, Sequoia?"

"I can't believe he *let* you," Holly said.

"I didn't give him a choice," Sequoia said. "And I shut off my phone."

"Wait," Jasmine said again. "Tell me again what you said."

"And also tell us why you're crying," Holly said.

It was Monday evening. Sequoia had called another emergency meeting of The Garden Club, and the girls were now gathered in her living room, only after her sisters paused on the front steps to ooh and ahh over the pumpkins.

Sequoia sat on the middle cushion of the couch, and her sisters sat on either side of her, handing her tissues and pieces of chocolate, alternately.

"I texted him that I couldn't see him any more, and that the experiment is over. I told him he'd found his answer, which was that I'm not capable of relationships, and therefore, we didn't need to continue seeing each other any longer."

"And you didn't give him a chance to respond?" Holly said.

"No," Sequoia said, blowing her nose again. "I told you, I shut off my phone."

"You're insane," Jasmine said. "He's clearly crazy about you."

"Yes," Holly said. "Clearly. You're insane and he's crazy about you."

"I'm not insane!" Sequoia said. She made a mental note to turn down the volume of her voice. "I cared about him. I enjoyed his company. But it could never work. I'd just end up hurting him in the end."

"Because you like your job?" Holly said. "Isn't that why Walt Walters thought you were a cold, uncaring workaholic?"

"Something like that," Sequoia said.

She didn't bother going into all the details, the ones about how Walt had never even inspired warm and fuzzy feelings in her. Not in the way Elijah had. Those details didn't matter, anyway. The story always turned out the same.

"But you were so cute with Elijah," Jasmine said. "I've never seen you carve pumpkins as an adult."

"It's only a matter of time before he starts driving me crazy," Sequoia said. "They always do. I think about a work-related call or topic on the weekend, and I get accused of being a workaholic. I want a day alone, and I get accused of being cold."

"But no one else has understood you like Elijah does," Holly said. "He's probably the same way."

"You've always dated jerks," Jasmine added. "Especially Walt Walters. I can't believe you're going to let a jerk like him ruin your chances at love."

Sequoia supposed that was meant to be a helpful observation, but it actually just made her feel even more inadequate.

"That's the problem," Sequoia said. "He's too nice for me. He's too good. He's kind and caring and warm and thoughtful. And I just can't deal with that. I'll mess it up. And that's that. I didn't call you here so you could change my mind," she added. "I called you here so you could bring me more wine and feed me chocolate and talk about inconsequential things like Navy blue versus gray curtains. It's over between Elijah and me, and that's that."

Just because she knew things were over didn't mean she felt ready to see Elijah the next morning. She'd heard through the grapevine Monday that Beth Hardwick had cleared him to come back to work. She dreaded seeing him.

By the time she walked into the office Tuesday morning, she still hadn't turned her phone on, so she had no idea how he'd responded to her text. But she had to turn it on for work, which meant she couldn't put it off for much longer.

But first, email.

Again, Xena seemed to sense her unease. The dog wouldn't sit still, even when Sequoia sat at her desk to check her email. And of course, Sequoia knew the instant Elijah came into the office because Xena tore away to greet him.

He approached Sequoia's desk at an unnaturally fast pace that made her shoulders rise in anxious anticipation.

"Outside," he said. "Now."

Although she didn't turn her head to look at him, she could see how he was standing: one hand on a hip, the other pointing at the door to the parking lot.

Did he think she was a child? Sequoia wasn't going to follow his orders. She remained seated, and he took the phone off her desk and turned it on. Then, he stood there while it booted up. Sequoia could practically hear the clock ticking, even though the only clock in the office was digital and didn't tick.

Elijah opened Sequoia's texting app and selected his conversation with her. He set the phone on her keyboard. She refused to look at it. Instead, she stood up (too quickly, hitting her thigh on the desk) and said, "I've got to get to work."

She grabbed the phone and marched out of the office. In a rare display of solidarity, Xena followed her.

Elijah didn't.

When she sat down in the driver's seat of her patrol car, she took a moment to catch her breath, and finally braved a look at Elijah's response to her text.

To her complete surprise, there wasn't one.

What did that even mean? Why had he come striding into the office to show her the conversation, if he hadn't even responded?

For some reason, Sequoia began to giggle. Then she howled. She howled with laughter until tears filled her eyes, spilled over, and ran down her cheeks. And then she started to cry. She put her head down on the steering wheel and sobbed, her eyes squeezed shut and her mouth wide open until she ran out of tears and sound.

Xena, who'd been whining from her spot in the back, stuck her head through the pass-through and sniffed at Sequoia's shoulder. Then, in a move that clearly required a lot of effort, the dog pulled her entire body into the front seat with Sequoia and climbed onto her lap.

Sequoia responded by wrapping her arms around the dog and crying into her fur.

CHAPTER TWENTY-THREE

The only way to adjust to a new normal, Sequoia thought, was to throw yourself into it. She would spend the next phase of her life becoming the best K-9 officer she could possibly be. She would get in the best shape she'd ever been in. She would take every overtime shift she could and put all that extra money in a savings account for Jasmine and Hudson's children (since she obviously wouldn't be having any children of her own).

She would be so busy she wouldn't even notice the space where Elijah used to be.

Wednesday morning, she woke up determined to immerse herself in this new life. Instead of wearing the running tights Elijah so loved, she pulled on baggy sweatpants that did nothing at all for her figure. As a purposely perpetually single woman, she didn't have to think about her appearance anymore.

"Maybe I should trademark that phrase and build a club around it," Sequoia said to Xena. "Purposely Perpetually Single Women unite!"

This thought bolstered her a little, but even Xena seemed put off by the sweatpants. She followed Sequoia around the house, her nose attached to Sequoia's knee, which she sniffed and sniffed until finally Sequoia made her lay down next to the front door.

"You can't smell ugly," Sequoia said to her.

When they finally got out of the house and began their run, habit had Sequoia running on the right edge of the sidewalk to leave room for a third body. When she realized what she was doing, she gave herself a little more space and talked herself into enjoying it. No one bumped into her arm or jostled her. She never had to change her pace to go single file.

She ran past Julie Sandusky's normal spot, and when her mind would have veered toward Elijah and their trip to Turn the Page, Sequoia instead thought about what she'd do now to find Julie and see if she was okay.

Actually, the store would open in a few hours, and a quick phone call to the owner or manager would at least reveal whether Julie had quit.

At work, Sequoia reminded herself that a silent phone allowed her to concentrate. No one sent her funny texts, and she preferred that to the constant distractions of thoughtful messages.

Xena was on fire at training, finding hides like she'd been doing it all her life. The dog acted like finding drugs was her lifeline. For the first time, Sequoia thought she might be able to use her on a stop.

Whenever Sequoia thought about Elijah—when the dog obeyed a command, when she checked her phone, when the office door opened and he didn't walk through it—she told herself to get a grip.

She repeated like a mantra, "He's not part of my life anymore."

Yet for some reason, no matter how many times she said it, her subconscious wouldn't accept it as truth. Her mind's eye saw him making coffee in her kitchen or sitting at the bar with a beer while she made dinner. She placed him on her couch, petting Xena's head. She walked into her bedroom and expected him to be sitting on her bed, reading.

Every time, she felt a tiny surge of surprise when she realized he wasn't actually there, and that she was still alone.

All this time, she'd thought it was her lack of warmth that made her unfit for relationships.

The truth was coming clear, now, though. She was incapable of relationships, but not because she was cold and detached.

The first time Sequoia met Walt Walters, she found him charming and sexually attractive. Who wouldn't? He was clever and complimentary, witty (to the point of making a real conversation almost impossible, she'd discover later). He had a smile as big as Alaska, and as brilliant as the northern lights. He was tall and broad-shouldered with a trim waist and a six-pack like cut crystal.

Not that she'd seen his six-pack right away, but she could tell it was there, underneath his silky black shirt.

She'd always enjoyed the sex, that was for sure. That aside, she'd never enjoyed his actual company. He was totally boring, and couldn't carry on a real conversation if Sequoia begged him to. And she had. This was probably because he was so narcissistic he couldn't think of anything to talk about (other than himself and his shiny white teeth).

Still, they seemed to fit together well. They were both good-looking, successful professionals, and her wit was a good match for his. Sure, their relationship lacked depth, but Sequoia, due to a startling lack of comparable material, thought it was normal. She had her sisters for friends, if she ever felt the need for that level of companionship.

Now, after having spent time with someone like Elijah, she had to laugh at herself. What she'd considered a "deep" level of companionship with Walt—your partner remembering your favorite restaurant or how you like your eggs cooked or which movie you wanted to see on a particular weekend—was really just basic relationship skills.

Walt had accused her of being cold and detached if she had to cover a co-worker's shift and missed one of Walt's many social engagements. He accused her of not caring about him if a call kept her at work late and she didn't make it home in time to watch his favorite TV show (which she hated—it was a cartoon made for adults and she just couldn't see the humor in it).

It didn't help that her sisters accused her of being "the mean one," always saying the most insensitive thing at the worst possible time. She knew they didn't mean it, that they all applied roles to each other.

The truth was, with the right person, Sequoia was warm and caring. She'd been both of those things with Elijah. But she was at once so convinced it wouldn't work, and so afraid of hurting him, that she couldn't accept his love.

She questioned everything he did, assigned ulterior motives to every kind act, and ruined anything that could possibly have happened between them.

She knew she was doing it, and she did it anyway. And if nothing else, that made her incapable of carrying on a romantic relationship with a decent man.

It also made her lonely.

For the past several weeks—since Xena had moved in—Sequoia had worn earplugs to bed every night to block out the sounds of Xena's whining, yipping and scratching. Even so, she could hear the dog's complaints in her dreams, and she hadn't gotten a good night's sleep since then.

So whether it was loneliness or the fact that Xena finally wore down Sequoia's resolve, she couldn't say. And fortunately, because she was alone, she didn't have to say.

Wednesday night, when she finally melted into bed after a hot bath and two glasses of wine, she left Xena's crate door open. As she expected, the dog leapt onto the bed and curled up beside her, faster than she had a chance to roll over and turn off the bedside lamp.

"Don't get used to this," she said, and Xena responded by curling into a tighter ball and sighing with contentment.

"It's temporary, Xena," Sequoia said.

Then she turned her back to the dog, closed her eyes, and fell into a deep, dreamless sleep.

When she woke up in the morning, Xena was splayed out on the other side of the bed, her head on the pillow. As she ate breakfast, the dog sat next to her with her head on Sequoia's thigh.

"We're not, like, new best friends or anything," Sequoia said to her. "And also, I am not talking to you any more. You're turning me into a crazy person."

If Sequoia was a dog person, she might say something shifted in that nine-hour period between going to bed Wednesday night and leaving the house Thursday morning. Maybe buddying up in bed was a good bonding technique. Whatever it was, she felt like Xena actually liked her.

Today, though, it put a little spring in her step.

"Maybe you'll do even better at work today," Sequoia said to Xena. "Maybe we can put this new connection to work. But don't tell anyone I said there's a new connection, okay?"

Xena, bright-eyed and pointy-eared, sat down next to Sequoia and wagged her tail. Sequoia almost expected her to speak.

"Let's go."

They drove to the office, where Sequoia checked her email before heading out. Once they were in the car, Sequoia said, "Okay, so practicing my people skills with a dog may be kind of a stretch. But I think it'll do me some good."

Xena responded by wagging her tail.

"Look, I already expanded my boundaries by letting you sleep in my bed last night. And you're already rewarding me by listening to what I say."

So far, all Sequoia had asked Xena to do was sit by her desk for a few minutes while she checked her email, and then follow her to the car and get in. But she'd obeyed each command the first time, and she'd looked so cheerful doing it. If Sequoia liked dogs, she might even say Xena looked cute.

As they drove up the highway onramp, Sequoia's phone signaled a text message, and her stomach lurched with nerves. It wasn't Elijah. It was Holly, and she'd sent the message to Jasmine, too: *Come over for dinner tonight?*

Holly rarely invited them over. Sequoia wondered about her motive, but decided not to ask. She'd been assigning motives to Elijah all along, and she was kicking herself for it, now.

She texted back that she'd be there.

Jasmine responded to both of them that she'd be there, too, and then sent Sequoia a separate text: *What the heck? Why is she inviting us over? Do you think she has an ulterior motive?*

Sequoia wrote back: *Haha. I know. But I'm giving her the benefit of the doubt. Maybe she just wants to hang out with us.*

Jasmine responded: *Who are you and what have you done with Sequoia?*

Sequoia wrote back: *Funny. See you tonight.*

See? She didn't need a man. She had her sisters. They were keeping her social calendar full.

Just then, an SUV sped by her as if she were standing still on the highway. When the driver noticed her, he slammed on his brakes, which she took as a red flag. She tossed her phone on the passenger seat and pressed down on the accelerator. The SUV swerved into the slow lane and began pulling onto the shoulder before she even switched on her lights.

She pulled up behind the SUV, called in the license plate, and approached the passenger side window, which was already rolled down. She noticed right away that the driver looked jumpy. His eyes darted from her face to the steering wheel, which his hands gripped so hard they shook.

"How are you doing today?" Sequoia said.

"I'm fine," the driver said.

She asked for his license and registration, and he dug them out of his glove compartment, shoving papers and candy wrappers onto the floor. He handed them to her.

"Do you know why I pulled you over?" she said.

"I was speeding." He looked chagrined.

She decided not to chastise him, and instead said, "Got anything in here I should know about?"

"Like what?" he said.

"Illegal substances, firearms, things like that?"

He nodded. "No, ma'am."

"Where are you headed?" she said.

"Just going to my cousin's house," he said.

"Where does your cousin live?"

He shrugged. "Over off Monte Vista."

"What's your cousin's name?" Sequoia said.

The driver shrugged again. "I forget."

Of course you do. "Do you mind if I run my dog around your car?"

"For what?" he said.

"Just to check things out," Sequoia said.

"Your dog a drug dog?"

Sequoia nodded, and resisted the urge to put a hand behind her back and cross her fingers. "Yep. She is."

"Go ahead." He shrugged again.

Now Sequoia was nervous. She was hoping he would tell her he didn't want her to run the dog, but now she didn't have a choice.

In a last ditch effort, she said, "Last chance. Anything in the car I need to know about?"

"Nope."

"All right. You're not under arrest, but I need to detain you while I run her."

He got out of the car, turned around, and put his hands behind his back. Sequoia handcuffed him, and led him back to her car.

"You can sit here," she said, letting him into the back next to Xena, who snarled and barked at him, showing her teeth.

"Good looking dog," he said.

Sequoia snorted. When she opened Xena's door, she lurched out of the car like she'd been closed in there with a whole swarm of bees.

Sequoia called her back and hooked the leash onto her collar.

She walked her over to the rear bumper and said, "Work."

Xena put her nose to the ground and circled the car. She stopped at the passenger side rear quarter panel, ears perked. Her entire body quivered. Then she alerted, her paws scratching and scratching at the panel. Sequoia rewarded her with the toy and loaded her back into the car. She walked around to the other side of her patrol car and told the SUV's driver, "She alerted, which gives me probable cause to search. So just sit tight."

She heard him swear as she walked away. Xena had done her job by alerting on the car, and now she had to do her part by finding the drugs. This had never happened before. In training, sure. Xena found the hide many times, but Sequoia never had to follow up.

She put in a quick call to the K-9 team and asked them to head out for support, and then she started her visual inspection. She knew she was going to have to take the car apart, which meant she definitely had to wait for the guys.

SEABREEZE PD'S K-9 Unit Lands $1.8 Million Cocaine Bust

SEA BREEZE, CA—Seabreeze Police Department's K-9 Unit landed a cocaine bust worth $1.8 million Thursday on Highway 1 near Monte Vista Road.

Xena, a four-year veteran of the squad, alerted on an SUV her handler stopped for speeding and reckless driving. The driver, 34-year-old Darren Yates, is in the Seabreeze County Jail on felony charges of possession of dangerous drugs for sale. Judge Oren Landis set bail at $250,000.

FOR THE REMAINDER OF THURSDAY, Sequoia felt like a celebrity.

The guys in the office came into the evidence building to congratulate her, giving her high fives and slaps on the back. She'd normally shy away from this kind of attention, but fortunately, Xena was receiving the spotlight's strongest beams.

By the time her shift ended, she was ready to drop … and she still had cocaine to package and put away, and the report to write.

Being personable and productive, at the same time, was exhausting, especially because she didn't finish her work until twelve hours into her ten-hour shift. If she could just gather her stuff and get out to the car, she could go home, have a big glass of wine, and savor the silence.

Xena, who hadn't left Sequoia's side all day, now followed her from the evidence room back into the office. She flopped down under Sequoia's desk with the same sense of relief Sequoia was anticipating once they got home.

"It's hard being a celebrity, isn't it?" Sequoia said.

Naturally, Elijah chose that very moment to come in. Sequoia supposed he'd heard about Xena's bust and then avoided the evidence room all day. He was probably here now to wrap up his shift just as Sequoia was doing.

He did look surprised to see her, the way he froze in the hallway when he realized she was there.

She hated the fact that she felt so drawn to him even though she'd mentally committed to getting over him. On one level, she couldn't wait to hear his praise for Xena. On another, she wanted to run to him and hug him around the waist and celebrate with him. On yet another, she wished he'd never come in this evening. She toyed with the idea of whether it was possible to avoid him for an indeterminate amount of time. Like forever.

Suddenly, Sequoia realized both of them had been standing frozen in place for way longer than necessary. She cleared her throat.

"Hey," she said.

"Hey," he said. Then he added, "Good work today. Both of you."

Xena, who'd apparently been faking exhaustion, shot out from under the desk to stand by Elijah's side. He scratched her behind the ears and let her lean against his leg.

The look in her eyes said to Sequoia, "Traitor."

Sequoia ignored her.

"Well, I'd better get going," Elijah said. "I have stuff to do."

"Yeah," Sequoia said. "Me, too. I was just wrapping it up."

"Did you ever find out what happened to your friend, Julie?" he said.

She was tempted to remind him that Julie wasn't her friend, but she stopped herself. No need to prolong the conversation.

"No," Sequoia said. "I called the store, but didn't get an answer. I'll probably stop by on my day off. I'm sure she's fine. You know how cops can be, always jumping to the worst-case scenario."

He nodded. "Yep. Well, I'll see you around."

When he would have just walked away, Xena continued to lean against him. Every time he began to step back, she leaned back further, her feet making little dancing movements towards him to maintain their closeness.

"She doesn't want you to go," Sequoia said, the words coming out of her mouth before she realized she shouldn't say them.

Her words came out short and harsh: "Well, I think it's obvious which one of you prefers me. I've gotta go, Xena girl."

He took one big step away from the dog, and she stumbled a

little before walking, head and tail lowered, back to her spot under Sequoia's desk. She flopped down and glared at Sequoia.

Sequoia looked at Elijah to see if he found this behavior as humorous as she did, but he was already gone.

By the time she made it to her personal car to drive home, tears blurred her vision. The street lights wavered before her, a beautiful painting left out in the rain.

All the way home, Sequoia considered her little run-in with Elijah. He'd seemed distant, but not in an angry way. He was sad. Disappointed, probably. Had he really thought he could convince her a relationship was a good idea, even though she'd warned him otherwise?

During their time together, he'd really seemed to care about her. She'd assumed that was because he was participating in the experiment, not because he actually had feelings for her. She'd thought he was acting like the relationship was real, just to gauge her response. But maybe the relationship was real to him.

Maybe she'd been operating under an incorrect assumption all this time.

Maybe she'd been wrong.

She scoffed at herself. *Sequoia Carr, wrong? Never.*

"Get a grip, Carr," she said. Xena whined from the backseat. Sequoia let her new train of thought sink in for a few moments as she rounded the corner and approached her house. What if he really cared about her? Could they enjoy a life together? Could they cook dinner together, relax on the couch together, share space in the washing machine?

Then she brought herself back to reality. Even if Elijah Sawyer had cared about her at one point, she'd fouled it up.

Experiment complete.

CHAPTER TWENTY-FOUR

When Sequoia's doorbell rang just before nine p.m., she slapped a palm to her forehead. It had to be Holly, who'd invited Sequoia and Jasmine over tonight. Sequoia had completely forgotten. She set her wine down and dragged herself off the couch to answer the door, surprised at how weary she felt.

"Oh, thank goodness you're alive," Holly said.

"I'm so sorry," Sequoia said, almost stumbling over the unfamiliar feel of the phrase in her mouth. "I got caught up at work today and completely forgot we were coming to your place tonight. Xena's first big bust."

She gestured to the dog, who was curled up on the couch, taking up an entire cushion.

Jasmine, who'd been silent until that moment, barged forward.

"Ohmygosh is your dog actually on your couch?"

Sequoia rolled her eyes. "I gave up the battle."

Jasmine put a hand on Holly's arm, and the two of them doubled over in hysteria.

"I can't believe it," Holly finally said, her voice a high-pitched squeal. "A dog on your couch!"

"Jasmine has a dog on her couch all the time, and I don't hear you making fun of her," Sequoia said.

"Wow, you're so defensive," Jasmine squeaked.

Xena hopped down and sauntered over to the girls, sniffing their hands as if they held the cause of all this giggling. When she didn't find anything, she walked back to the couch and hopped up.

"Geez," Holly said, wiping her eyes, "it looks like she owns the place. How long has this been going on?"

Sequoia rolled her eyes. "First time. Anyway. Holly. I'm really sorry I forgot about coming over tonight. What's up?"

"I think I'm going to try online dating," Holly said. "I wanted you guys to help me set up my profile."

"Online dating?" Sequoia said. Jasmine nodded. So obviously, Jasmine and Holly had already talked about this.

"Bring me up to speed," Sequoia said, meanwhile thinking this sounded dangerous.

"Look," Holly said. "I know you're thinking worst-case scenario. You're thinking the online dating world is full of psychos who use fake names so you can't Google them and discover their criminal records."

"True story," Sequoia said. "I've seen it happen."

"You've seen everything happen," Jasmine reminded her. "You see the worst of everybody so you see the worst in everybody. This could be good for Holly. Seabreeze doesn't have the best dating pool, as you know."

Holly was now wringing her hands, which Sequoia recognized as a nervous habit. She wondered, briefly, whether Holly was starting this new activity to distract them from thinking about her personal training certification.

"And plus," Holly said, "that's why I wanted your help. So you could guide me in weeding out the psychos."

"Fine," Sequoia said. "But I want to reiterate that I think this is a bad idea."

"But you'll still help me?"

"Fine. Get your profile set up and we can peruse the losers and child molesters."

Holly's shoulders slumped.

"I went into Taco Don's today, by the way," Jasmine said.

"Yeah?" Sequoia said.

She had a feeling she knew where this was going.

"Yeah," Jasmine said. "Luis said Elijah came in crying because you dumped him."

Sequoia felt the heat of embarrassment rushing to her face, even though she was positive Elijah hadn't cried to Luis.

"First of all, I'm sure Elijah didn't go in there crying," she said. "Second of all, how could I dump him when we weren't even together?"

"You were together," Holly murmured. "You're just too dumb to realize it."

Sequoia felt her mouth drop open. Holly never said things like that, even if they were true.

"You're not surprised at what she's saying," Jasmine said. "You're surprised that she had the audacity to say it."

"True," Sequoia said. "So true. But still. The whole relationship was built on the premise of it being an experiment. That's hardly a basis for real romance. The same way online dating is hardly a basis for real romance. Yet, you have your mind set on proceeding. So let's begin."

"Holly brought her laptop," Jasmine said, "but she was too scared to bring it in. She left it in the car."

Sequoia shook her head. "Go get it. Let's get to work."

While Holly was gone, Jasmine said, "So, you gonna shack up with a dog for the rest of your life? Why are you so afraid of romance?"

"No, I'm not going to shack up with a dog for the rest of my life," Sequoia said. She gestured at Xena. "This is temporary. And I'm not afraid of romance."

"Oh-kaaaay," Jasmine said.

Holly returned with the laptop, and Xena jumped off the couch and went into the bedroom.

Setting up Holly's online dating profile went as well as could be expected, although Jasmine and Holly complained about the strict restrictions Sequoia put on the men with whom Holly could communicate: piercings and tattoos were okay, smoking was not. Self-proclaimed born-again Christians were out, and so were non-fathers who claimed to love kids. Sequoia also axed Boy Scout leaders, although Jasmine said she thought that was going a little too far.

At one point, Holly accused Sequoia of hating everyone, to which Sequoia replied that Holly had asked for her help and could take it or leave it. Of course, Holly took it, and left the house that evening ready to storm the (now considerably smaller) online dating world.

Even though she'd planned on going to bed early, Sequoia now felt reenergized. She decided to give the house a quick cleaning before she changed into her pajamas. After all, she thought, cleaning always felt so … well, so cleansing.

Especially when bleach was involved.

She put on some rock music and began dusting, lifting the very small collection of photo frames off her bookshelf and wiping the surfaces beneath them before spraying and scrubbing her kitchen counter tops and dining room table.

Suddenly it dawned on her that this would be the perfect time to call Turn the Page, so she turned down her music and dialed.

Her hands were shaking, and her breath caught when someone actually answered. Sequoia knew right away that it was Julie … her breathy, smoky voice was so unique Sequoia would recognize it anywhere.

"You're still alive," Sequoia said, before realizing how stupid that sounded.

First of all, she hadn't even identified herself. Julie had no idea who'd apparently been worried about her. Secondly, it's not like they were actually friends. It wasn't really Sequoia's place to worry about her.

"Sorry," Sequoia said before Julie could answer. "It's Sequoia. Sequoia Carr. I haven't seen you on my run route since you started the job, so I was just wondering how things were going."

Sequoia heard Julie changing her grip on the phone, and when she spoke again, her voice was quiet. "I'm fine. You didn't have to send your boyfriend, you know. He just left."

"My boyfriend?"

"Yeah, that guy I saw you running with."

"He was there? I mean, he's not my boyfriend. Did you talk to him?"

"Yeah, I told him I moved into a different shelter on the east side to get away from my ex? Trenton? He said he would let you know."

"Oh, I guess he just hasn't called yet."

"What do you mean, he's not your boyfriend? I saw the way he looked at you."

Sequoia had the urgent need to shut this particular vein of the conversation down. Right away.

"Where are you staying? Do you need anything?"

Julie exhaled, and Sequoia imagined her laughing. "Well, I guess that boyfriend of yours is a touchy topic."

Now, at this astute observation from an almost-stranger, Sequoia felt herself softening to the point that she was smiling, too.

"It is. We're not really, um, you know, together. Especially now. But when I told him I was concerned about you, he offered to help track you down."

"You gave him the old brush-off, did you?"

"I'm about to give you the brush off," Sequoia said, hoping Julie would realize she was joking. "Really, though, it just wasn't working out."

"Why not?"

Sequoia had the urge to snap, "It's none of your business!" but then her memory flashed on the worry she'd felt around Julie's disappearance and she said, "I don't know. It's just that I'm not really cut out for relationships."

"Huh."

Sequoia's phone vibrated, which meant she had a text. She put it on speaker and brought up the message, which was from Elijah: *I talked to Julie. She's safe. She's still working at the book store. She moved to an apartment on the east side to get away from her scum ex. Just thought you'd want to know.*

She sighed.

"What do you mean, 'Huh'? Wait. Never mind. Don't answer that. We were just trying things out as a kind of experiment."

"Okay," Julie said, and Sequoia heard doubt in her voice. "But just so you know, I saw something there. As a bystander."

"Thanks for the info, Julie," Sequoia said. "And I'm really glad to hear you're okay."

"You running tomorrow?"

"Yeah. Gotta get rid of some of this tension, you know?"

"I'll see you then."

"You don't have to—"

But Julie hung up before Sequoia could finish her sentence. Again weary from everything that had transpired during the past couple of days, Sequoia turned off all the lights in the house and fell into bed.

Then she remembered she hadn't responded to Elijah's text, so she sat up and without turning on any lights, wrote back, *Thank you so much. I talked to her tonight, too, apparently right after you left the store. I really appreciate you going over there again.*

Her fingers hovered over the phone's keyboard, because she was uncertain of whether to say anything else. She wanted to, but she just didn't know exactly what that something else was. So she put her phone on silent and set it on her nightstand.

When Sequoia laid back down, Xena rested her chin on the side of the bed. Sequoia patted the empty spot, and Xena hopped up, turned around about twenty times, and didn't move again.

Sequoia spent the entire night awake, staring into the dark, listening to the dog snore beside her.

XENA SEEMED to enjoy running with Sequoia now. When Sequoia put on her running clothes each morning, the dog pranced behind her, stopping every time Sequoia stopped, picking up the leash between her teeth and following Sequoia all over the house until she clipped it on.

When it came time to get in the car, she bolted out the door and waited for Sequoia, then hopped in and perched on the backseat, staring, hyper-focused, out the windshield. Then, when they arrived at the police station, Xena got out and stood ready, positioned in the direction they always went.

If Sequoia were a dog person, she might find this behavior endearing. In fact, it was a tiny bit charming when Xena started their run before Sequoia was really ready, tugging just a bit at the leash until Sequoia followed.

On her way into work, Sequoia had stopped at the Quickie Mart to grab a sandwich for Julie, even though it was probably unnecessary since she had gotten a job.

Now, as she rounded the corner near the Seabreeze Transit Station, she saw that it had been unnecessary, but not for the reason she thought. Julie wasn't there.

"Huh," Sequoia said to Xena. "The way she talked, I thought she would be here."

Most likely, Julie had changed her mind because Sequoia was so rude on the phone. Or maybe Trenton Washington had been lurking around here, had seen Julie at her normal spot, and had taken her somewhere. From that point, the possibilities were endless.

Julie's dead body could be lying in a broken-down shed somewhere, right now.

"Hey," Sequoia said to another of the regulars, a woman whose dirt-lined face resembled that of an apple doll. "You seen Julie? The woman who usually sits right here."

"Yeah, I seen her," the woman said. "But not for a long time, now. She ain't been around here much at all. I hear she got a job or something."

Sequoia nodded. "Thank you."

"I know you always bring her food," the woman said, her beady eyes looking out from under a big, faux fur-lined hood. "You can give it here."

She put out her hand, and Sequoia couldn't help but notice the dirt under her fingernails and smeared into the crevices of her skin.

"Give me a few minutes to find her," Sequoia said. "If she doesn't turn up, you can have it."

The woman's jaw worked up and down, side to side, and she nodded before hobbling away.

As she walked around the platform, Sequoia weaved between bodies wrapped in heavy blankets and draped in multiple layers. Trenton Washington was not usually homeless, but he'd have an easy time disguising himself here.

She sighed.

Then, just as she made her final turn to head back to the beady-eyed woman and her own running route, another homeless man came toward her. He walked like an old sailor, his sea legs bowed and wobbly. Long dark hair flowed behind him, and he wore an eye patch around his neck.

"I saw your friend," he said. "She walked off with that gargantuan guy that just come back from the dead, or from prison. You know the one? Seven feet tall, eyes and nose gathered so close together on his face you think they're the last three bowling pins standing?"

"Oh, yeah," Sequoia said. "I know the one."

Aside from being impressed with this man's spot-on description of Trenton Washington, Sequoia experienced a growing sense of panic.

"When did this happen?" she said.

"Just about two minutes before you showed up in your fancy pants. Nice looking dog."

"Did she seem upset?"

"Nah. He probably told her not to make a scene. You know how those guys are. He had a hold of her elbow. You know what I mean?"

"I do," Sequoia said.

"I'll bet you can run and catch up with 'em," the man said. "You're pretty fast, faster than that piece of crap car he was driving, I reckon."

"Do you remember what it looked like?"

"I told you. It looked like a piece of crap. It was an eighty-eight Mustang. Red. Seen better days. License plate ended in eight, eight, three, but he had the first few letters blacked out. You could get a stop on him for that."

"Very astute," Sequoia said to the man.

He tapped the side of his head. "Used to be a cop," he said. "Still got the skills."

"Did you retire?"

"No," he said. "Went ten ninety-six." Now he twirled a finger next to his temple. "Law enforcement'll do that do a person."

He grinned at her.

"Thank you," she said.

"Any time," he said. "The name's Don."

Sequoia gave Julie's sandwich to the beady-eyed woman and then hightailed it back to the office. She could start working a bit early today.

"Of course he's the first person we see when we get back," Sequoia said to Xena when they ran into the parking lot and saw Elijah getting out of his car.

When she would have pretended not to see him, he stood there, arms crossed, waiting for her to pass him. When she did, which happened despite the significant slowing of her pace, he greeted her without smiling.

"You're here early," she said.

She stopped herself from adding, "Yes, I still have your schedule memorized."

"What's the matter?" he said.

She wanted to say, "Oh, nothing. It's just that Julie, yet another person who has a quasi-relationship with me, is suffering. This time it's life-threatening. Obviously, I'm like poison," which is what she'd been thinking as she ran from the transit station back to the police department. But that would take too long, especially because Elijah would feel obligated to refute her. So she said, "I think Trenton Washington kidnapped Julie from the transit station."

"Wait. She told me she hasn't even been hanging around the transit station."

"I know," Sequoia ground a foot into the asphalt like she'd grind out a cigarette. "When I called her last night she said she'd see me today. So I think she was making a special trip there just to put my mind at ease. I came back to change so I could go look for her."

"Anybody see her leave?"

"Weirdest thing. One of the regulars? Turns out he's a retired cop. He gave me a great description of Trenton and the car he took Julie in."

"Old Don," Elijah said. "One of my favorites. He warned me about law enforcement. Said it made him go crazy. I told him only women can drive a man crazy."

Sequoia narrowed her eyes at him.

"Look," Elijah said. "I'm dressed. Why don't you give me the description and I'll head out. You can meet me after you change. Although it's a pity. You should consider doing a shift in your running tights."

"Funny guy," Sequoia said, rolling her eyes when she felt like wrapping her arms around him.

She gave him the description Don had given her. Then she had to resist the urge to kiss him. Instead, she squeezed his arm and said, "Thank you. Really. I'll be right behind you."

She felt ridiculously touched by his offer to help track Julie down, but again, she attributed it to professional courtesy. And again, reading her thoughts, he said, "I wouldn't do this for anybody else, Sequoia. Only you."

His eyes flicked down to her mouth and back to her eyes before he got into his car and drove away. Xena whimpered, and because Sequoia felt like whimpering, too, she jogged into the office to change.

Within five minutes, Sequoia and Xena were in the patrol car. She called Elijah on the radio to find out where he was.

"I think they're parked at the bridge on Riverfront Street," he said. "I did a quick ATL and someone reported seeing an old Mustang there."

"On my way."

Sure enough, the Mustang was parked right in the middle of the bridge, which, Sequoia thought, didn't bode well. Trenton Washington was probably on a suicide mission. Sequoia drove along High Street, which ran perpendicular to Riverfront and overlooked the bridge.

She watched from a distance as Elijah drove his patrol car onto the bridge, then stopped it fifteen or so yards from Washington's Mustang. She was far enough away that she couldn't hear whether he was calling them out on the bullhorn. Still, her sixth sense was going off, so she upped her speed with the hopes of pulling in next to him before anything crazy went down.

Elijah got out of his car. Sequoia could see him standing there between the open driver's door and the body of the car, his gun pointed at the Mustang.

The driver's door of the Mustang opened, and Trenton Washington, all six feet, five inches of him, stood up. Sequoia rolled down her window, and was close enough now that she could hear Elijah giving Trenton commands to step away from the car with his hands raised. He wasn't listening. Instead, he was motioning wildly for his passenger—Julie—to get out of the car. She did, and he used his left arm to pin her body against the front of his.

Sequoia growled and turned onto the bridge. Trenton Washington adjusted and readjusted the position of his arm around Julie's shoulders. Julie's eyes were wide, and although she struggled against him initially, he said something close to her ear and she dropped her arms.

Then he pulled a knife out of his pocket.

Sequoia doubted he'd use it. Washington was one of those people who did a lot of talking but rarely took action. He was probably just trying to get the upper hand, and Sequoia doubted Elijah would give it to him.

She pulled her patrol car up next to Elijah's, and Washington turned toward her, jerking Julie's body with his as he did so. Julie stumbled and started to fall. Her neck must have scraped against the knife blade, because a trickle of blood made its way from her Adam's Apple down to the V of her collarbone.

Elijah didn't take his eyes off of Washington and Julie, and Sequoia wondered if he knew she was there.

"Drop the knife," Elijah said to Washington.

"Make me," Washington yelled, like some idiot kid on a playground.

From her car, Sequoia weighed her options. She could call in a negotiator, which would take time. She could send Xena after Washington, which would be risky. With Sequoia's luck, Xena would attack Julie rather than Washington. She could charge Washington, herself, but not without a putting Julie in danger.

She sighed. Xena whined.

Then Washington pulled out a gun and aimed it at Elijah.

Time stopped. Sequoia's vision blurred at the edges, and became a tunnel that brought Elijah's face into hyper-focus. Why had she ever thought she could live without him? She needed him. He wasn't perfect, but he was perfect for her. He cared about her and she—well, she felt quite strongly about him.

She may have passed out from that revelation if Washington hadn't grinned then, his wide-spaced teeth and close-together eyes standing out against his dirty face. His body emitted a crazed energy that made Sequoia sick. His finger, which had been resting against the barrel of the gun, now curved around the trigger.

Sequoia got out of her car and drew her own weapon at super-human speed. She knew it was risky, but she'd grabbed her bullhorn instead of her gun.

"Trenton Washington, drop that gun right now unless you're prepared to die."

"I'll kill her before you can kill me," he said.

She could practically feel the rage-induced spittle flying out of his mouth.

"No, you won't," Sequoia said. "You love her. You want to be with her. That's the only reason you took her from the transit station, isn't it? Because you love her. You missed her so much when you were locked up. All you thought about was getting back to Julie."

She could see his resolve softening. The arm around Julie's shoulders relaxed, and the knife moved away from her skin. Washington's focus was on Sequoia, but still, he kept the gun pointed at Elijah.

Sequoia continued, "And then you got out and she didn't want anything to do with you."

Washington tightened his grip again. Julie gritted her teeth.

"Shit," Sequoia whispered.

She snapped her mouth closed when she realized Washington could probably hear her whispered swearing through the bullhorn.

"And you're finally with her, right now. We don't want to hurt you. We just want to talk with you, to help you and Julie work through this."

Her mind added, *In other words, get you back to prison so she can get on with her life.*

Washington nodded. "I love her, man," he said.

Then he sniffled, calling up images of a little boy, sniffling at his mother's hem. "I just wanna be with her."

"I know you do," Sequoia said. "I hear you. But we need you to drop your weapons. Can you do that for us? I'm afraid you or Julie is going to get hurt, and then you won't be able to be with her."

Washington's knife arm relaxed again, and Sequoia exhaled. Julie was breathing hard. Washington kept the gun raised, but he took his finger off the trigger.

"Nice and easy, Trenton," Sequoia said. "Nice and easy. Just put the gun on the ground, okay? Just set it down. And then the knife. And then we can talk. Would you do that for me? For Julie?"

"I can't, man. You don't understand what I'm into."

"We can help you," Sequoia said. "There are programs we can get you into. People who know how to help you start over."

"Nah, man, you don't get it. I can't start over."

He dropped the gun, and started pulling Julie toward the side of the bridge. Julie tried to move her feet fast enough to keep up, but she kept tripping over Washington's feet so he half-dragged her across the bridge.

Sequoia had seen this before. Next thing they knew, Washington would hoist them both onto the railing and then lean back, taking them down into the fast-flowing Fremont River. It would take a matter of seconds.

"You don't have to do this," Sequoia said. "We can stop right here and start over."

"You don't get it," Washington said again.

CHAPTER TWENTY-FIVE

SEABREEZE, CA—The Mayor of Seabreeze is hailing two Seabreeze Police Department officers as heroes after they rescued a kidnapping victim and arrested her kidnapper.

According to a police report, Trenton Washington, 35, a welder who returned to Seabreeze this past week after a year in prison on felony drug charges, allegedly kidnapped Julie Sandusky, 30, from the Seabreeze Public Transit station.

Acting on a tip, police followed Washington's car to the Riverfront Bridge, where he allegedly held Sandusky at knifepoint and pointed his gun at a police officer before threatening to jump off the bridge.

Police officers were able to negotiate with Washington until he dropped his weapons and released Sandusky, who, aside from a small cut on her neck, escaped injury.

"This is policing at its finest," said Mayor Tony Strunk. "Our officers were able to save two lives today, thanks to their courage and professionalism. They're true heroes."

"SO, Elijah and I have now shared space on the front page," Sequoia said to Jasmine and Holly the following evening as they sat at Starboard, a bar overlooking the beach. Nighttime lights shone off the water's surface, undulating like magic.

"I guess that means your lives are forever intertwined," Jasmine said.

"Gag me," Sequoia said, even though, or maybe *because* she didn't mean it. She felt like Elijah Sawyer had left an impression on her life. His fingerprint would remain there forever. In the twenty-four hours since Trenton Washington surrendered, Sequoia had relived the moment when she thought he was going to shoot Elijah. She saw a whole series of images, moments in time: the way Elijah had responded when they first bumped into each other in the office; the way he looked at her when they finally started talking, like she was a puzzle to figure out; his feet next to hers on the coffee table; his body above hers in bed.

She could force herself to live without him in *her* world, but she couldn't live without him in this world.

When she made that realization, she felt herself snap.

"Trenton Washington," she said. "You let go of that woman right now and get down on your knees."

It worked. He was just a foot from the edge of the bridge. He let go of Julie and stood there, his shoulders slumped, before falling onto his knees and putting his hands behind his head.

She wondered if Elijah had heard her give Washington that final command and thought that's how she'd talk to their future children.

"You don't mean it," Holly said, reaching across the little table to touch Sequoia's hand. "You really liked him. You've just got way too much baggage."

Typically, Sequoia would have responded by flicking Holly's hand away from her own, and probably shooting out some remark about Holly's own baggage. But tonight, she felt so exhausted she didn't bother responding at all.

"Wow," Holly said. "She's depressed."

"I know," Jasmine said. "I've never seen her like this."

"I'm sitting right here, you guys," Sequoia said.

"I think we need to get you drunk," Jasmine said. "Help you forget about your woes."

She signaled to a server, and when he came to the table, she ordered two shots of tequila for each of them.

"I don't need to get drunk," Sequoia said. "I just need to come to terms with—"

She wanted to say, "losing Elijah," but instead, she finished, "being perpetually single."

"I thought you'd already come to terms with that," Holly said. "I mean, you always give me a hard time because I haven't come to terms with your being perpetually single."

The server came back, and Sequoia took her two shots in rapid succession. Holly and Jasmine exchanged yet another meaningful glance.

"Geez, you guys, it's not like two shots are going to put me under the table or anything."

Almost immediately, though, she began to feel the warmth spreading down her neck to her shoulders, to her belly and the tips of her fingers.

"You know what it is?" she said, then, her tongue feeling just a bit too thick in her mouth, her chest filling with emotion.

Holly grinned and Sequoia smiled back before continuing, "It's just that I let myself feel, for one minute, that it might be possible."

"That what might be possible?" Jasmine said. "Romance?"

"Yeah," Sequoia said. "I mean, I knew it was an experiment and everything, but it felt so … I don't know. So real, I guess. I mean, even though I was playing along at first, doing all the things I knew I should do if we were in a real, actual relationship, the feelings I had for him started to feel real. You know?"

"I do know," Holly said. "I think they *were* real."

"And just as importantly," Jasmine said, holding up her pointer finger, "I think Elijah's feelings for you were real, too. I think you guys really had a thing going on."

Sequoia felt herself swaying on her stool. Maybe two shots were enough to put her under the table, after all.

"Not that it matters," Sequoia said. "I went and messed it up."

"You totally did," Jasmine said.

"Wow, aren't you the straight shooter tonight," Sequoia said.

Holly shrugged. "Why don't you go talk to him?"

"I said the feelings started to feel real," Sequoia said. "Not that they were real. I think I fooled myself into believing they were real, but they weren't. I can't even stand the thought of him, now."

She almost choked on the lie, but she picked up Holly's shot glass and took a sip of tequila. "I mean, he brought me pumpkins to carve. Like we're kids or something. Ridiculous."

Now tears threatened, and Sequoia knew the two shots were too many. She signaled for another round.

"You're so weird," Holly said.

"Tell me about it," Sequoia said. She took the next shot straight from the server's hand and tossed it back.

"Enough about me, other than to say that you girls are going to have to get me home somehow. How's that online dating going, Holly?"

The girls ended up staying at the bar until long after closing, nursing coffees the bartender put in to-go cups for them, watching the ocean swirl under the lights.

By then, Sequoia was able to drive home, so she dropped her sisters off and greeted Xena with half the enthusiasm the dog had— which was twice as much as she normally showed.

"Okay, I pet you, now go away," Sequoia said.

Maybe her sisters were right. Maybe she should call Elijah and see if he'd forgive her. Maybe she should invite him over to dress up in Halloween costumes and have kinky costume sex.

"That's the tequila thinking," Sequoia said to herself. "The kinky sex would be okay, but I'm not calling him."

What if he just came here without her calling? What if he showed up and rang the doorbell? That would be perfect. Then she wouldn't have to grovel. She would never have to actually say she'd been wrong to question his feelings for her.

After brewing a half-pot of coffee, Sequoia sat on the couch and waited for Elijah to ring the bell or knock on the door. He'd stand there, a bouquet of flowers in his hand, and tell her how much he missed her. He'd tell her suggesting an experiment had been stupid, and he'd tell her he wanted to date her for real this time.

She hated flowers.

Every time a floorboard creaked or Xena thumped her tail, Sequoia's eyes landed on the front door. Of course, these sounds never panned out. Elijah never knocked or rang the bell or texted or called.

"I guess it's officially over," Sequoia said to Xena as they went to bed that night. And for the second time, she hugged her dog and cried into her fur.

CHAPTER TWENTY-SIX

At work, Sequoia immersed herself in calls, meanwhile enforcing her own personal Zero Tolerance Policy on speeders, stop sign runners, and non-signaling lane changers.

She managed to avoid Elijah at the office by coming in extra early and leaving a bit late, and noticed the sting of missing him decreased ever so slightly when she didn't have to see him in person. Yes, images of him still walked across her conscious and subconscious during every waking and sleeping moment, but she couldn't help that.

In addition to avoiding Elijah, Sequoia somehow managed to avoid Beth Hardwick over the course of the next several days. At first, she thought it was just timing, but then she overheard someone in the office mention Beth's name.

"What's going on with Hardwick?" she demanded, loudly, as she came around the corner to find Mack and a couple of guys standing around the coffeemaker. She thought again of how perfect Mack would be for her sister, but again, the thought was fleeting thanks to the way the conversation halted as the guys turned to look at her.

She realized it was probably the first time she'd ever joined in the water cooler (or coffeemaker) gossip with her co-workers.

Mack cleared his throat. "Uh, hey, Carr."

The rest of the guys remained silent. Sequoia plastered on a big smile. "Hey, Mack."

"So. Uh, Hardwick. We were just talking, you know, and we realized we haven't seen her in a few days. We're thinking she must have gotten time off, you know? Forced time off? While somebody investigates all the accusations in the *Daily Trumpet*."

"Huh," Sequoia said. "I figured I was just missing her."

She saw a couple of the guys exchange a glance and knew what they were thinking: *Just like you've been "missing" Elijah Sawyer every shift.*

She lifted her chin a fraction of an inch and waited for Mack to reply.

"Uh, maybe. But none of us have seen her."

"Huh," Sequoia said, taking note of her new tendency to repeat herself. "I guess we'll find out soon enough."

SEABREEZE POLICE DEPARTMENT LIEUTENANT FIRED, Charged With Embezzling Money

SEABREEZE, CA—Seabreeze Police Department this Thursday fired Lieutenant Beth Hardwick, according to a press release.

County prosecutors have charged Hardwick with embezzling more than $15,000. Last month, detectives with the California Highway Patrol opened an investigation into Hardwick's possible involvement in the death of former Seabreeze PD public information officer Earl Little. The investigation is ongoing.

Hardwick was a 15-year veteran of the police force, having spent the past year in her position as lieutenant. She would have been eligible to retire in five years.

SEQUOIA'S first reaction to Jasmine's article was a strong desire to call Elijah. A week ago, she would have invited him over to share a bottle of champagne. Or wine. Or even a couple of beers.

But today, after waking up too late to go for a run, too late to get to work early to avoid Elijah, she walked to her car, her movements weary, and drove to the police station without remembering much about the drive. She saw Elijah in the office, getting coffee, and she avoided him, skipping her morning email-checking routine in favor of heading out right away, lest their paths cross. The mood in the office was rather celebratory—Sequoia didn't know of anyone who actually liked Beth Hardwick—and she was sorry to skip out so quickly.

Still, she experienced a deep sense of relief when she saw Elijah watching her leave. She may be incapable of maintaining a relationship with him, but she could still keep his interest.

She went through the motions, pulling people over, stopping to help a young mother change a tire, directing traffic at an accident scene, running Xena on a carful of seedy-looking characters. Her heart just wasn't in it.

Maybe she should make a new list, she thought as she ran a teenager's license through the system after she stopped him for going eighty-five in a fifty-five. The headings would read: *Love Him* and *Leave Him*.

Come to think of it, though, she'd already left him, hadn't she?

She might have to get more creative with the headings.

The speeding teenager had a few prior tickets for criminal speeding, so she'd have to write him another.

"Hey, bud," she said when she approached his window. "You've got to stop speeding. Think of all the money you've spent on these tickets. You're going to need that when you go to college. For stuff like computers and text books. Why the hell are you wasting it on speeding tickets?"

His eyes grew as round as coins, and his mouth formed a tiny *O*.

"I don't know, ma'am. I hadn't thought of it like that."

"I have no choice but to write you a ticket. If I don't, I could lose my job. And *I* have things to pay for, like a mortgage. But stop speeding, okay?"

The kid nodded, signed his ticket, and drove off.

Why couldn't she think that reasonably about her own life?

She pulled back into traffic and began compiling a mental outline of her feelings for, and reaction to, Elijah.

She'd already taken note of his actions, and judging by those and what her sisters said, he really did care about her. It didn't have to be Love, but the feelings were real.

What *were* those feelings, exactly?

She'd let him come running with her, which symbolized how she'd let him into her own private life. She never ran with anyone. She felt a foreign sense of satisfaction and contentment when she saw their gun belts side by side on the counter and his toothbrush in her bathroom drawer. She looked forward to telling him things about her day, to confiding in him.

She imagined him naked. Like, all the time. That had to mean something.

She'd even turned down her other two regular booty calls—Alex Light and George Harrison—when they'd called or texted recently. When she considered meeting up with them, she pictured Elijah. She pictured him standing in her kitchen, cooking bacon.

Cooking bacon, of all things.

The answer was simple: she was in love with Elijah Sawyer. Not just love, but Real Love.

But the next step was not so simple. What should she do? Should she resolve to get over him, to move past any notion of the two of them being together? Or should she beg for forgiveness?

That night, Sequoia drove to Elijah's house. She parked along the street near the walkway, and Xena followed her to the front door.

He opened it before she even knocked.

"Hi," he said.

Sequoia took a deep breath. "Hi."

"What's up? Want to come in?"

He opened the door wider and stepped back. On autopilot, she walked in.

"Everything okay?" he said.

He reached out to take her hand, but let his arm drop before he actually made contact.

"Yeah," she said, and her voice came out in a drawl. "I mean, yes.

Yes, everything's fine. Great, actually. I'm sure you've heard Xena is kicking ass at work."

"Yes, I've heard. Good work."

He shut the door.

"So…" he said.

"So."

"What can I do for you?"

Sequoia scratched the back of her neck. "This is awkward, isn't it?"

Elijah scratched the back of his neck. "Uh, yeah. A little bit."

Xena, sitting between them, ears perked, gave a little yip.

"Sorry," Sequoia said. She patted Xena on the head. "I didn't mean for this to be awkward. I just wanted to explain, I guess, why I ended things."

"Oh!" Elijah said. He sounded so jovial. "No need. I know why you ended things. You believed the experiment was over."

"It was. I believed your actions were a result of your experimentation, not your actual feelings for me. I couldn't believe that your feelings might be real. Therefore, the answer to the experiment's question is: No, Sequoia Carr is not capable of a relationship. Ergo, it's unfair of me to continue the relationship."

Elijah shrugged one shoulder. "I hadn't quite finished the experimentation."

Sequoia's ever-imaginative mind brought up an image of the two of them in kinky costumes.

"Wait," Elijah said. "Are you smiling right now? You are. You're trying not to smile. It's because I said experimentation, isn't it?"

Sequoia didn't bother trying to hide her smile, now. "Yeah, it is."

She opted not to tell him about the costumes. Xena laid down.

"So anyway, I'm sorry. I could have handled it better. But I've never experienced this before, where someone actually has real feelings for me. Where someone brings me pumpkins to carve, for goodness' sake. I just don't want to hurt you, that's all. I thought it was better to end things quickly, like taking off a Band-Aid."

Elijah was nodding now, and the look on his face reminded her of the way he'd looked at her when they first met.

"Say something," she said. Then she added, "Actually, you don't have to."

"No," he said. "I do have something to say. I'm just formulating it right now."

Sequoia sighed.

Elijah said, "You know, I think I was upset because I felt like you didn't give us a chance. But then I realized, you did. You acted out of character because of the experiment. You were more open to the way I treated you. I know you hate it when men open doors for you or offer to pay for meals, but you let me do that, in the name of science. And guess what? You liked it. And then you hated the fact that you liked it."

He was right. He was spot on. And she hated him for it. Well, kind of. She also loved him for it. But that just simply wouldn't do.

"I liked it," she said. "I did. But it'll never work between us. Pretty soon, you'll have me all figured out, and then your feelings for me will change."

Now he smiled, a mega-watt smile that made her want to lean in and kiss him.

"You're wrong," he said. "I already have you all figured out."

That was probably true.

So she did the only sensible thing she could think to do: she opened the front door and walked out, Xena trotting along behind her.

A growing sense of satisfaction made Sequoia's movements purposeful as she strode down the walkway to her car.

He wasn't coming after her, which proved her right. Yes, they'd had feelings for each other, and they could both admit it. The truth was that their relationship simply wouldn't last. They could be adults about it and move on now, before either of them did serious damage to the other.

Just as she opened the driver's side door, though, Elijah grabbed her arm and spun her around to face him.

"This isn't over," he told her, and then he put one hand behind her head and kissed her. She could feel so much in that kiss—urgency, passion, anger, and a kind of tenderness that surprised her.

When he stopped, she had two equally opposing urges: to kiss him again, or to sink down into the car and drive away as fast as she could.

He made the choice for her when he framed her face with both hands and then curled a tendril of her hair around his finger and tugged on it. He leaned forward and kissed her again, this time so gently she wanted to cry. Again.

"Go on, now," he said. "I'll be seeing you."

With that, he turned around and walked back to the house. Xena watched him go, her head cocked so far to one side Sequoia almost laughed. Speechless, herself, Sequoia gestured for the dog to get in the car, then sank down into her seat, pulled her legs in, and shut the door. She started the engine but couldn't bring herself to drive away.

CHAPTER TWENTY-SEVEN

Sequoia continued to surprise herself.

She sat in front of Elijah's house for a few moments after he went back inside, and then drove home, changed clothes, and took Xena for a run. Afterward, the two of them sat on the couch watching cheesy romance movies on the women's movie network she always made fun of. She even shared her trail mix with the dog, tossing raisins into the air for Xena to catch.

"I never thought I'd be sharing my snacks with a dog," she said at one point. "Much less cheering when she caught pieces of it out of the air. Very athletic, Xena, really. But I'm sharing only because I don't like raisins. You're not getting the cashews."

After a moment, she added, "I'm so glad Jasmine and Holly aren't here. I'd never live this down."

Sleep didn't come easy that night, even though Sequoia felt exhausted from all the excitement of the past several days. She laid in the dark, her thoughts consumed by Elijah Sawyer, his kiss, and his promise that things weren't over between them.

The next morning, she rose at dawn and took Xena for another run.

"You're going to get into good running shape, one way or another," she told the dog, whose endurance was finally within throwing distance of her excitement level.

When they arrived at work, Mack greeted them in the parking lot.

"I have good news," he said when Sequoia got out of the car.

"Are we all getting raises now that they found out where all that money went?" Sequoia said.

"Ha. No," Mack said. "That would be nice. But this is even better. You know I'm taking over for Hardwick, right? Temporarily, anyway. Well, I know how you feel about Xena, and I did some thinking. I can transfer Joey Billings to the canine squad and you can go back to regular patrol."

Sequoia froze. Did *she* even know how she felt about Xena? Why was Mack approaching her now? Was it really because he was trying to be nice, or was she doing a bad job with the dog?

"Well, well, well," Mack said then, before she could answer. "You don't know what to say, do you? Just say, 'Thanks, Mack. I sure appreciate it. You're the best.' That'll do."

Sequoia smiled at him, and hoped it didn't look angry.

"You are the best, Mack," she said. "But I can hang onto her for now."

Xena chose that moment to hop out of the car door, which Sequoia had left open. She looked at Mack, but for the first time, she didn't run over to him. Instead, she came to sit next to Sequoia's left leg. Then she pushed on Sequoia's hand with her nose, asking to be pet.

Out of reflex, Sequoia rubbed the dog's head and scratched behind her ears. Mack raised his eyebrows.

"What do we have here?" he said. "Do I see that some bonding has occurred? Wait. Don't tell me. You let her sleep in your bed, didn't you? You kicked Sawyer to the curb and replaced his body heat with Xena's."

This was embarrassing. Did everyone know Sequoia had ended the experiment with Elijah?

"I didn't replace him, Mack," Sequoia said. "I just took your advice, that's all."

She wanted to add, "And it's not because I was lonely," but she didn't, since it *was* because she was lonely.

"Anyway," Mack said. "I know putting you in canines was Hardwick's idea. Now that she's gone, we can fix it. You can start as soon as today, if you want. Billings works today."

Sequoia's heart started beating fast. If anyone had asked her, before this moment, if she'd welcome the chance to offload the stupid dog, she'd have said, "Absolutely!"

But now that the decision was staring her in the face, her answer changed. She didn't want to hand Xena off any more than she wanted to end things with Elijah.

And even though ending things with Elijah had been the right decision, ending things with Xena wouldn't be. It's not like she could break the dog's heart.

"You know," Sequoia said, trying to play it cool, "it's all right. I can keep her. I don't want her to get moved around again. It's probably traumatic for her."

Mack didn't respond for a moment, and Sequoia knew something was brewing. Sure enough, he started to laugh. He opened his mouth and tipped his head back and roared as if this was the funniest joke he'd ever heard. Sequoia could have sworn tears leaked out of the corners of his eyes.

"What's so funny?" she said when his laughter died down.

That was a mistake. He started laughing again, and then he turned around and walked away, chuckling and shaking his head. Before he went inside, he called over his shoulder, "The whole world's gone crazy, Carr. But you can keep her."

In the silence that followed, Xena hit Sequoia's hand with her nose again, and Sequoia rubbed her ribcage, then kissed her on the head. After Sequoia glanced around to make sure no one had seen that display of affection, they walked together into the office.

Of course, Elijah was the first person they encountered.

"So, you're keeping Xena, huh?"

Sequoia could see a mix of humor and something else in Elijah's eyes, and she wasn't sure how to respond. So she kept it short. "Yep."

"Mack's getting a real kick out of it. Said you said you didn't want to traumatize her by handing her off to someone else."

Sequoia nodded. She'd kill Mack if she didn't have plans brewing to set him up with Holly. Xena bumped Elijah's hand with her nose.

"Can we talk outside?" he said.

"Um, well, I just got here. My shift's starting."

"I know. It'll just take a minute."

He was already moving toward the door, and Xena, the traitor that she was, followed him. Sequoia fell in line. When they stepped outside, Elijah kept walking, straight through the parking lot.

"Where are we going?" Sequoia said.

He motioned to the corner, where two benches sat at a right angle to each other. His affect—commanding, serious, purposeful—left no room for discussion. Normally, Sequoia might suggest walking while talking, because it would get rid of her nervous energy. Today, though, she just followed Elijah to the benches. When he sat down on one, she sat down on the other. And she waited.

"Look," Elijah said.

Sequoia didn't think it was possible for conversations that started with, "Look," to end well.

"I think it's clear that my experiment failed."

"Aha!" she said. "I knew you'd come around."

"Wait. Just because my experiment failed doesn't mean I didn't get an answer to my question."

"What?"

Xena hopped up onto Sequoia's bench and leaned against her.

"What I mean to say is that I believed that by completing my experiment, you'd realize you were in love with me."

When her mouth dropped open, he held out both hands, palms up.

"I know. It was stupid. I was stupid. But that's what I'd hoped. The experiment's failure has nothing to do with your ability to participate in a healthy, long-term relationship. Scientific evidence proves that you are completely capable. More than capable. You'd be excellent at it. But I skewed the real results by telling you about the experiment."

He rubbed both hands over his face. "I'm not doing a very good job at explaining this."

She put a hand on his shoulder. "No, you're not. Terrible, actually."

"What I'm trying to say is that I should not have gone full-disclosure with you. I should have asked you out, made it clear I was interested in you. But the problem is that you wouldn't have given me a chance."

"That's true," she said. "I wouldn't have."

"But why not? Don't tell me you weren't attracted to me."

"Oh, I was attracted to you," Sequoia said.

"But you wouldn't have wanted the hassle at work, right? You wouldn't have wanted to worry about hurting my feelings, damaging my ego, whatever."

"Right. But the experiment made it seem safer. Like you weren't invested emotionally. Yes, you were conducting research, but I wouldn't be able to hurt your feelings."

"Right," Elijah said. "But now, despite the experimental nature of our relationship, you've gone and hurt my feelings."

"Thanks for reminding me."

"I know you didn't do it on purpose."

"Of course not," she said.

"What do you mean, 'Of course not'?"

"I mean, of course I wouldn't hurt you on purpose."

"Why not?" he said.

This was making her very uncomfortable. She squirmed on the bench just like she'd squirmed in her third grade desk when Mrs. Wharton chastised her for blowing her nose too many times. "Um, because I'm a nice person?"

Elijah made a buzzer sound. "Wrong answer."

"Because you're a nice person?"

He made a buzzer sound again. "I am a nice person. But wrong answer."

She sighed.

"Try again," he said.

Now she bounced her right heel, jiggling her leg up and down, a habit she despised. She crossed her left leg over her right to stop it.

"Because I don't like hurting people? God knows I've been accused of enjoying it my whole life, being the oldest of three sisters. Now I'm extra sensitive to it. I try so hard not to say hurtful things, but that doesn't always pan out."

The buzzer sound again.

"That's getting really annoying," she said.

"Then give me the answer I'm looking for. The right answer. The truth."

"The truth? All of my answers have been the truth. You know as well as I do that there is always more than one truth."

"True," Elijah said. After a pause, he held up a finger, apparently pleased at his own cleverness. "But you haven't given me the one truth I'm looking for."

Suddenly, it dawned on her. He wanted her to admit she had feelings for him.

"Why are you doing this?" she said.

"I'm doing this because you kept Xena. You kept her because you've changed. You've changed because of our relationship. Whether you want to admit it or not, that's one truth I won't let slide by."

"Wait. You're doing this because I kept Xena?"

"You're twisting my meaning all around. I'm doing this because the fact that you kept Xena proves that you aren't as hard-edged as you think you are. And if you can admit, more or less, that you want to keep the dog, then I think you can tell me the truth I'm looking for, right now, so we can get on with our day. And our life together."

This last bit brought Sequoia up short. What was wrong with her? Why was it so difficult for her to admit that she loved him? Hadn't she enjoyed their time together? Hadn't she felt so at ease, so at home, around him? Hadn't she missed him when he was gone? Yes, she had. And it's because she was in love with him. She took a deep breath.

"I said, 'Of course I wouldn't want to hurt you' because I'm in love with you."

A giddy feeling of relief, joy, excitement, came flowing up from Sequoia's stomach and into her chest, and she felt like crying and dancing all at the same time.

Elijah sat on his bench, smiling, but he didn't say anything.

So she said it again. "I'm in love with you, Elijah Sawyer."

Now he stood up and pulled her to her feet. Xena remained sitting on the bench. Elijah wrapped his arms around Sequoia's waist, and she wrapped hers around his neck.

They kissed, long and slow and deep, and she wondered why on earth she'd ever thought walking away from this man was a good idea.

Suddenly, she heard applause, and she stopped kissing Elijah long enough to shake her head at Mack and the other guys who were starting their shift. They stood in a small group just outside the office door, grinning like idiots.

"The show's over," Elijah said. "Thank you for your support. We'll be signing autographs in about three minutes, after we take care of some private business in the back of my personal vehicle."

To a chorus of catcalls and more cheers, the guys turned around and walked back into the office, leaving Elijah and Sequoia—and Xena—alone.

"You told everybody I kicked you to the curb," Sequoia said, bringing her face close to Elijah's again.

"I did," he said. He kissed her lightly on the mouth. "And I told them I was going to get you back again. When Mack came into the office in hysterics over you wanting to keep the dog, I knew this was my chance. I had to catch you when you were feeling all soft and emotional."

"Well, it worked," she said. She kissed him again. "I'm still feeling all soft and emotional."

"Should we take that three minutes in the back of my personal vehicle?"

"I'm going to want a lot longer than three minutes, Mr. Sawyer. Why don't we take a rain check for this evening. You can come over to my place."

"THIS IS SO RIDICULOUS," Sequoia said. "I can't believe I asked you guys for help with this."

"Why?" Holly asked, all innocence. "Isn't this what sisters are for —helping you choose sexy lingerie for the man you love?"

She stood in front of the sex shop's dressing room mirror, holding a bright pink feather boa across her chest.

"I wasn't exactly thinking feathers," Sequoia said.

Jasmine, who was in the store hunting for "the sexiest possible outfit," returned and knocked on the dressing room door.

"Didn't I tell you I would choose lingerie for you to wear when you had hot, steamy, incredible, mouthwatering sex with Elijah Sawyer?" she said. She draped a leather-and-lace teddy over Sequoia's torso. "This will look great with fishnet tights. And heels."

"No!" Holly said. "With your work boots."

Sequoia rolled her eyes, and Jasmine disappeared again, this time, "On the hunt for some killer toys."

"This is too much for me, all in one week," Sequoia said. "First I'm getting in touch with my emotional side, and now I'm choosing over-the-top lingerie with my little sisters. Never in a million years would I have expected this."

Holly said, "I have a feeling my own dating life is about to pick up speed, and when it does, I'm going to need your help with stuff like this all the time."

"All the time? Stuff like this? I certainly hope not. Unless you find someone you want to date long-term."

"Okay, not all the time," Holly said. "But it's fun, right?"

"I'm not sure yet," Sequoia said. "I'll tell you after tonight. Or maybe I won't."

Jasmine returned with her arms full of toys.

"Actually, you can keep the details to yourself," Holly said. "But I admit, I'm getting kind of jealous."

Sequoia felt her body waking up, thrumming with the anticipation of this evening with Elijah. Would things feel different now that they were officially together? Now that she'd admitted she loved him?

She'd never really loved anyone before, so she couldn't be sure. But she was definitely looking forward to finding out.

"Don't be jealous, Holly," Sequoia said. "We'll help you find a guy you can dress up for."

Jasmine snorted, and Holly picked up the feather boa Sequoia had discarded. She wrapped it around her neck, and then leaned over and kissed Sequoia on the cheek.

"Right now, I'm just enjoying watching you fall in love."

CHAPTER TWENTY-EIGHT

W‌HEN S‌EQUOIA OPENED HER FRONT DOOR LATER THAT EVENING, HER entire body filled with happiness that was at once fizzy champagne and glowing embers. Elijah stood on the steps, looking freshly showered and gorgeous.

She took his hands in hers and leaned forward to kiss him.

"I'm so glad you're here," she said when she came up for air.

"Me, too," he said. "Thanks for inviting me."

She stepped back to allow him inside, and inhaled the spicy scent of his cologne as he passed.

"I have a surprise for you," she said.

"I hope it's your famous spaghetti," he said.

"I don't even have a famous spaghetti," she said, "but I did make dinner. But first, there's something I want to show you. Meet me in the bedroom."

Elijah whistled, long and low, and walked into her bedroom. Sequoia went the opposite direction, into the bathroom, to change into the leather-and-lace lingerie Jasmine had picked out. She draped the feather boa around her neck and stepped into her highest heels.

When she came out of the bathroom, Xena was sitting next to the door. She sniffed the lingerie, and kept her nose plastered to

Sequoia's hem line as they walked across the living room to the bedroom.

"I know, it's weird. You're not used to it," Sequoia said. "But don't worry. I'm sure I won't be wearing it for long."

When she stepped into the doorway of the bedroom, Elijah stood up from where he'd been sitting on the edge of the bed.

"Wow," he said.

She smiled. "I know. A little over the top, right?"

He closed the distance between them with two strides. The next thing Sequoia knew, they were on her bed, tangled up in one another so completely she couldn't form any coherent thoughts but one: *This.*

THE END

TURN **the page for a sneak peek of *Just Holly*, the third book in the Garden Club series.**

Chapter One

At first, Holly Carr thought the flickering red and blue strobe lights dancing around the inside of her convertible were meant for someone else.

So when she saw them bouncing off her dashboard, she put on her turn signal to indicate she was getting out of the way, so the police could pursue the driver they were really after. It didn't even occur to her to be nervous until she realized the lights remained behind her … even when she came to a complete stop.

Then she thought about the two double margaritas she'd downed with dinner, one with a side car of some sweet orange-flavored liqueur of which she couldn't even recall the name. She also thought about the way her insides felt warm and liquidy as she traipsed out of the restaurant, and the way her heels didn't seem quite steady on the parking lot pavement. She'd blamed the gravel. Cara, her drinking buddy for the night, had asked her several times whether she was okay to drive. The first time was when she twisted her ankle walking back to the table from the bathroom. The second was just before they ordered their final round of drinks. And Holly had said, "I'm fine! That's why I'm ordering a beer, to chase those margaritas down!"

Had she really said that? Yes. Yes, she had.

The third and final time Cara had asked her whether she was okay to drive was just before Holly got into her car … after accidentally locking the driver's door rather than unlocking it, and then trying to open it three times before she realized she'd turned the key the wrong way.

And again, she'd answered, "I'm fine!"

And truly, she felt fine. She'd consumed the margaritas and beer over the course of several hours. Things *were* a bit fuzzy around the edges, but Holly attributed this to the camaraderie she was sharing with Cara.

The two of them had gone out on this crisp November evening to celebrate being single in a sea of happily-paired-up women in their thirties. Sequoia, the oldest Carr sister, had (surprisingly) settled down with another cop, Elijah Sawyer. And Jasmine, Holly's middle sister, had pledged her undying love for Hudson Parker, photojournalist, just recently. Cara, a newcomer to the newspaper where both Jasmine and Hudson worked, had witnessed the budding romance firsthand.

Then, on a whim, they'd planned a shopping date for the following morning. Cara had declared she needed a makeover, and Holly, who loved nothing more than revolutionizing people's wardrobes, offered to act as her personal stylist.

But now, Holly was going to end up in jail. She waited for the policeman to approach her car, a horrible, cold feeling of foreboding taking root in the pit of her stomach. She should have taken a cab, like Cara had, just to be safe.

Holly put her forehead on the steering wheel. Going to jail wasn't the worst-case scenario. The cop who pulled her over could be her sister, Sequoia, rather than some random patrolman. "Oh, God," she said. "Please don't let it be Sequoia."

After what seemed like an interminable wait, she heard a tap on her driver side window. Holly jerked upright and, half-blinded by the flashlight that was now shining in her eyes, rolled the window down.

Although she could make out nothing other than a trim waist, she knew right away that it was a man, and therefore, not her sister. She exhaled, then, with a tiny shred of hope that he'd pulled her over for something like not using a turn signal, she turned on her best mega-watt grin.

"How can I help you, officer?"

The flashlight clicked off, and Holly blinked to let her eyes adjust. The police officer put his hands on the bottom of her open window and bent down so they were eye-to-eye.

The first thing she noticed—well, the first thing she noticed after noticing this guy didn't look like a police officer at all with the tattoos lining his forearms—was that he didn't look charmed. Not one tiny bit.

I guess the Carr Sister Charm isn't going to work in this scenario. She toned down the smile.

"You wouldn't happen to be related to Sequoia Carr, would you?"

Uh oh. Holly's toned-down smile turned into a grimace. She did the weird, noncommittal nod-head-shake thing Sequoia always made fun of her for. *No, never met her. She's only been bossing me around for the past thirty years.* She couldn't deny it, though. The three Carr sisters shared a strong resemblance from their oversized teeth to their pointy noses.

"You're not going to tell her you pulled me over, are you?"

"You been drinking tonight?"

"You taking me to jail?"

Even in its state of panic, Holly's brain took an automatic profile: the cop had skin the color of coffee with cream, and thick, dark eyelashes that made her envious. His lips were full, and if they'd been in any other shape—something besides the thin line of disapproval—she would have thought them quite kissable. Her eyes skimmed over his name tag—Bravo—and landed on the very well-defined bicep just beyond that name tag?

He cleared his throat. "Ah—"

"You do lots of curls?" she said.

Shut up, Holly. Shut up. She hadn't felt drunk, but this must be some kind of delayed response to that final beer. Mr. Bravo flashed a smile at her, and his teeth were straight and so white they practically glowed. He spoke into the radio at his shoulder.

"You speaking code?" she said.

Shut up!

"Have you been drinking tonight, Ms. Carr?"

She nodded, then, her head moving up and down so quickly her vision blurred. "Just a couple of margaritas, really. You know."

Mr. Bravo cocked his head to the side as he listened to a tinny voice coming through his earpiece.

"There's three of you?" he said to Holly.

"No, but there are three of you," she said, and she couldn't stop herself from giggling. "Just kidding. Totally kidding."

"Your sister—Jasmine?—is coming to get you. Carr, well, Sequoia, I guess is what you call her, is working. As you probably know. She called Jasmine."

"Oh, thank *goodness,*" Holly said. She could hear her heart beating in her ears and she could feel relief flooding her veins.

"What?" Mr. Bravo said. "You thought you were going to the drunk tank?"

"No," Holly said. "I thought Sequoia was coming to get me."

When Jasmine pulled up behind Holly's car, her headlights hit the rearview mirror. Holly winced, then watched as the Jeep's passenger door opened. Hudson appeared. He opened her door and offered a hand.

"I hope you know we just saved your ass," he said. "Sequoia's off in twenty minutes and said she'd come get you if we couldn't."

"I'd rather go to jail," Holly said. She tested her legs and found that her heels still felt very unsteady. *Must be the pavement.*

"I'll drive your car home," Hudson said. "But first I'm going to walk you back to Jasmine's Jeep."

Holding her under one elbow, Hudson navigated her right into the passenger seat and even pulled out her seatbelt and handed the buckle to Jasmine, who buckled it.

"See you in a minute," she said to Hudson. He nodded and closed the door.

"I miss your Golf," Holly said to Jasmine, who pulled onto the road only after Hudson had. "I wish you hadn't crashed it."

"Holly," Jasmine said.

Holly flinched. She hadn't expected *Jasmine* to lecture her. Sequoia played her role as the oldest sister by lecturing, and Jasmine played the role of the middle sister by keeping the peace.

"Well, I just wish you hadn't crashed it, that's all," she said.

"We both know I wasn't talking about the Golf."

"Oh. Yeah, I guess so. Thanks for coming to get me."

Jasmine sighed. The streetlights passing overhead made Holly dizzy. She closed her eyes, but then she saw a whole kaleidoscope of colors and had to open them again.

"Holly, what were you thinking?"

Holly shrugged. "I don't know. Cara and I had a few drinks and—"

"Oh, Cara, was it? You're blaming Cara for your debauchery?" Holly glanced at Jasmine and saw that her lips were twitching. In an undertone, she added, "Although, that girl has gotten me drunk on margaritas, too, I admit."

"It isn't—wasn't—debauchery! It was just a few drinks, okay? Honestly, we were there for hours. I didn't feel drunk."

"Imagine if this got leaked to the press, Holly," Jasmine said. "Seabreeze Police Department is still recovering from a public relations nightmare. Imagine the sister of a cop, thrown in jail for drunk driving."

"Do I have to remind you that you *are* the press, Jas?"

Hysteria hit, and Holly felt tears leaking out the corners of her eyes. They were tears of shame—who gets pulled over for drunk driving at the age of thirty?—and they were fat and juicy and rolled down her cheeks and plopped onto her jeans.

"The only reason I'm not lecturing you right now is because of the state you're in," Jasmine said. "But rest assured that you can look forward to a good talking-to."

"I mean," Holly said, her voice coming out as something between a squeal and a wail, "couldn't you just not report on that particular news item?"

She glanced over at Jasmine and saw that a slight smile had formed on her lips. In her role as the youngest sister, Holly had always been able to perform, to entertain her sisters.

"What would your headline be, anyway? Sister of Sequoia Carr riots at jail after being forced to wear state-owned underpants while sleeping off a bender?"

Jasmine's smile grew, just the tiniest bit, and she shook her head. "You interrupted a perfectly lovely movie night, you know."

"Did I? I'm sorry. You can get right back to it. When you and Hudson have been married for forty years, you can look back and remember this night as the night you had to save my life."

"Save your life? Save your ass, more like. I just saved you from a verbal lashing by Sequoia, is all I saved you from. We were in the middle of *City of Angels*."

They'd stopped at a red light, and Holly looked out over the ocean to her right. Nighttime lights from the harbor sparkled on the water's surface, which undulated peacefully.

"I'm sorry," she said. "Really, I am. I had just run into Cara at the store, and we were both lamenting the fact that we were buying Hungry Man frozen dinners to eat alone on a Saturday night, and wondering why they don't make Hungry Lady dinners, and we decided to go out to eat, instead. I drank too much, thought I was fine, and started driving home. And again, thank you. Seriously."

"Does it really bother you that you're single?" Jasmine asked. "I mean, tonight obviously went beyond dinner. You're sloshed. This borders on binge drinking as a pity party."

Holly shrugged. Her sister had a point.

"I admit, I was feeling kind of down," she said. "It's not so much being single. It's just that everyone else seems so settled, and I don't even know what I'm doing with myself, you know?"

Jasmine nodded and made a humming noise in the back of her throat. The discussion about what Holly was doing with herself was ongoing.

This would be a good time to tell Jasmine she'd been living a lie, Holly thought. For the past several months, she'd told her sisters that she was pursuing a personal training certification. And she had been. But a month ago, she'd dropped out of the program.

Personal training didn't feel like a calling or a passion, and she felt like she was old enough that whatever she did next *should* be. The problem: she wasn't sure what would feel like a calling or passion.

It certainly wasn't waitressing, which is what she'd been doing at the Broken Egg for years. She was good at it, for sure, but she didn't want to to it forever.

If she told Jasmine about dropping out of the personal training program now, she'd have to tell Sequoia later. She didn't look forward to telling either them, at all. It seemed even worse to have to tell it twice.

"What are you thinking?" Jasmine said. "You're doing that finger-tapping thing."

Holly pulled her finger in, making a fist.

"Did you see that cop who pulled me over?"

"I didn't get a good look at him, no," Jasmine said. "Why?"

"Just wondered," Holly said. Even to her own ears, her voice sounded unnaturally high.

Jasmine gave Holly an uncharacteristically caustic response: "I'm sure he thought you were hot, Holly, especially as he thought about taking you and your blue hair to jail."

Jasmine pulled the Jeep up to the curb in front of Holly's house, and Hudson pulled Holly's convertible into the driveway. Just as Holly swung her legs down onto the pavement, which, she noticed, was still wobbly, another set of headlights came around the corner. Sequoia. Holly and Jasmine realized who it was at the same instant, and emitted identical gasps of surprise and horror.

Holly heard Hudson bark out a laugh. She could have sworn he muttered, "This is getting good," but it may have been a figment of her drunken imagination.

"Well," Jasmine said. "I'm out of here. I can tell you right now this isn't going to be pretty."

Before she could get back into the Jeep, Sequoia's voice broke through the quiet evening air.

"Oh, no you don't," she said to Jasmine. "You're not leaving me alone with Holly."

Holly yelped. "You mean, she's not leaving *me* here alone with *you*."

The alcohol was wearing off, and Sequoia's appearance was siphoning the last of its warm, calming, soothing effects right out of Holly's bloodstream. In fact, this November nighttime air was chilly. Holly noticed that Sequoia was wearing a pair of running tights. She thought about how Sequoia's boyfriend, Elijah, had remarked more than once that a similar pair of pants played a role in his falling for Sequoia.

"Those pants look good on you," Holly said.

Jasmine snickered.

"Thanks," Sequoia said. "They do. What the—"

"Is Xena with you?" Holly said. Xena was Sequoia's K-9 partner at work. Although their relationship had gotten off to a rocky start, it had developed into a cute friendship.

"No," Sequoia said. "I didn't want her to witness this. What the hell were you thinking?"

Sequoia was now leaning against the spare tire on Jasmine's Jeep, her arms crossed. She pinned Holly with her stare, her bright green eyes intense and without even a hint of humor.

"It's cute that you're worried about Xena's sensibilities," Holly said, trying to keep the mood light. When Sequoia continued staring at Holly, Holly blanched.

"I don't know," she said. She leaned back against her passenger door so she didn't have to look Sequoia in the eyes any more. She mimicked her oldest sister's pose and glared out into the darkness. Jasmine, apparently convinced she wasn't leaving, sat down on the curb.

Hudson held up Holly's keys and shook them so they jingled. "Beer?"

"No, thanks," Holly said, at the same time as Sequoia said, "I think she's had enough."

"I meant for me," Hudson said.

"Oh," Holly said. "In the fridge. Help yourself."

A beat of silence passed. Jasmine picked at her shoelaces. Sequoia took a deep breath. "What's going on with you, Holly?"

"I don't know, honestly," Holly said.

She thought:

I'm single and lonely.

I'm keeping a huge secret from you.

I don't know what I want to be when I grow up.

I'm thirty years old and almost just got arrested for drunk driving.

I hate my life.

Where Sequoia would have waited her out, stood there in silence until Holly broke, Jasmine jumped in with questions. Two completely different interviewing techniques for two completely different professions.

"What do you mean, you don't know?" Jasmine said. "I mean, something must be going on. You look miserable."

Holly nodded. She felt her throat constricting, and bit her bottom lip to keep herself from crying. Her sisters had lived to tease her about being a crybaby.

"I'm not miserable in general," she managed in a strangled voice. "I'm just embarrassed, I guess. I should have shared a cab with Cara or something, but I didn't realize how drunk I was."

"You know, with all the hair dyeing you've been doing recently," Sequoia said, and Jasmine jumped in, "You think chemicals are seeping into her brain?"

"No," Sequoia said. Apparently she wasn't in the mood to joke around. "I think this might be a symptom of a bigger problem."

Jasmine looked away.

"Why do things always come down to my hair dyeing?" Holly said. "At first it was funny. But now you're saying it points to emotional problems. I just like changing my hair color. I mean, I could come up with a psychoanalysis based on your overuse of the French braid."

"I know I make fun of your hair all the time," Sequoia said. "I mean, most big sisters would, right? One day it's pink, one day it's leopard print, and one day it's banana sunset. But I sometimes think your failure to settle on a single color is indicative of a lack of direction in your whole life. I think you're having an identity crisis."

"Ohmygosh," Holly said. "I just like changing my hair color. The hair dye, the drunk driving, they're not symptoms of a bigger problem."

Now Jasmine stood up. "Holly, don't get irritated. She's just asking, okay? I'm not talking about the hair dye" (here she shot Sequoia a Look) "but I do think a drunk driving incident, at our age, is pretty serious stuff. Especially when you're on the cusp of a new career and everything."

Why did Jasmine have to bring up the new career issue? There *was* no new career. Holly was a tiny boat, a dinghy without a rudder, bobbing on the surface of the ocean, following the tide wherever it took her. A tiny, rudderless boat with a hole in it. Maybe this would be a good time to tell them. She could just blurt it out. She could say, "About that. I'm not actually getting a new career. Did you know I'm still waitressing at the Broken Egg. It *is* a career, actually. Want to hear the breakfast special?"

Or she could say, "Actually, I've decided to become a gypsy. I'll change my residence as often as I change my hair color."

But she didn't. Instead, she said, "I know. It was a one-time deal, okay? I promise. You guys don't have to worry about me. I've got it all together. Thank you both, so much, for showing up tonight. Now get home and get some rest. *City of Angels* is waiting, Jas. And Sequoia, I'm really sorry for getting pulled over."

Alone in her quiet living room, a blanket draped over her lap and a cup of too-hot tea in her hands, Holly tried to find some mindless distraction to watch on TV. But every show she put on seemed to mirror her life. Not a regular mirror, but one of those bendy ones that shows a grotesque version of reality.

First, there was a soap opera where a woman woke up from a coma and didn't recognize her life, at all. She didn't recognize her friends or family members or the people at her job. Holly felt as if she'd just woken from a coma and was realizing she didn't recognize any of the choices she'd made.

Then, she found a based-on-real-life movie where the hero got his arm caught between two rocks, and he had to saw it off to get free. She wondered if that was the predicament she'd gotten herself into. One where changing the course of her career—after spending an arm and a leg on a certification she didn't plan to use—meant the metaphorical sawing-off of a limb.

She came across a show where contestants ran an obstacle course that tried to knock them off kilter. She turned off the TV when she saw a mechanical arm extend, the boxing glove on its end punching a woman off a narrow, raised walkway and into a pit of mud.

With nothing to distract her from thinking about tonight, Holly sighed. She took a sip of her tea and felt her face twist into an involuntary grimace. She didn't even like tea. She was drinking it now only because Jasmine had made it for her before leaving.

Holly stood up, marched to the kitchen, dumped the tea in the sink, and set the empty mug down on the counter. Then she went to bed.

Chapter Two

The next morning—the day after what Holly was now calling the Drunk Driving Incident—Cara picked Holly up for their shopping date.

"I think you need coffee, first," Cara said, and they didn't speak until they were seated at a little table at The Grind, the coffee shop overlooking the ocean.

"When you texted me last night," Cara said, "I thought you were joking."

Holly, having just filled Cara in on all the details, just shook her head.

"I wish. That was the most humiliating event of my life."

"Was Sequoia mad?" Cara wanted to know.

"She seemed worried, more than anything," Holly said. "Surprisingly. She thinks the hair dye and the drunk driving are indicative of a deeper problem."

"I have to ask," Cara said. "Are they?"

Holly shrugged. "I mean, I've never thought about it that way, but now that I am, maybe they *are*. I'd never admit it to Sequoia. She's always so sure of herself and I think it frustrates her that I'm not."

It felt good to say the words out loud.

"Have you tried to talk to her about it?"

Holly shook her head, which only made it pound more severely. Sequoia's home remedy of two glasses of water and three aspirin wasn't quite kicking the hangover. Holly watched through the window as a couple strolled by on the sidewalk, pushing a baby in a stroller.

Cara took a sip of her coffee and a bite of her muffin before speaking again: "I hate to say this, but—"

Holly groaned. This sounded like something Jasmine would say. Cara held up a hand. "Just hear me out, okay? I know we were talking dating strategy last night. And I know you want to fall in love, start a family, and go for walks on cool fall mornings. But I think maybe you should just take some time to, you know, find yourself. That's what I'm doing."

Even as Holly said, "What does that even mean?" she drew the parallel between Cara's words this morning and her own thoughts the previous night.

"Okay, don't kill me," Cara said. "But you know I'm a straight shooter. It just seems like you're so unsure of yourself all the time. You struggle to make decisions on your own about even the simplest things."

Holly felt herself sitting up straighter. Her mouth dropped open.

"Don't get indignant," Cara said, misreading Holly's reaction. Her blue eyes, framed by thick black eyeliner, twinkled with humor. "Just listen. Take, for example, this morning. Just like every time we have coffee or lunch or drinks, you made me choose the spot. And then you had me order first. And then you ordered the same thing as me. You haven't even touched your muffin. You don't even like blueberry muffins, I think you told me once. But when it was your turn to order, you said, 'I'll just have what she's having.' And it's not just this morning. You do it all the time. I mean, you drive a convertible."

Okay, so the muffin thing was true. But the convertible? "What does that have to do with anything?" Holly said.

"You can't decide whether you want a roof or not." Cara shrugged. "It's symbolic."

Arguing was Holly's natural inclination, but not after last night.

"You know," she said, "you might be on to something."

Cara tilted her head, waiting.

"I did a lot of thinking last night. Did you know I don't even like tea? That's what started it. Jasmine made me tea before she left, and I was just sitting there, drinking it."

"You have tons of tea in your cabinet," Cara said. "I never would have guessed you don't actually like it."

"Hate it," Holly said. "I'm no good on my own, Cara. I can't make plans or decisions or form an opinion."

"Ever?"

"Well, when I do, they flop. When Sequoia and Jasmine and I were little, we'd always make these little stands, and we'd sell cookies or lemonade or hot cocoa in our cul de sac. One weekend, the two of them both had birthday parties to go to, and I thought, 'I'll show them.' I set up the stand, and I went inside to make cookies. We always made the cookies together, you know? With one of us reading the recipe and one of us gathering ingredients and one of us measuring. Divide and conquer, you know?"

Cara nodded and sipped her coffee.

"Well, they weren't there that day, and I messed up those cookies. Badly. The ones I didn't burn to a crisp were flat and as hard as bricks. So I thought, 'I'll just make lemonade. Scoop and stir. What can go wrong?' But believe me, a lot can go wrong. At first, I underscooped and ended up with lemonade that tasted like water. And then I overcompensated. As I was pouring the powder into the pitcher, my elbow slipped and all the powder went in. It tasted horrible. I went outside to clean up our little stand, and the whole thing had crumpled to the ground. I'd forgotten to latch the legs of the table, so when a gust of wind blew by, they folded in."

Once Holly started talking, she couldn't stop. She'd never verbalized any of this before, and Cara was such a good listener (probably thanks to the years she'd spent as a journalist).

"And then there was this talent show. The three of us had done a little performance every year in elementary school, when we were all there together. Sequoia aged out first, of course, and then Jasmine didn't want to do it without her. But I did. I wanted to do a little dance. Alone. Big mistake. It was *Singin' in the Rain*. And what did I do? I practiced and practiced at home, torturing the entire family to no end with my singing and dancing and humming. And then I got up on stage and ruined the entire thing. Can you believe I forgot my umbrella? And I know it's because they weren't there with me."

Holly told Cara about how going solo—and failing at it—became a pattern in her life.

At Sequoia's urging, she'd joined the track team her freshman year. She quit halfway through the season because she didn't have either of her sisters to cheer her on (Jasmine was playing chess or something and Sequoia was in college by then).

When it came time for Holly to choose a college major, she chose English. But midway through her second year, Jasmine made an offhand comment about how Holly should find a career that would make a positive difference in the world. Holly, with both sisters at different colleges and no one there to give her direction, suffered an identity crisis. She took a wide variety of classes but never earned her degree.

Meanwhile, she started working at the Broken Egg, and in her free time she became what Sequoia called a "gym bunny," making best friends with free weights and elliptical machines.

"You spend so much time there, you should just become a personal trainer," Sequoia had said at one point.

Holly, like a hunting dog who spots a fox, had looked up, ears pointed and eyes sharp, and grasped onto the idea as if it were her own.

Only, it wasn't.

"And now," she told Cara, who'd listened, rapt, to the long list of Holly's failures, "here I am. Rock bottom. I've quit the personal training program and all signs point to me being a lifelong waitress at a mid-scale diner. Which isn't bad, but it's not what I'd say if you asked me about big dreams I have for for my life."

"What would you say?" Cara said.

"I have no idea," Holly said. "That's the problem, isn't it?"

"Let's shop," Cara said. "A little retail therapy never hurt anybody."

It was true: as soon as they stepped into the air-conditioned sanctuary of the mall, Holly felt her entire body relax.

"I love it here," she said.

Cara snickered. "I'm glad you do. It gives me anxiety. Which I'm pretty sure is the reason I started wearing all black."

"I think it's time we did something about that," Holly said. "This way."

Since the moment they met, Holly had envisioned a different wardrobe for Cara, one that showed off her curves and brought out her eyes. Of course, she hadn't proposed a shopping spree until they'd become closer, but when Cara said, "Yes," Holly had leapt out of her chair and given Cara a big hug.

"Here?" Cara said. Her forehead wrinkled as she looked up at the entrance to Flair, a women's boutique where mannequins dressed in multi-colored outfits lined the walkways, and sweaters in reds, oranges and greens sat on tables. "Holly, I don't see a single black sweater on that table."

"You'll be fine," Holly said. "Trust me."

While Holly's stride became longe and more confident, Cara lagged behind. But only for a few seconds, because Holly started piling her arms with sweaters, pairs of jeans, and shirts.

"You're going to run my bank account dry, woman," Cara said, her voice muffled from behind an infinity scarf Holly had added to the pile.

"You're not going to buy all of it," Holly said. "Just try stuff on. Okay?"

"Okay," Cara said, drawing the word out. "If you say so."

The sales girl raised an eyebrow when Holly asked for a dressing room.

"I'll wait out here," Holly said. "But you have to promise to show me everything."

"Everything?"

"Everything."

"There's so much. I don't even know where to start. And I can't guarantee I'll wear any of it. You're going to make me look like a lollipop," Cara said.

"Better than looking like the angel of death," Holly said.

Cara set the clothes down on the dressing room bench, and Holly began separating them into outfits: jeans and a sweater, a sweater and a scarf, a blouse and a pair of corduroy pants.

"Hit it, sister," she said, gently pushing Cara into the dressing room. "You can do this."

When Cara emerged, wearing the first outfit, she had a shy smile on her face.

"I'm not sure about the color of this sweater," she said, "but I'm digging it."

Holly sat on her stool, stunned, her mouth hanging open.

"You look so…"

"Terrible?" Cara said.

"No!" Holly said. "You look great, Cara. Amazing. That sweater brings out the color of your eyes, and the fit is so good on you. Turn around."

Cara obeyed, but her posture suggested she was still nervous.

"Your ass looks so good in those jeans," Holly said. "You know, I don't think I've ever seen your ass."

"Funny," Cara said, her voice flat. But by the time she'd finished her revolution, her smile looked more confident.

"Okay," Holly said. "I've given that one a score. Try the next one."

Cara's self-assurance increased with each showing, and by the time she'd tried on the final pairing—a pencil skirt with a floral blouse—she was glowing.

"This is the prettiest I've felt in years," she said. Then she clapped a hand over her mouth. "And I never thought I'd say that."

"You look great," Holly said. "I mean, you always look pretty—

you are pretty—but I feel like you hide behind all those dark colors. These brighter colors, they make you shine."

Cara grabbed Holly's hands and pulled her to standing, then gave her a big hug. "Thank you so much, Holly. This means so much to me. You have no idea."

Hours passed. They conquered several more stores, adding shoes, accessories, and makeup to Cara's bounty. When they were done, Cara said, "You ran my bank account dry and I'm starving. Take me out to lunch."

They opted for the sushi place across the street, and when the hostess seated them, Cara slid into her side of the booth with a sigh.

"I don't think I've ever been more exhausted in my life," she said.

Holly leaned forward. "So, tell me. Which outfit are you going to wear to work on Monday?"

Cara smiled, but didn't answer.

"Don't tell me these clothes are going to sit in your closet," Holly said. "You wouldn't."

"No," Cara said. "But I'll admit, I'm scared. I've worn all black for the past five or six years. That olive-green skirt? Totally foreign. But I'll do it."

"If you wear it on Monday, with that blouse, I'll buy you a present."

"Wait. Are you bribing me? Like a little kid?"

"Totally," Holly said. "Wear it Monday."

"You know," Cara said, her tone of voice and her expression turning serious, "you're totally in your element right now. Remember earlier, when I was saying how you never form your own opinion?"

"I do remember," Holly said. "And you're right."

"But not when it comes to this. You were on fire today. I mean, I've never seen you like this. You turned into some kind of wardrobe drill sergeant. It was amazing."

"Ha," Holly said. "Too bad I can't spend all my time shopping. Unless you want to pay me some kind of stylist fee."

"I can't," Cara said, deadpan. "Like I said, you ran my account dry."

The bell above the restaurant's door tinkled, and both Holly and Cara turned to see who'd entered.

Of all the people in Seabreeze, it had to be Mr. Bravo. In this setting, he looked even less like a police officer and more like a surfer getting ready to head to the beach.

Holly wished she could slide down in the booth and hide under the table. She had the insane thought that maybe if she closed her eyes, he wouldn't see her.

Still, as she turned her head away from the door he'd come through, she noticed the way his light blue t-shirt showed off his muscular, tattooed arms. And those jeans! She'd never seen a guy look absolutely edible in jeans before.

She licked one corner of her mouth and looked down at her menu.

Holly had seen Sequoia scan a room upon entering, and she was positive Officer Bravo was doing the same thing. She could practically feel the moment his eyes skimmed over her, and almost involuntarily, she made eye contact with him—and saw the recognition dawn on his face.

His expression went completely blank, and he gave her a curt nod. After giving him what she hoped was a polite smile in return, she spent a full second wondering what his blank expression meant. Probably that he found her reprehensible after last night's Incident. When she realized her own face probably looked like a Botox nightmare, she turned her attention back to Cara, who was leaning forward, her eyes boring into Holly's.

"Hey, do you know that guy?"

"Huh?" Holly said. "What guy?"

Cara rolled her eyes. "That guy, with all the tattoos. The one that just turned your brain to mush."

Fortunately, or unfortunately, Mr. Bravo didn't seem prepared to stay long. He took his order in a to-go bag, and walked toward the door. Holly took another long look at his tapered waist and his toned back muscles and sighed before she could stop herself.

"Nope," she said. "Don't know him at all."

Cara leapt into questioning mode. Since Jasmine had become a real reporter (Sequoia's words, not hers) after meeting Hudson, Holly was used to it.

"What are you thinking right now? You don't know him, but you'd like to, wouldn't you? You've met him before, haven't you? Wait—wait. Don't tell me. You had a one-night stand with him and never called him again."

Holly shook her head.

"Okay," Cara said. "Let me think. He's the one who got away, like in high school or something."

"Nope," Holly said.

Then, Holly could practically see the realization dawning in Cara's eyes, a lightbulb on a dimmer switch, gradually brightening.

"He's the cop who pulled you over last night, isn't he? His face—your face—it's all making sense."

When all Holly could manage was a nod, Cara said, "You know, Holly? I'm surprised. He doesn't seem like your type."

Holly shrugged, and Cara said, "What *is* your type, anyway?"

"You know, Cara," Holly said. "I don't actually know."

Although shopping and lunch with Cara had bolstered Holly's mood temporarily, she found herself sinking back into low spirits when Cara dropped her off at home. The whole afternoon and evening loomed ahead of her, as empty as a two-lane highway running through the desert. If she were still pursuing a new career, she'd have plenty to do. But she wasn't. So the truth was, she would probably end up sitting on the couch, binge watching reality TV shows.

No, she couldn't waste even another hour watching women make fools of themselves vying for a man's proposal. She would be productive. She would vacuum. And dust. This place could use a good deep cleaning. She got the vacuum out of the closet and plugged it in, letting her thoughts wander as she picked up discarded shoes and socks to clear the carpet.

Maybe she should get a dog. Jasmine had Ruby and Sequoia had

Xena. Those relationships seemed to be working out well. Holly turned on the vacuum. The thought of Sequoia and Xena made her smile. As a police officer on graveyards, Sequoia had always relished her alone time. She'd never cared for dogs, in their hairy, slobbery existence. So when her boss assigned her to the K-9 unit, and she was suddenly stuck with a four-legged companion, twenty-four-seven, they all thought she'd lose her mind and resign. Grudgingly, though, she grew to like Xena, and surprised Holly and Jasmine with how quickly she adapted to having a dog in the house (and, to hear her tell it, in her bed). Holly wasn't sure whether it was Xena or Elijah who had helped transform Sequoia's personality from brusque to ... well, to a gentler brusque.

Sequoia paired up with Elijah after Xena came along. And just before that, Jasmine had met and fallen for Hudson while working with him at the paper.

Both of her sisters seemed so happy, so calm and centered and sure of their places in this universe. It wasn't just about finding a man, Holly thought. It was about knowing who you *were*. Of course, finding a man would be wonderful. But how could she find a man when she didn't even know herself?

At this rate, she'd be alone, lonely, and rudderless indefinitely. Was this night representative of her future? Pathetic and alone every weekend, vacuuming the carpet, debating between dishes and TV, while thinking about getting a dog for company?

She was looking forward to a pretty sad existence. She decided to wash the windows after all. If she was going to live a sad existence, at least it would be in a clean house. Was it possible that she was just meant to be alone?

"Maybe I should get a cat."

How many cats would it take to earn her official Cat Lady status?

Three? A dozen? She began assigning them favorite spots. One could sit there, in the picture window overlooking the street in front of the house. She could buy it one of those hammocks that hang on the windowsill. Another—two more, actually—could sit on the back of the couch. Some cats liked sleeping in house plants, so she'd have to get a new house plant, too, one she could keep alive. Maybe if there was a cat living in it, she'd remember to water it.

Sequoia would just die. If there was one thing worse than dogs, it was cats, with their long, shedding fur and their sharp, scratching claws.

At that very moment, Holly's phone dinged, signaling a text message from Sequoia: *What are you doing?*

Holly shook her head, and replied with a lie: *Studying.*

Why couldn't she just be honest? Why couldn't she just tell her sisters she'd decided not to pursue personal training? Holly set her phone down. Then, when she realized it was strange for Sequoia to text her with that kind of unimportant question, she picked it back up and added, *Why?*

Sequoia responded immediately: *Just wanted to make sure you're safely at home.*

Holly wrote: *Where else would I be?*

She fully expected her sister to write some snarky response related to the Drunk Driving Incident, but instead, she wrote, *Are you sure everything's ok?*

Holly wished for the confidence to tell her sister everything. But confidence doesn't develop overnight. *Everything's fine. Promise.*

Okay, Sequoia wrote. *If you promise.*

Cleaning gave her too much time to think, Holly decided. She'd cleaned the entry window, and that was good enough. Watching TV would stop this madness. And she'd watch something stimulating, like the news. She threw away the wad of paper towels, sat down on the couch, and turned on the TV. She picked up her phone and opened the Blackbook app to see what her friends had been up to.

Then she got a sign. From a Blackbook advertisement. It was a video: the camera panned the beach in Seabreeze. Holly could tell from the watercolor sky and smooth-as-glass ocean that it was sunrise. The dawn of a new day. Text started scrolling over the image: *Are you at a crossroads in your life? Are you searching for purpose and meaning?*

Holly sat up straight, nodding. "Yes," she said quietly, and then more loudly, as a seagull flew through the frame, "Yes!"

The camera had finished panning the beach, and now there was a view of the forest.

If you want to discover your true life's purpose, the scrolling text read as the sun rose over the horizon and shone through the branches of the redwoods, *then you are in the right place, right now. Introducing … Compass Coaching with Tristan Compass.*

A photo came up into the frame—a photo of a very, *very* good-looking guy. *Award-Winning Life Coach Tristan Compass.*

Tristan Compass could be Holly Carr's compass any time. Yes, he was wearing a tank top in the photo, which her sisters would say proved he had a big ego, but he deserved to, didn't he? With that physique?

We're scheduling complimentary Find Your Way consultations right now to help you determine whether Tristan is a good match for you … whether he can guide you towards a life filled with purpose, meaning, and true joy, starting in the New Year.

The text directed Holly to a link where she could sign up for a consultation. Holly realized she was literally sitting on the edge of her seat. She tapped the link, and the web browser opened. There it was, the web page for Compass Coaching … and the form to sign up for a consult.

Yes, this was a sign. It had to be.

The next evening, Holly, Jasmine, and Sequoia met at Jasmine's house for the weekly meeting of The Garden Club—the term they'd coined as kids when they realized their parents had named them all after flora.

Things were a little quiet as they settled in around the table, and Holly blamed the Drunk Driving Incident. Jasmine's dog, Ruby, who sat in her customary spot at Holly's feet, yipped, probably anxious for a piece of carrot or bell pepper. Holly tapped her fingers on the edge of the table. She had been looking forward to tonight, but now that they were all together, she was afraid to tell her sisters about Tristan Compass.

"You're tapping," Sequoia said.

"Sorry." Holly curled her hands into fists. "How are you?" she asked.

Sequoia shrugged. "I'm good."

Holly didn't press for further conversation. Instead, she said, "Should we dish up?"

She decided that this moment, while her sisters were distracted by serving themselves salad and meatloaf, she'd tell them.

She cleared her throat. "So," she said. "I've had a sign from the universe."

She went on to explain how she'd taken a break from cleaning on Saturday, and while scrolling through Blackbook, she'd seen the Compass Coaching advertisement and was considering signing up for a complimentary Find Your Way consultation.

Later, she would reflect on this moment and wonder how stupid she looked to both of her sisters, as she sat there bright-eyed at the table, accidentally revealing to them that she'd neglected, for months, to tell them she'd stopped pursuing her personal training certification. She was sure that in a few years' time they would all find the memory humorous: her expression changing from expectant, like she deserved a cookie, to surprised—when she remembered her sisters didn't even know she didn't have a life's purpose— to disappointed that she'd have to explain herself.

"Wait," Sequoia said, at the same time as Jasmine said, "A life coach?" and added air quotes.

They both said, "I thought you—"

Jasmine motioned for Sequoia to continue, and Sequoia said, "You said you were studying."

Jasmine held up a finger. "I thought you *had* a life's purpose. I thought personal training was, like, your thing. All those tofu burritos and everything."

"Look at that face," Sequoia said. "Deer in the headlights. What's going on, Holly?"

"Shit," Holly said. She scooped some more salad onto her plate.

"You weren't getting your personal training certification, were you?" Sequoia said.

"She wasn't," Jasmine said. "Her face just confirmed it."

Holly found herself slightly bent at the shoulders, looking at the lettuce like she was reading tea leaves. She had the urge to talk to Ruby, to bemoan the fact that her sisters were talking about her like she wasn't here, but she knew that would only make matters worse.

"I have so many questions right now," Sequoia said. "Like, why you didn't tell us you didn't want to be a personal trainer and what do you plan to do, instead? But what I really want to know is, a life coach? I mean, those people charge you thousands of dollars, Holly. Thousands. You're a waitress. A waitress! Are your tips really going to cover the expense of hiring some slick, hair-gelled prima donna to ask you deep, probing, thought-provoking questions that will ultimately lead to your life's purpose? Why not just ask yourself those questions?"

"This is exactly why I didn't want to tell you guys," Holly said. "And Tristan doesn't wear hair gel. At least, not in the photo they showed on the advertisement."

"Tristan?" Sequoia said. "I see why you didn't want to tell us. Because we'd think it's ridiculous. Especially with a guy named Tristan. Tristan!"

"You're right," Holly said. "It probably is ridiculous."

"Now, now, ladies," Jasmine said. "Let's keep it civil here, okay? Holly, I think Sequoia is just concerned that you're wasting your money."

Sequoia and Jasmine had no way of knowing Holly had built a serious savings account over the course of the past several years—one a bank teller told her she should be proud of.

"All I said was that I was thinking about signing up for the free session," Holly said. "It's free! You can't waste money on something that's free. I thought it would be good timing, with the New Year approaching and everything. I haven't even signed up yet! And I didn't sign up for the coaching."

"But you're going to," Sequoia said. "I can see that light in your eyes. You're excited about this in the same way you were excited about losing your virginity to Dylan Sanderson your sophomore year of college. You had already decided on it, before you even went on that date to the drive-in."

Holly sighed. It was true. She'd already decided she'd sign the life coaching contract. Just like she'd decided she'd sleep with Dylan Sanderson at the drive-in well before they were laying in the backseat, his pants around his thighs and her panties shoved off to one side.

"I can afford it."

"I still can't believe you lost your virginity at the drive-in," Jasmine said. "But that's not the point. Sequoia's right. You do get this light in your eyes."

"It's like the bright, shiny object thing," Sequoia said.

Jasmine must have stomped on Sequoia's foot under the table because she winced and pressed her lips together before Jasmine continued speaking, undoubtedly presenting the same idea Sequoia had planned on, only with nicer delivery. "You find something new to focus on, and you're all excited about it for, like, a minute, and then it loses its luster and you want to move on. Like the personal training thing."

If she was being honest with herself, Holly couldn't think of a single way to refute what they were saying. Even if she could, they'd just argue. She wasn't sure they were wrong.

Before she left that evening, Sequoia put a hand on Holly's arm and said, "Don't waste your time, Holly. You don't need a coach. You just need to decide what you want to do with your life."

As if it were that easy.

When she got home from Jasmine's, she walked through the house turning on lights—in the entryway, the clean living room, and the kitchen—to camouflage the fact that she was alone, again. On autopilot, she filled her teakettle (a gift from Jasmine) and put it on the stove. Then, abruptly, she turned off the burner, moved the kettle to the back of the stovetop, and marched over to the pantry. She pulled a couple of teabags out of each box to save for Jasmine, and threw the rest of the tea in the garbage. And so what if she felt a little thrill when the lid slammed shut?

Then she poured herself a generous glass of wine and sat at the counter twirling the glass between her forefinger and her thumb. If she was, in fact, easily distracted, how would she find the focus and perseverance to stick with any particular project for a decent length of time?

Wasn't life coaching the answer? She took a sip of wine.

In her research about Compass Coaching, Holly had learned that coaches didn't focus on why you employed a certain behavior or fell into a certain pattern; rather, they identified action steps for creating positive change from wherever you were.

Isn't that exactly what she needed to do?

The wine hit her bloodstream. She felt warm, her limbs heavy and pliable.

True, she hadn't been able to find a price tag for coaching programs with Tristan Compass, and that probably meant he cost a lot, like jewelry on display at Tiffany & Co. But maybe what it said on the web page was *also* true—she was investing in her own happiness, her own future.

Right?

Right, she told herself, draining her glass. She felt emboldened, and wasn't sure whether that was due to the wine or to the possibility of a new path to purpose.

She slid her phone across the counter and opened up the web browser again. Tristan Compass's face popped up, his blue eyes staring intensely at her from the screen.

She'd just sign up for the free consultation. It was free, and the website promised she'd walk away with at least one action step she could take to move closer to her biggest goal. Besides, she reminded herself, the end of the year was approaching, which meant that she'd start off the New Year with momentum and enthusiasm. And action.

What did she have to lose? Nothing but an hour of her time—or a complete lack of purpose and direction, she thought wildly as she typed in her name and email address and tapped on *Schedule My Session!*

ACKNOWLEDGMENTS

Innumerable friends and family members have supported me in the writing of "Studying Sequoia" … too many to list. A special thank you to my husband for supporting my crazy writing schedule, and to my mom for always being excited to read my first drafts!

Big thanks to my Advance Review Team, proofreader Donna Rich, and my cover designer, Bree.

ABOUT THE AUTHOR

Hilary Dartt loves great adventures, whether she's writing, reading, or living them. The author of nine women's fiction novels, Hilary lives in Arizona's high desert with her husband, their three children, her Weimaraner and running partner, Leia, a failed barn cat, and a flock of chickens. She loves camping, exploring in the Jeep, and dance parties with her kids. Learn more at www.hilarydartt.com.

www.ingramcontent.com/pod-product-compliance
Lightning Source LLC
Chambersburg PA
CBHW051654180726
48284CB00006B/1995